PART II

THE MINDBENDING MINECRAFT GRAPHIC NOVEL ADVENTURE!

GOING VIRAL

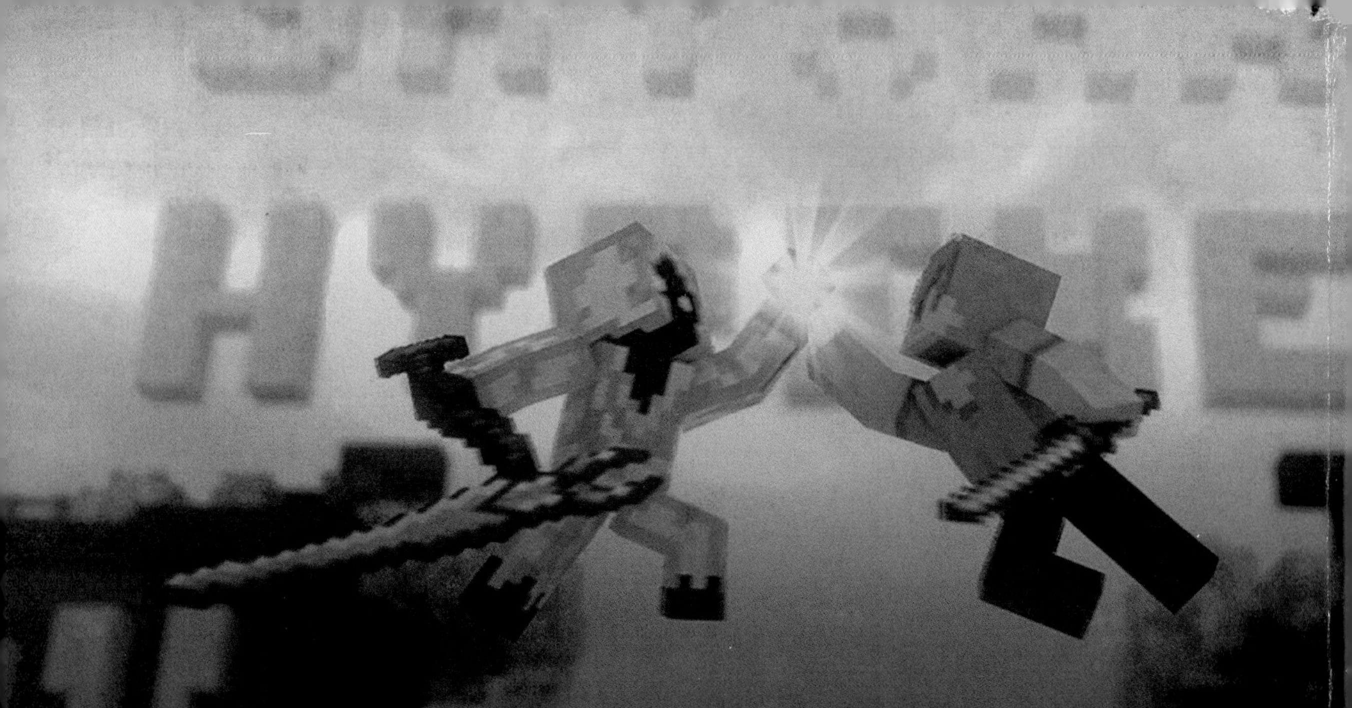

THIS IS A MORTIMER CHILDREN'S BOOK

Published in 2021 by Mortimer Children's Books Limited
An imprint of the Welbeck Publishing Group
20 Mortimer Street, London W1T 3JW

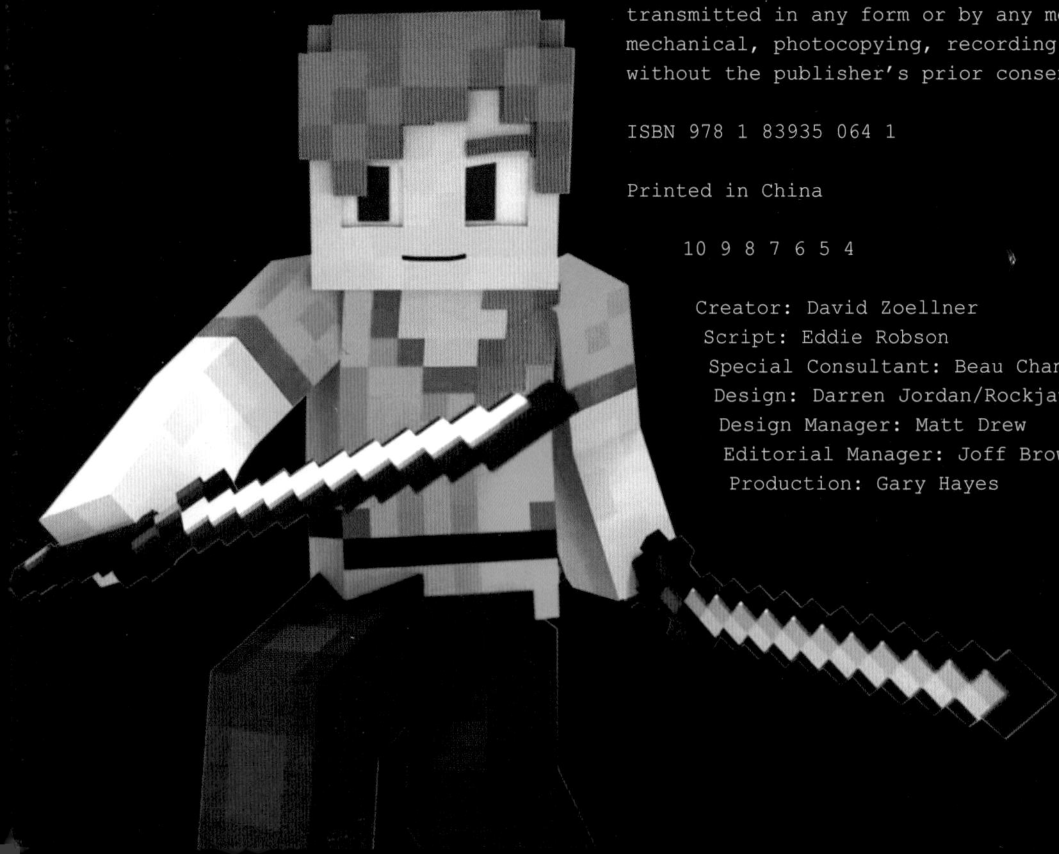

ISBN 978 1 83935 064 1

Printed in China

10 9 8 7 6 5 4

Creator: David Zoellner
Script: Eddie Robson
Special Consultant: Beau Chance
Design: Darren Jordan/Rockjaw Creative
Design Manager: Matt Drew
Editorial Manager: Joff Brown
Production: Gary Hayes

INDEPENDENT AND UNOFFICIAL

PART II

THE MINDBENDING MINECRAFT GRAPHIC NOVEL ADVENTURE!

GOING VIRAL

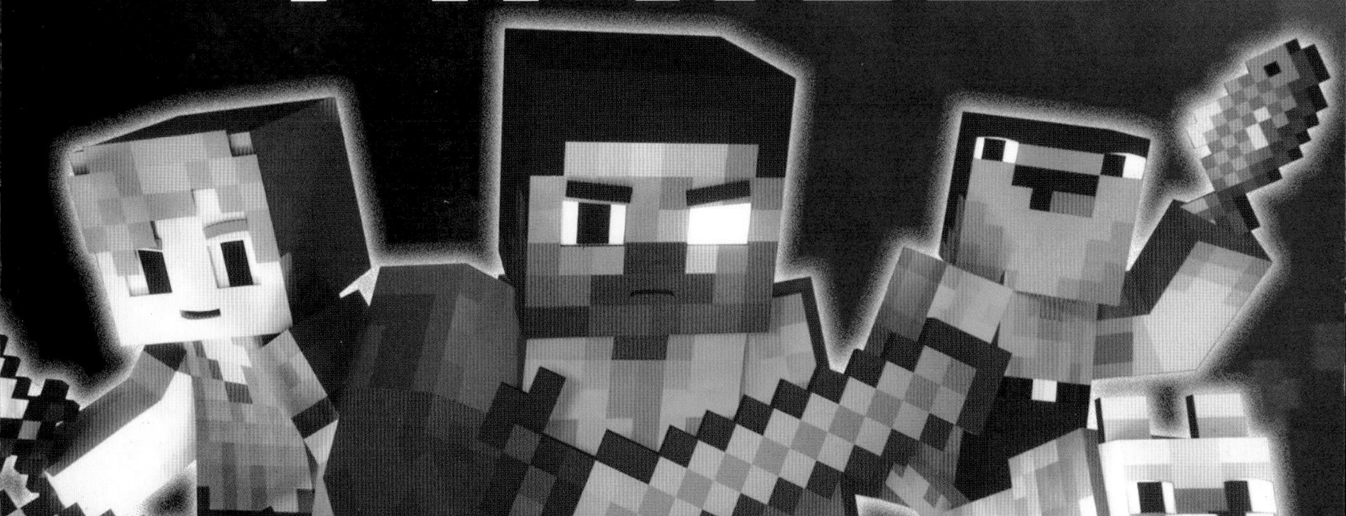

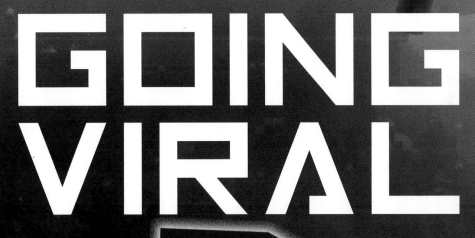

MORTIMER

THE STORY SO FAR...

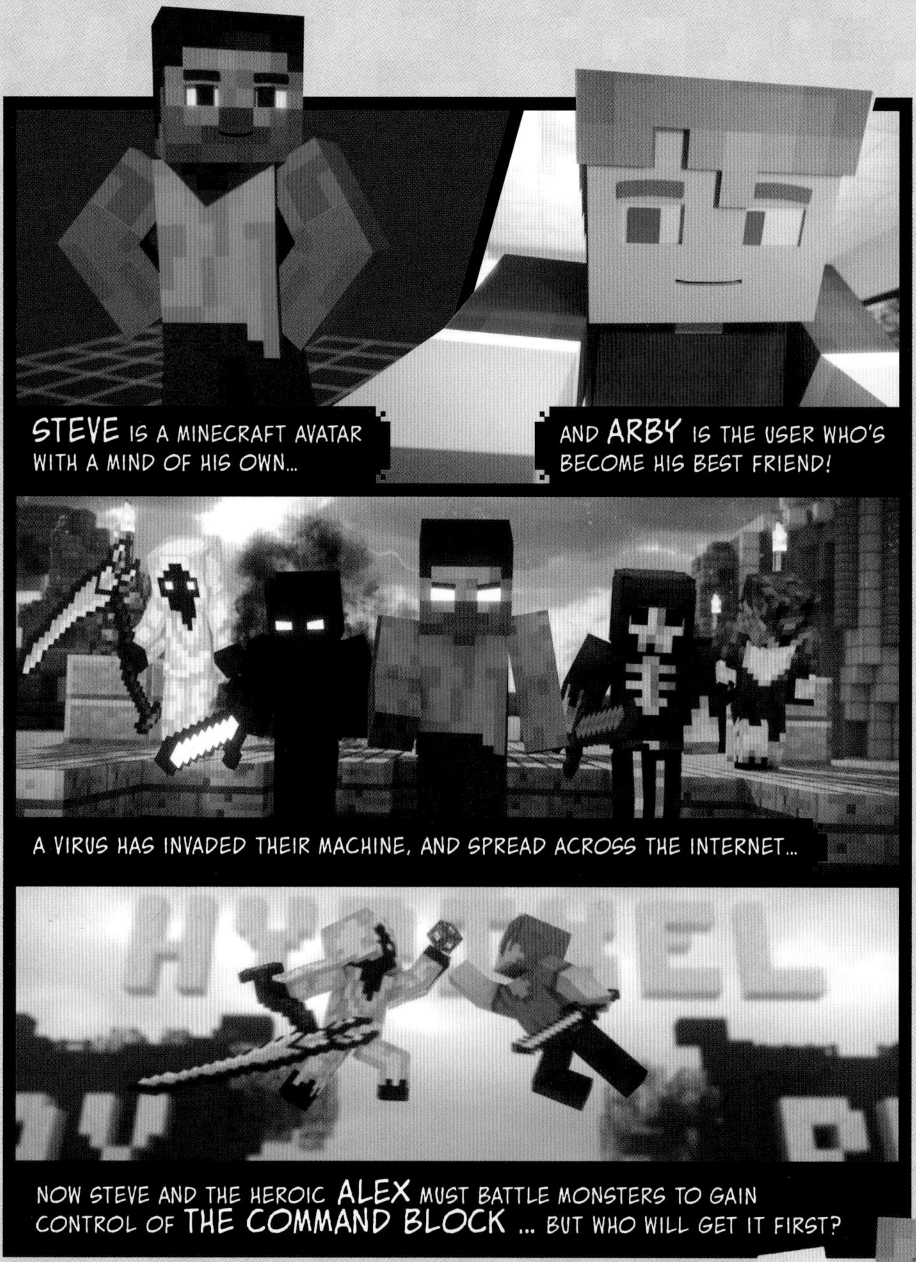
STEVE IS A MINECRAFT AVATAR WITH A MIND OF HIS OWN...
AND ARBY IS THE USER WHO'S BECOME HIS BEST FRIEND!
A VIRUS HAS INVADED THEIR MACHINE, AND SPREAD ACROSS THE INTERNET...
NOW STEVE AND THE HEROIC ALEX MUST BATTLE MONSTERS TO GAIN CONTROL OF THE COMMAND BLOCK ... BUT WHO WILL GET IT FIRST?

ABOUT THE CREATOR

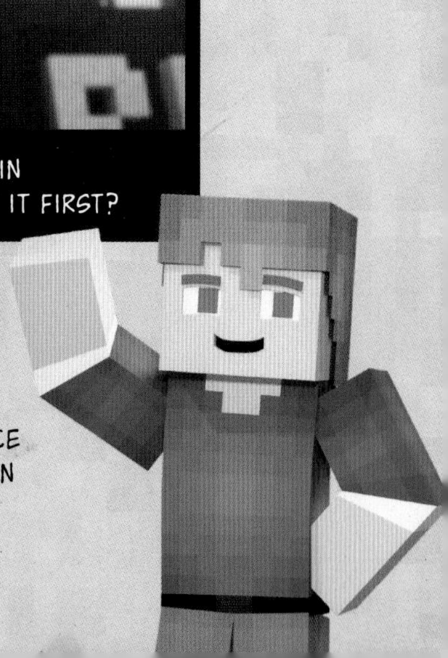

DAVID ZOELLNER, BETTER KNOWN AS ARBITER 617, IS THE DRIVING FORCE BEHIND BLACK PLASMA STUDIOS, THE BLOCKBUSTER INTERNET ANIMATION POWERHOUSE THAT HAS CREATED VIDEOS WITH OVER 32 MILLION VIEWS. HE LIVES IN THE USA.

CHAPTER 5

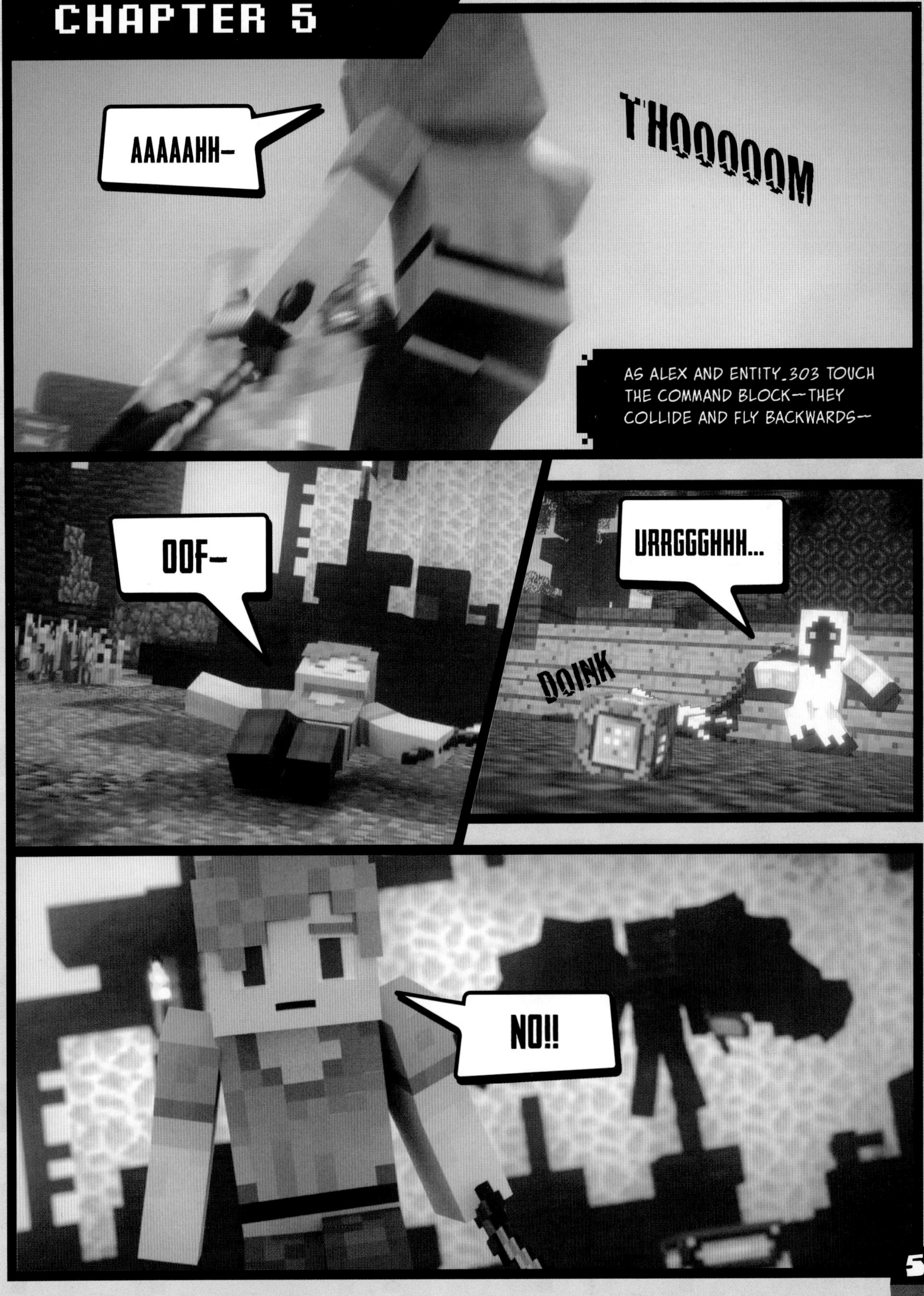

AAAAAHH–
THOOOOOM
AS ALEX AND ENTITY_303 TOUCH THE COMMAND BLOCK—THEY COLLIDE AND FLY BACKWARDS—
OOF–
URRGGGHHH...
DOINK
NO!!

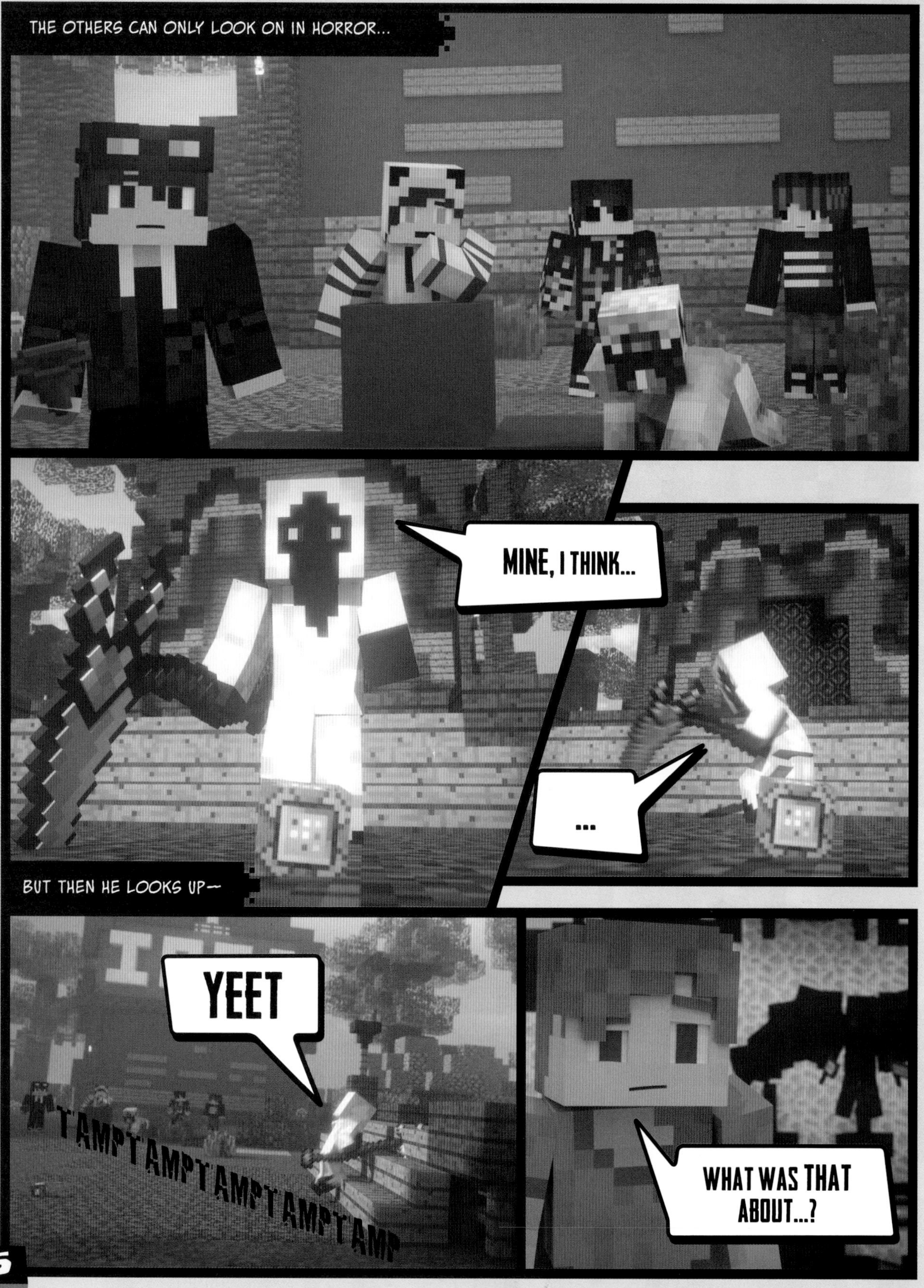
THE OTHERS CAN ONLY LOOK ON IN HORROR...
MINE, I THINK...
...
BUT THEN HE LOOKS UP—
YEET
TAMPTAMPTAMPTAMPTAMPTAMP
WHAT WAS THAT ABOUT...?

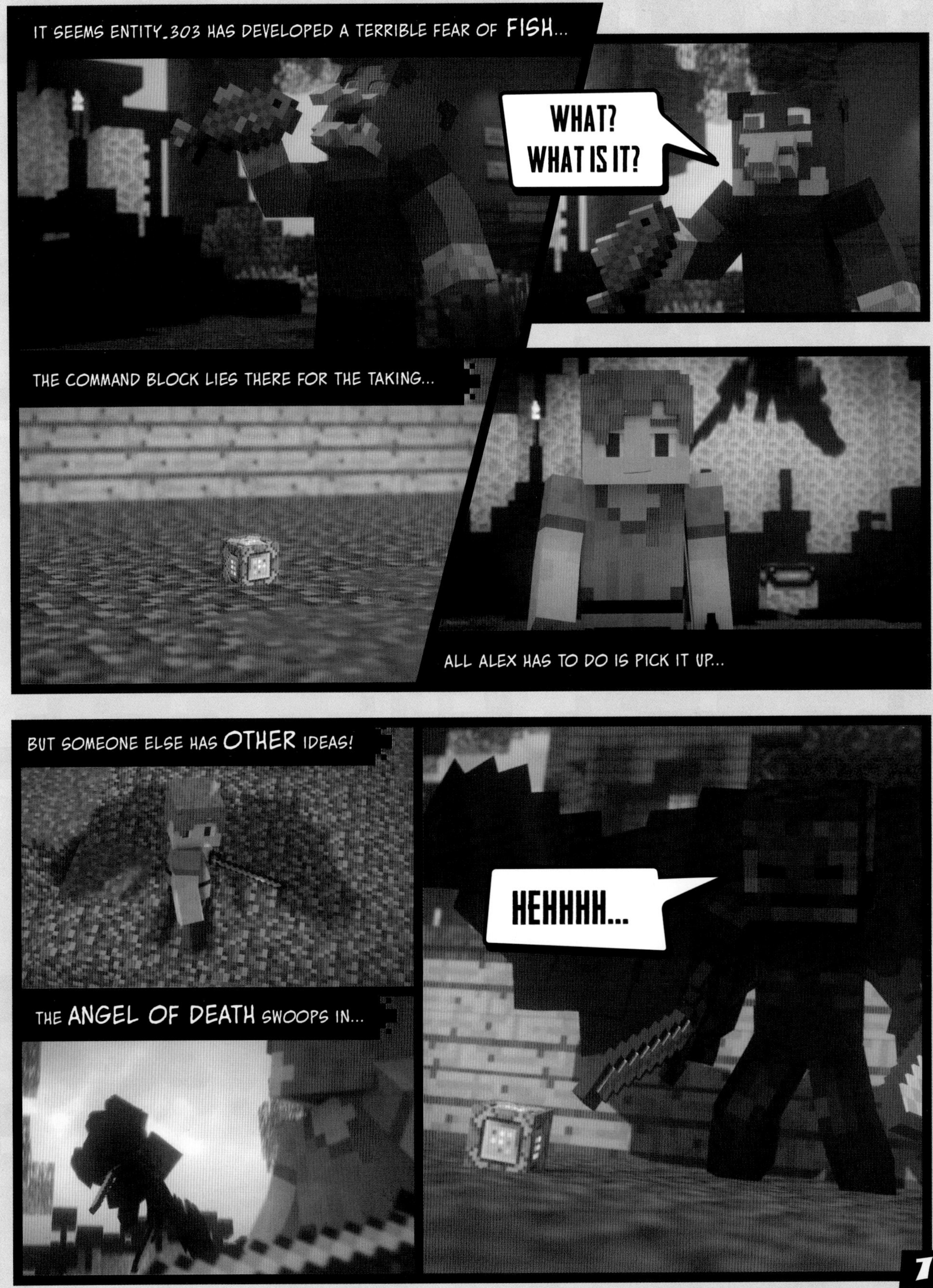
IT SEEMS ENTITY_303 HAS DEVELOPED A TERRIBLE FEAR OF FISH...
WHAT? WHAT IS IT?
THE COMMAND BLOCK LIES THERE FOR THE TAKING...
ALL ALEX HAS TO DO IS PICK IT UP...
BUT SOMEONE ELSE HAS OTHER IDEAS!
THE ANGEL OF DEATH SWOOPS IN...
HEHHHH...

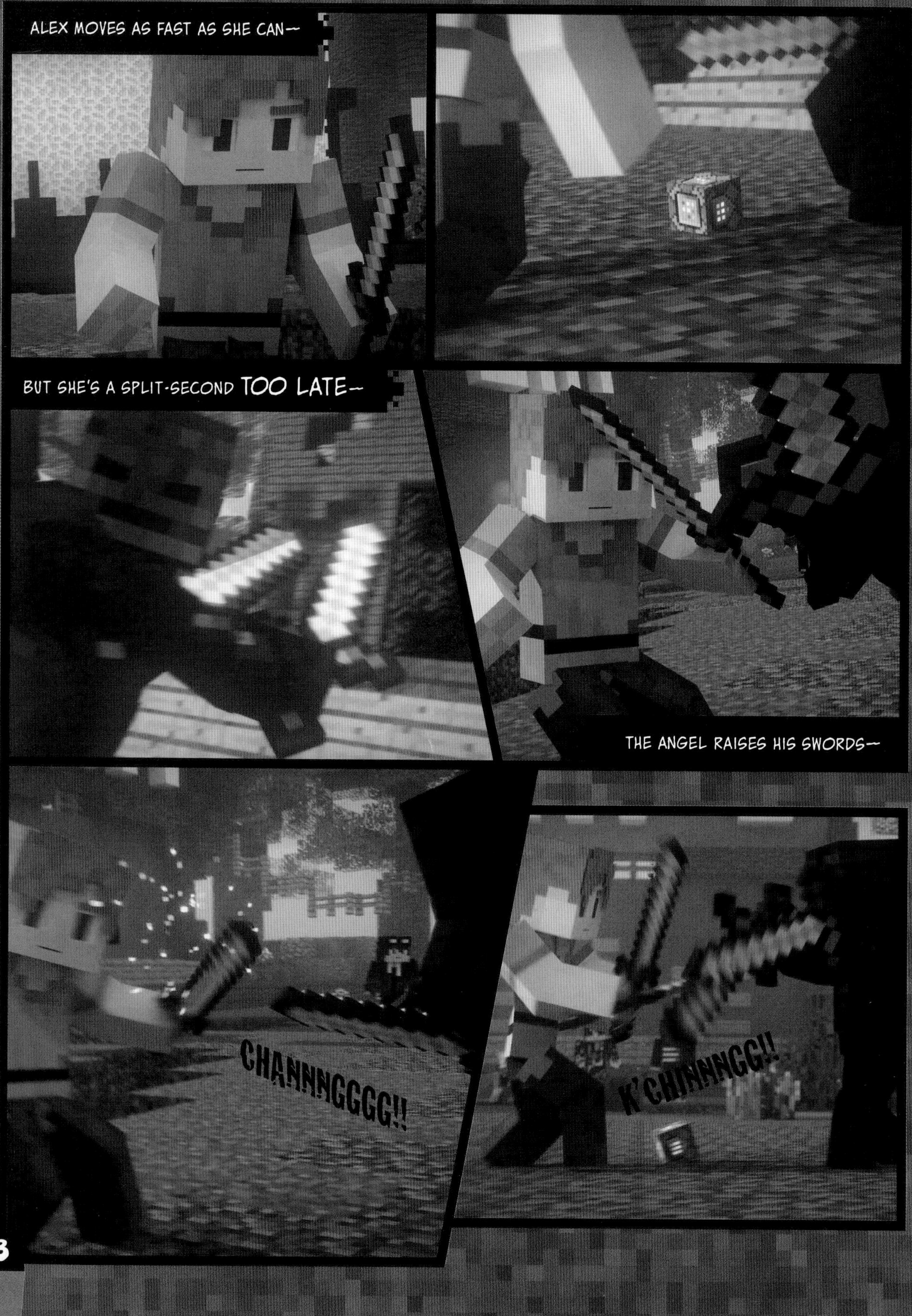
ALEX MOVES AS FAST AS SHE CAN—
BUT SHE'S A SPLIT-SECOND TOO LATE—
THE ANGEL RAISES HIS SWORDS—
CHANNNGGGG!!
K'CHINNNGG!!

MEANWHILE, **STEVE** IS STILL HOPPING FROM PLACE TO PLACE, LOOKING FOR ALEX...

ANY OF YOU GUYS SEEN A BUNCH OF PEOPLE FIGHTING OVER A COMMAND BLOCK...?

GUYS...?

ALEX DRIVES THE ANGEL BACK~

CRRSSSHHH

HEY!

DEMOLISHING DEFENSES SET UP BY **SPAWN779**~

UP TO THE TOP OF THE STEPS~

BUT THE ANGEL OVERPOWERS ALEX, THROWING HER AGAINST THE WALL~

NGGGHHH...

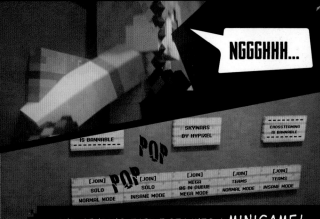

POP

POP

IS BANNABLE

SKYWARS
BY HYPIXEL

CROSSTEAMING
IS BANNABLE

[JOIN]
SOLO
NORMAL MODE

[JOIN]
SOLO
INSANE MODE

[JOIN]
MEGA
86 IN QUEUE
MEGA MODE

[JOIN]
TEAMS
NORMAL MODE

[JOIN]
TEAMS
INSANE MODE

AND SENDING THEM BOTH INTO A **MINIGAME!**

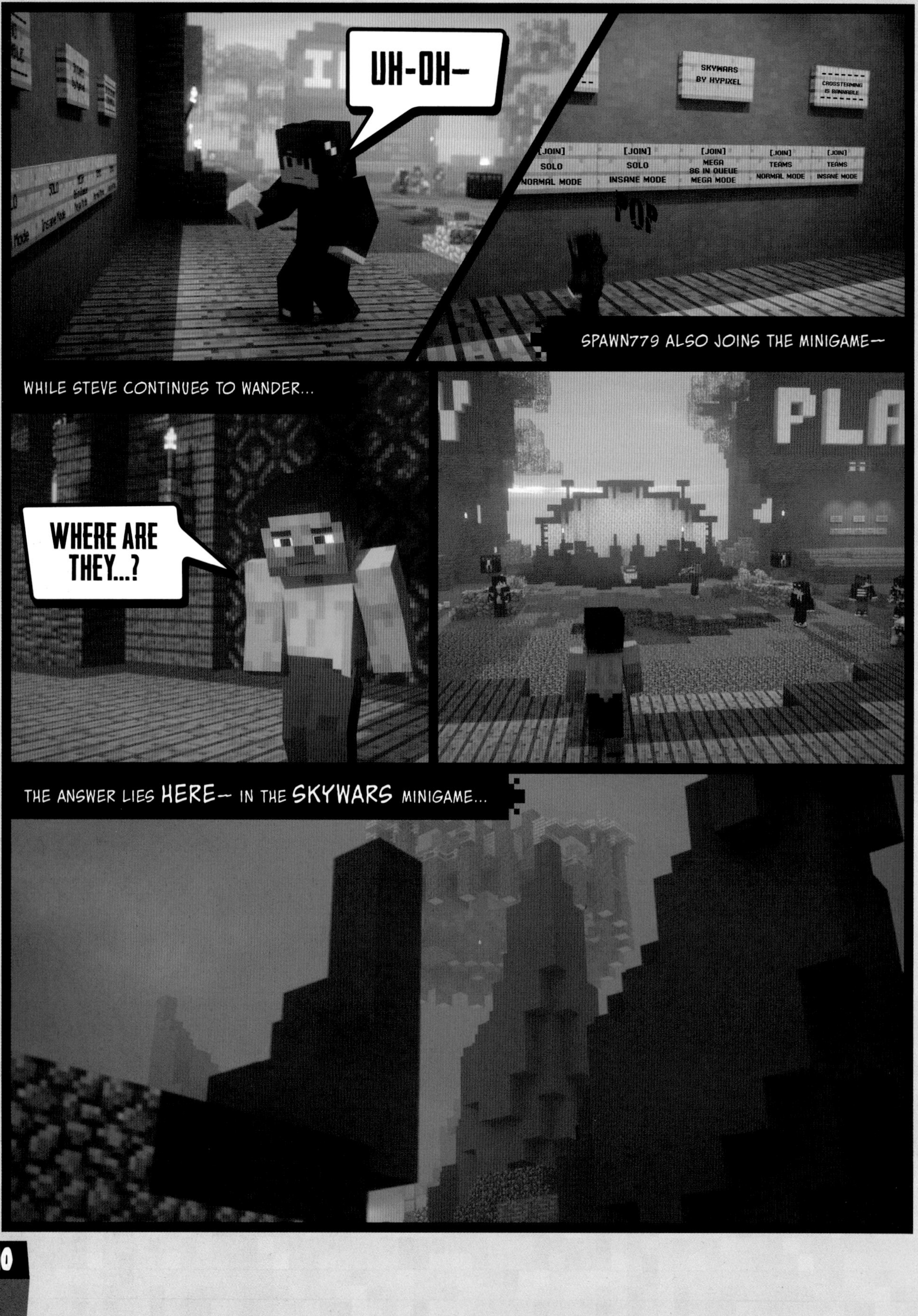

UH-OH–
SKYWARS
BY HYPIXEL
CROSSTEAMING IS BANNABLE
[JOIN] SOLO NORMAL MODE
[JOIN] SOLO INSANE MODE
[JOIN] MEGA 86 IN QUEUE MEGA MODE
[JOIN] TEAMS NORMAL MODE
[JOIN] TEAMS INSANE MODE
POP
SPAWN779 ALSO JOINS THE MINIGAME–
WHILE STEVE CONTINUES TO WANDER...
WHERE ARE THEY...?
PLA
THE ANSWER LIES HERE– IN THE SKYWARS MINIGAME...

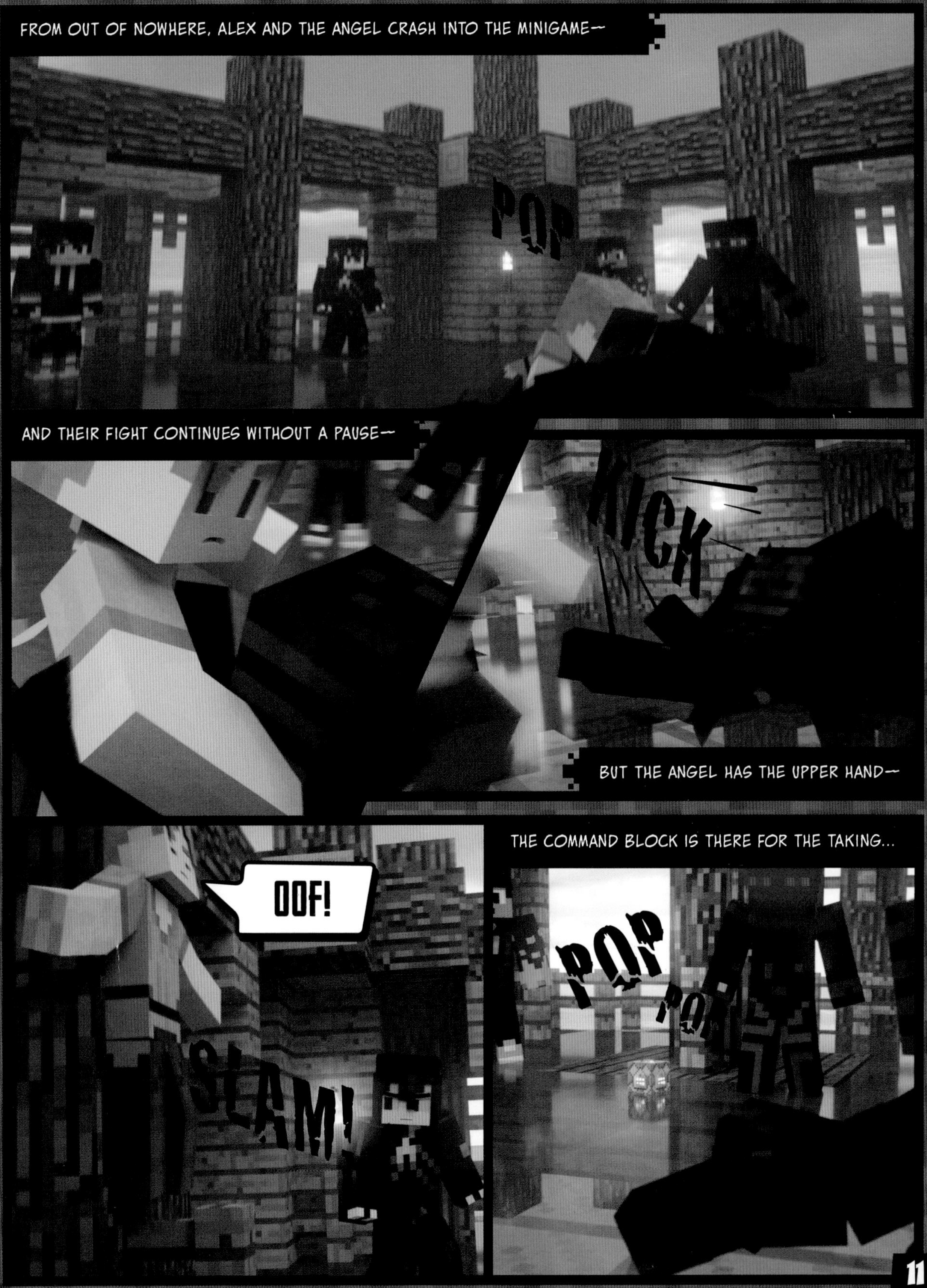
FROM OUT OF NOWHERE, ALEX AND THE ANGEL CRASH INTO THE MINIGAME—
POP
AND THEIR FIGHT CONTINUES WITHOUT A PAUSE—
KICK
BUT THE ANGEL HAS THE UPPER HAND—
OOF!
SLAM!
THE COMMAND BLOCK IS THERE FOR THE TAKING...
POP

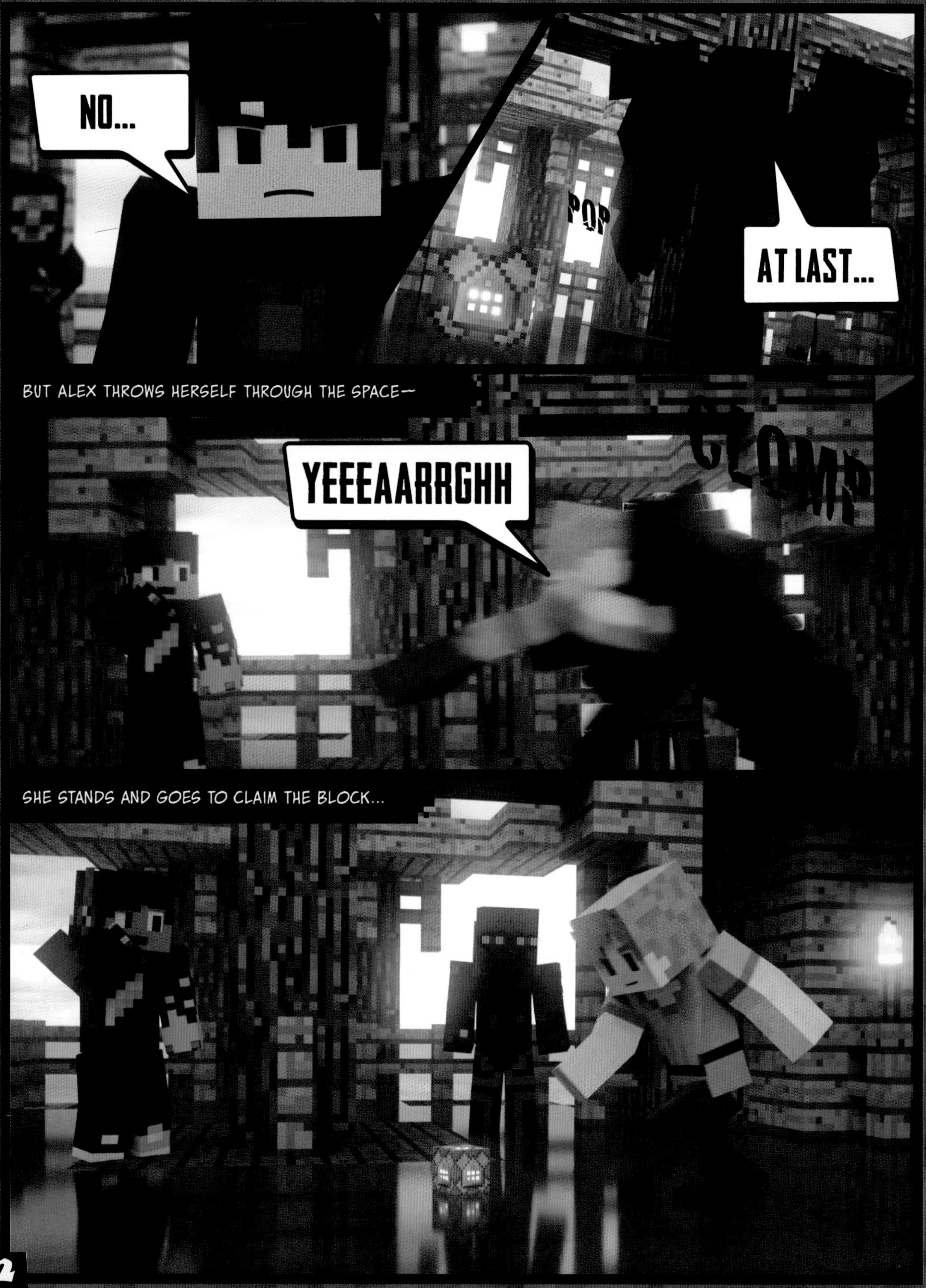
NO...
POP
AT LAST...
BUT ALEX THROWS HERSELF THROUGH THE SPACE–
YEEEAARRGHH
CLOMP
SHE STANDS AND GOES TO CLAIM THE BLOCK...

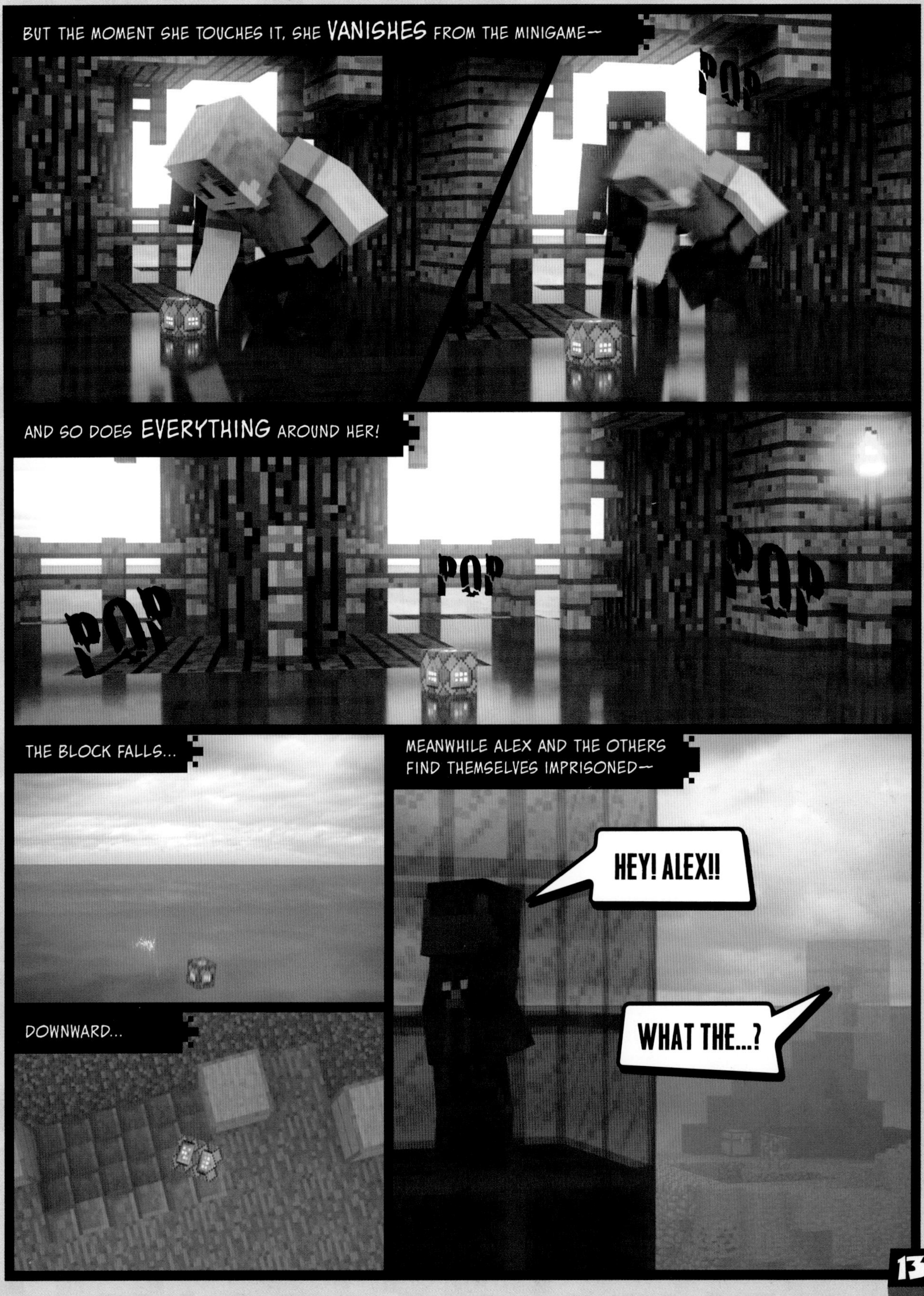
BUT THE MOMENT SHE TOUCHES IT, SHE VANISHES FROM THE MINIGAME—
POP
AND SO DOES EVERYTHING AROUND HER!
POP
POP
POP
THE BLOCK FALLS...
DOWNWARD...
MEANWHILE ALEX AND THE OTHERS FIND THEMSELVES IMPRISONED—
HEY! ALEX!!
WHAT THE...?

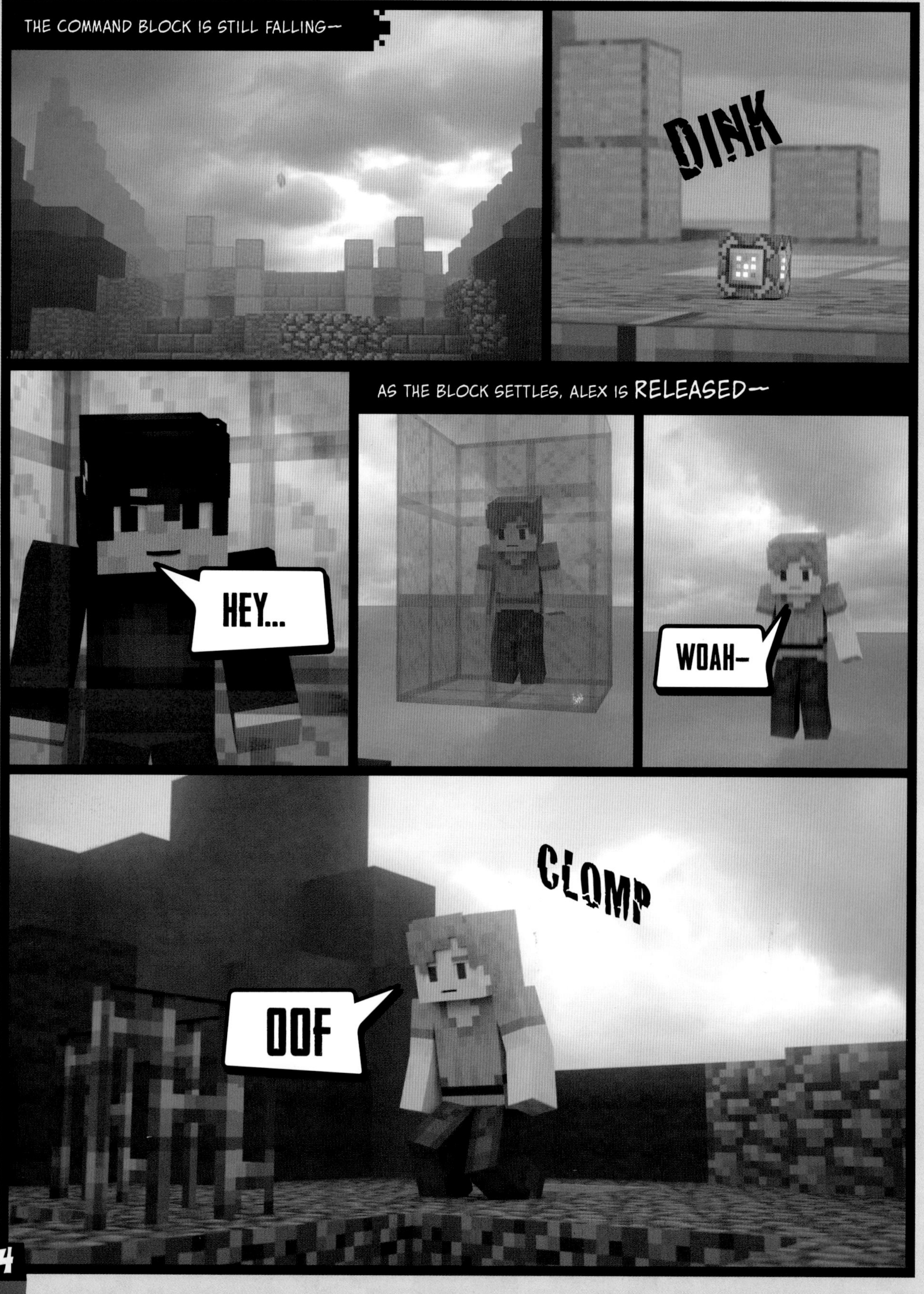
THE COMMAND BLOCK IS STILL FALLING—
DINK
HEY...
AS THE BLOCK SETTLES, ALEX IS RELEASED—
WOAH-
CLOMP
OOF

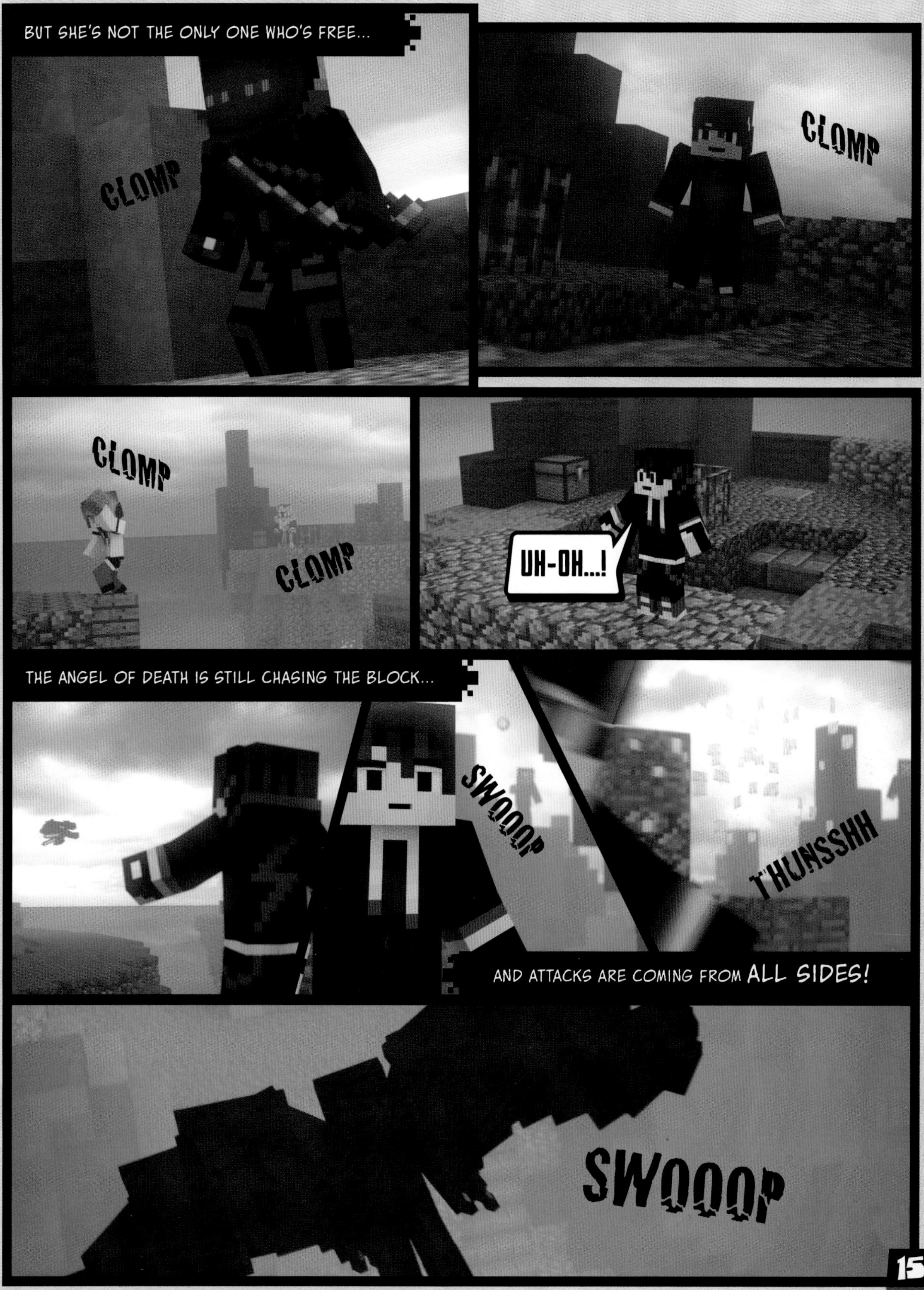
BUT SHE'S NOT THE ONLY ONE WHO'S FREE...
CLOMP
CLOMP
CLOMP
CLOMP
UH-OH...!
THE ANGEL OF DEATH IS STILL CHASING THE BLOCK...
SWOOOP
THUNSSHH
AND ATTACKS ARE COMING FROM ALL SIDES!
SWOOOP

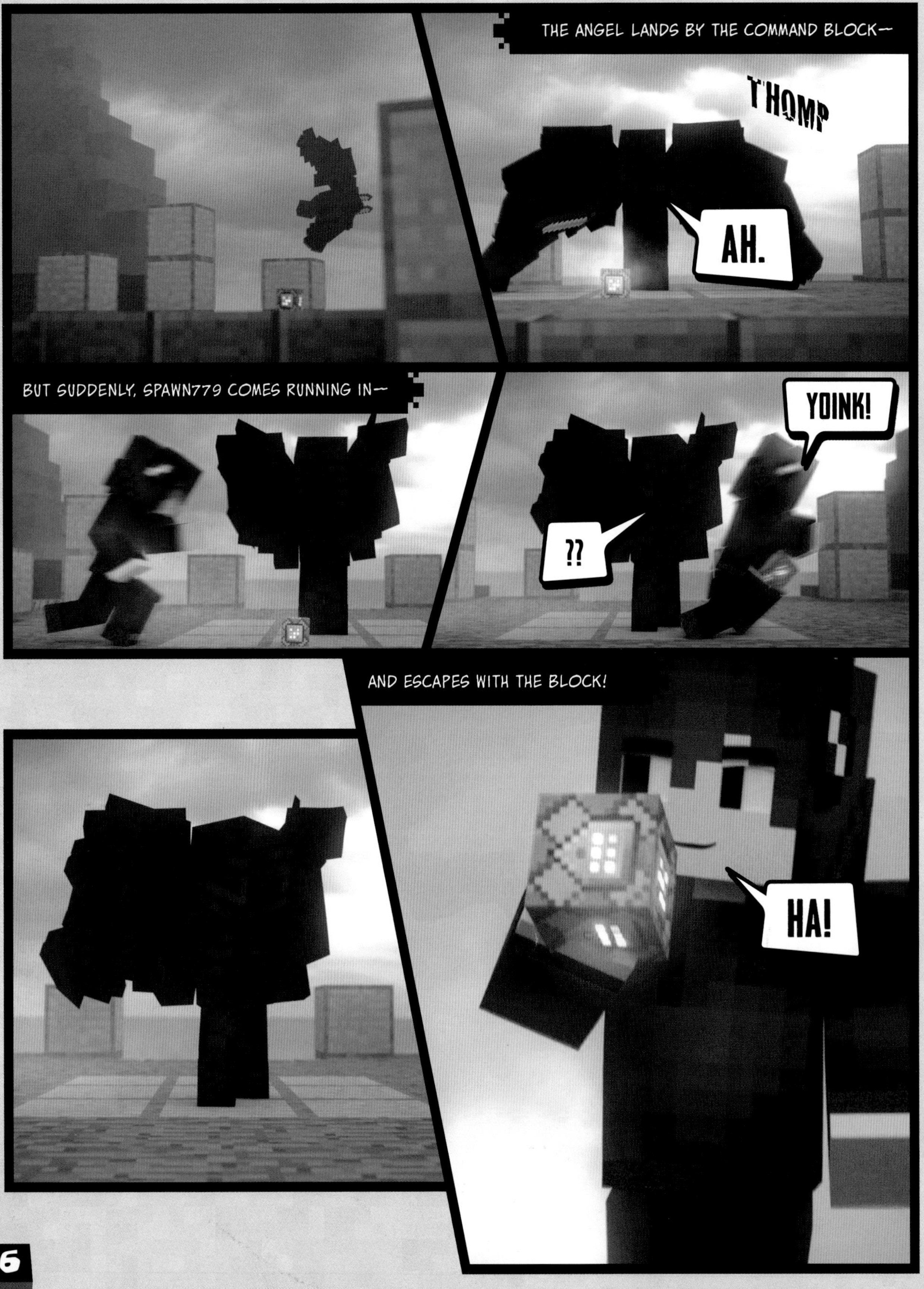
THE ANGEL LANDS BY THE COMMAND BLOCK—
THOMP
AH.
BUT SUDDENLY, SPAWN779 COMES RUNNING IN—
YOINK!
??
AND ESCAPES WITH THE BLOCK!
HA!

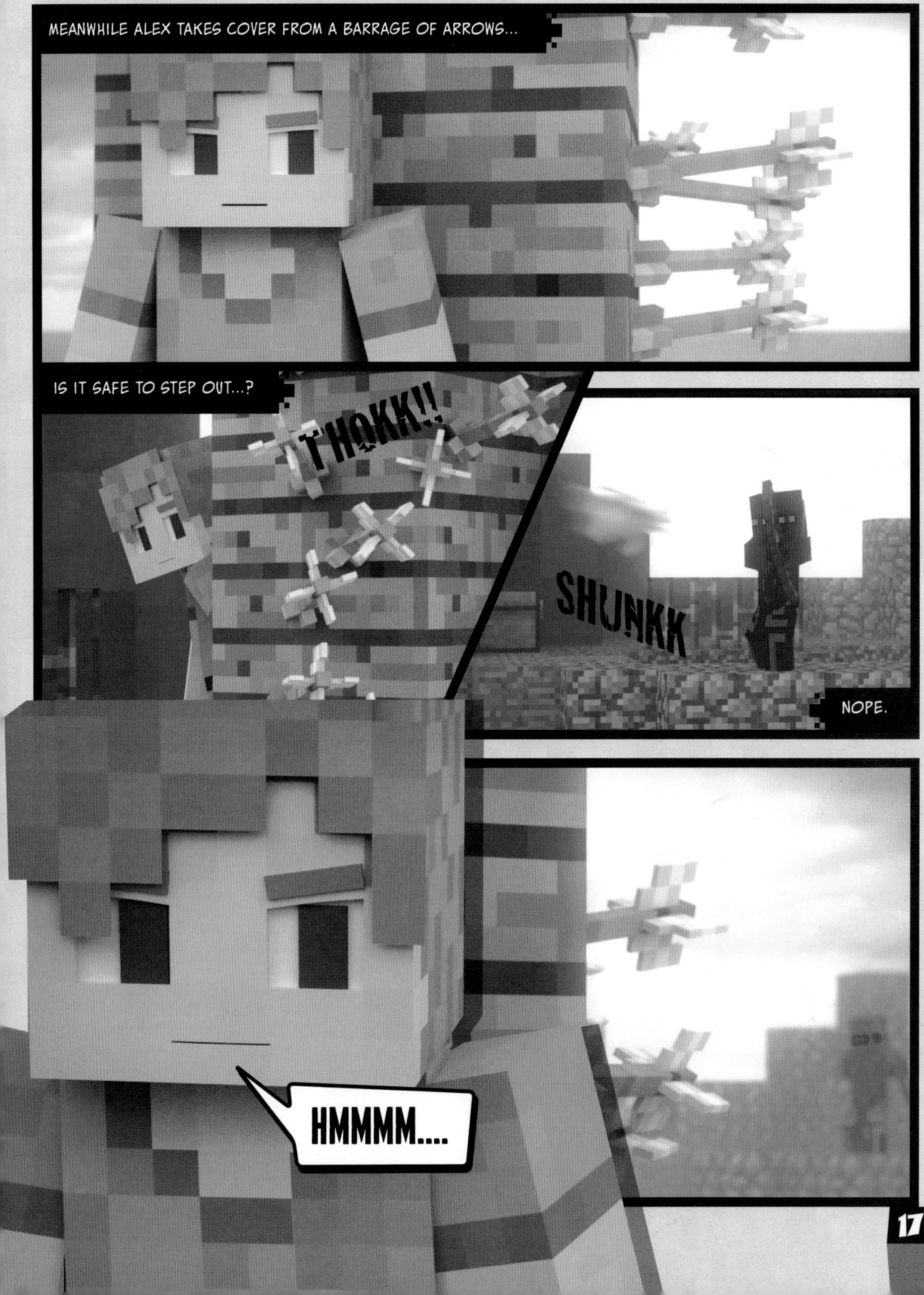
MEANWHILE ALEX TAKES COVER FROM A BARRAGE OF ARROWS...
IS IT SAFE TO STEP OUT...?
THOKK!!
SHUNKK
NOPE.
HMMMM....

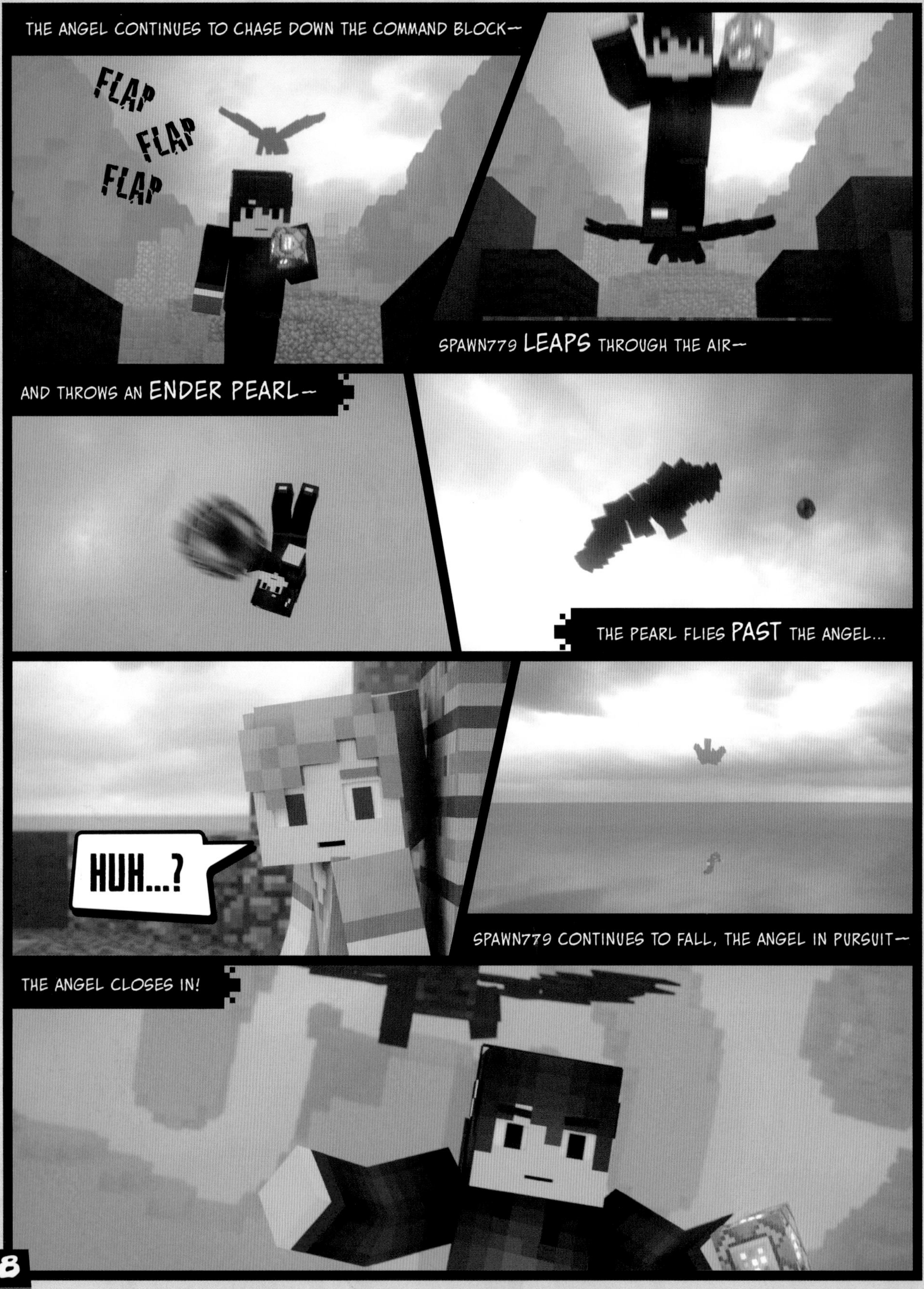
THE ANGEL CONTINUES TO CHASE DOWN THE COMMAND BLOCK—
FLAP
FLAP
FLAP
SPAWN779 LEAPS THROUGH THE AIR—
AND THROWS AN ENDER PEARL—
THE PEARL FLIES PAST THE ANGEL...
HUH...?
SPAWN779 CONTINUES TO FALL, THE ANGEL IN PURSUIT—
THE ANGEL CLOSES IN!

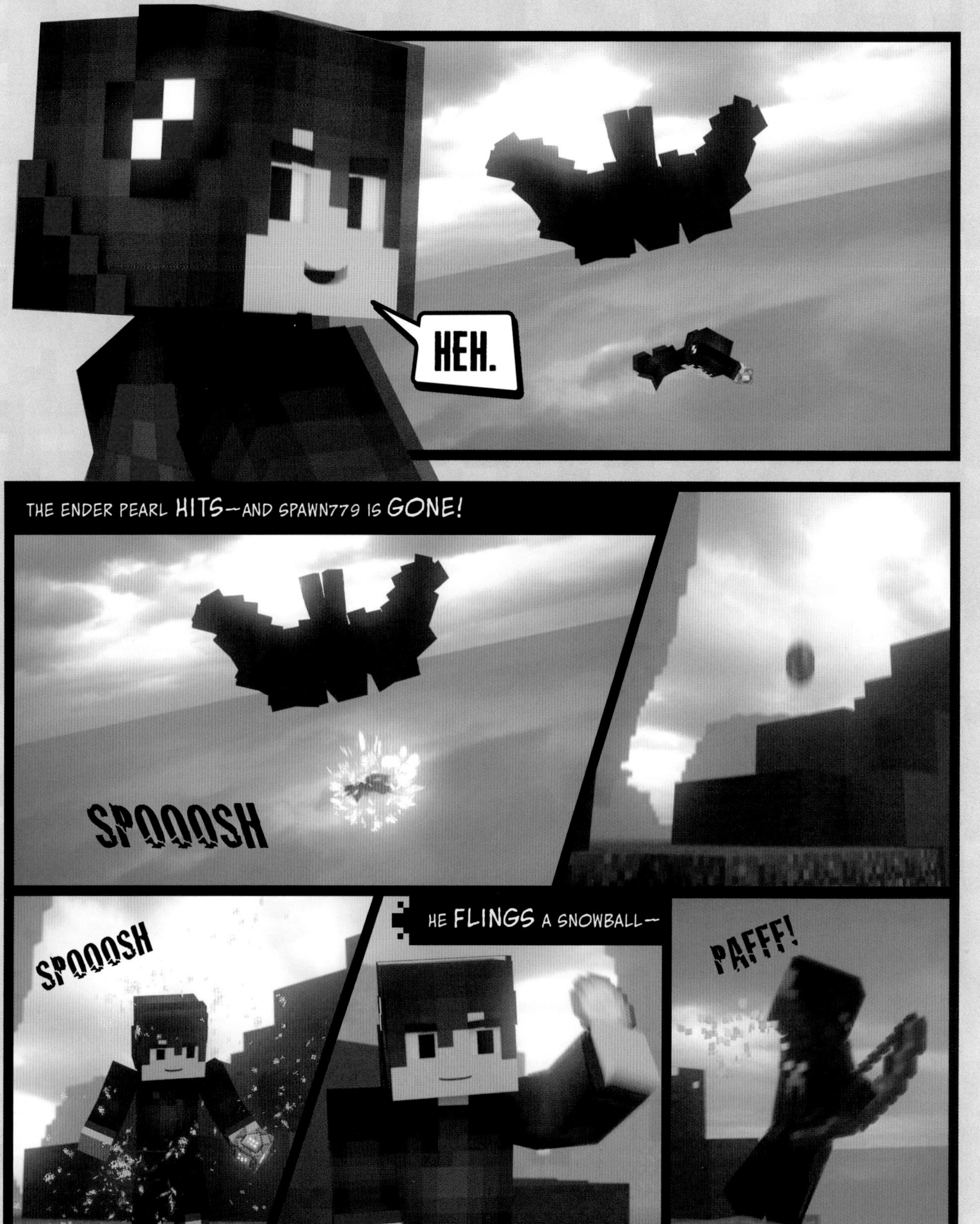
HEH.
THE ENDER PEARL HITS—AND SPAWN779 IS GONE!
SPOOOSH
SPOOOSH
HE FLINGS A SNOWBALL—
PAFFF!

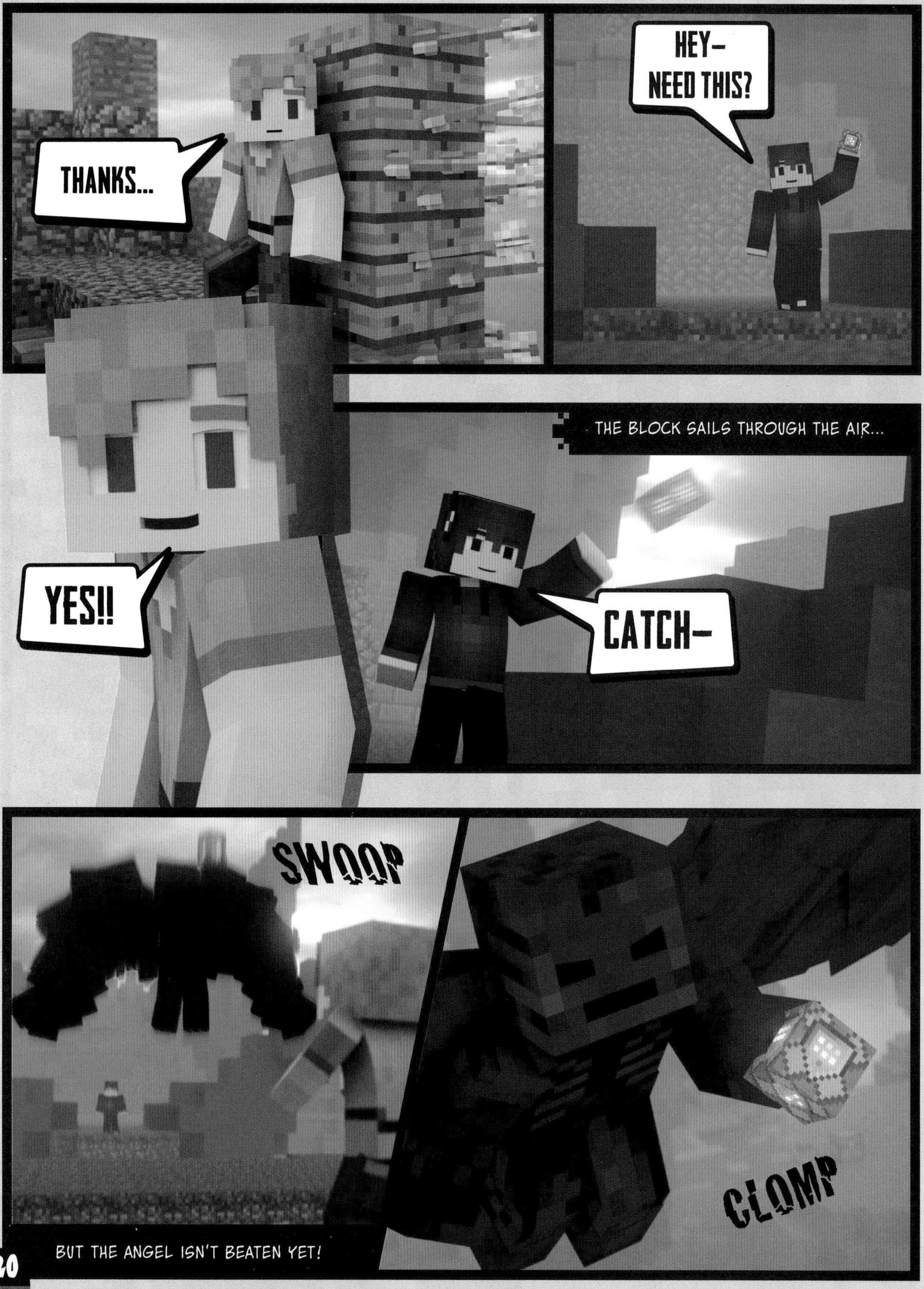
THANKS...
HEY– NEED THIS?
THE BLOCK SAILS THROUGH THE AIR...
YES!!
CATCH–
SWOOP
CLOMP
BUT THE ANGEL ISN'T BEATEN YET!

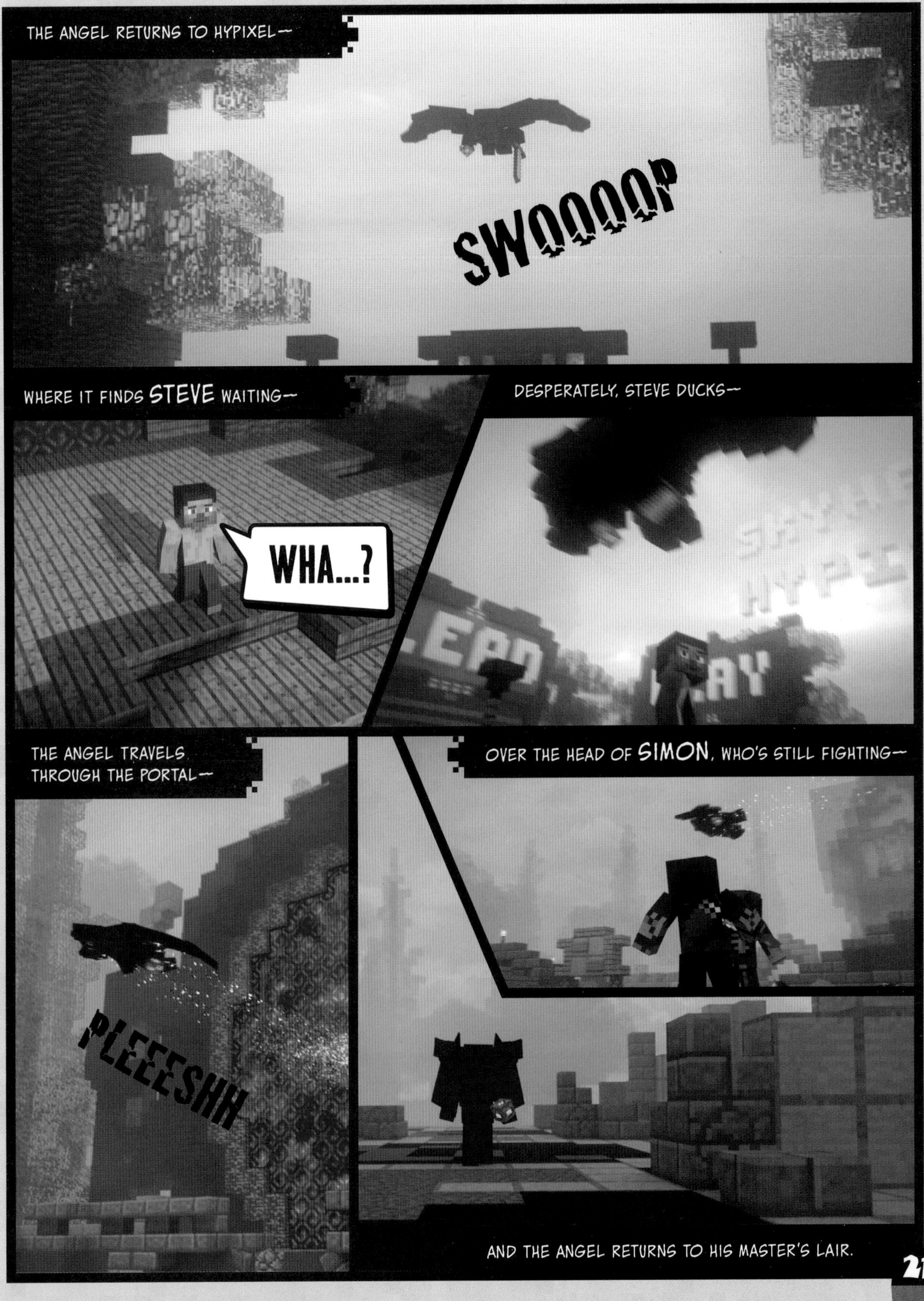
THE ANGEL RETURNS TO HYPIXEL—
SWOOOOP
WHERE IT FINDS STEVE WAITING—
WHA...?
DESPERATELY, STEVE DUCKS—
THE ANGEL TRAVELS THROUGH THE PORTAL—
PLEEESHH
OVER THE HEAD OF SIMON, WHO'S STILL FIGHTING—
AND THE ANGEL RETURNS TO HIS MASTER'S LAIR.

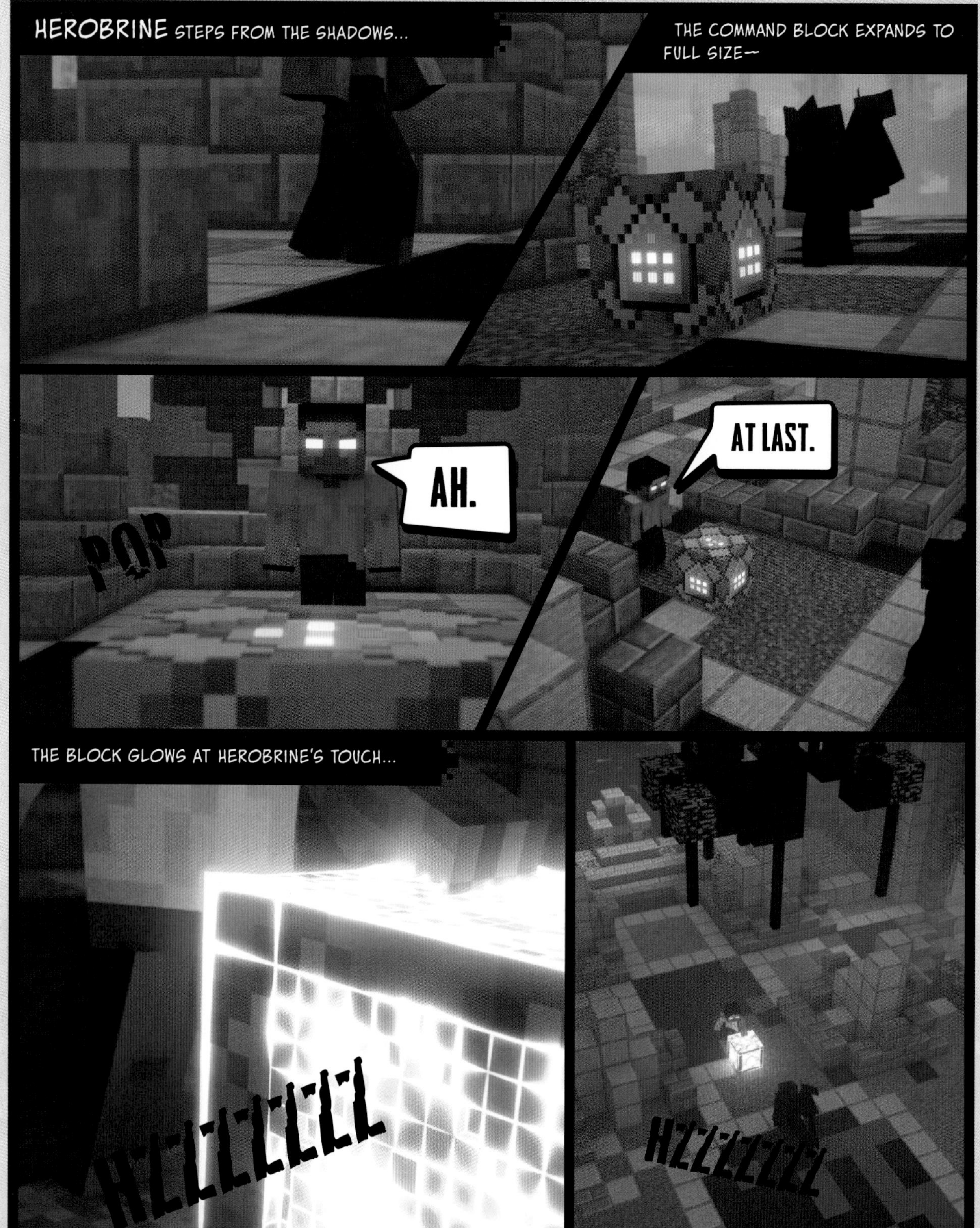
HEROBRINE STEPS FROM THE SHADOWS...
THE COMMAND BLOCK EXPANDS TO FULL SIZE—
POP
AH.
AT LAST.
THE BLOCK GLOWS AT HEROBRINE'S TOUCH...
HZZZZZZZ
HZZZZZZZ

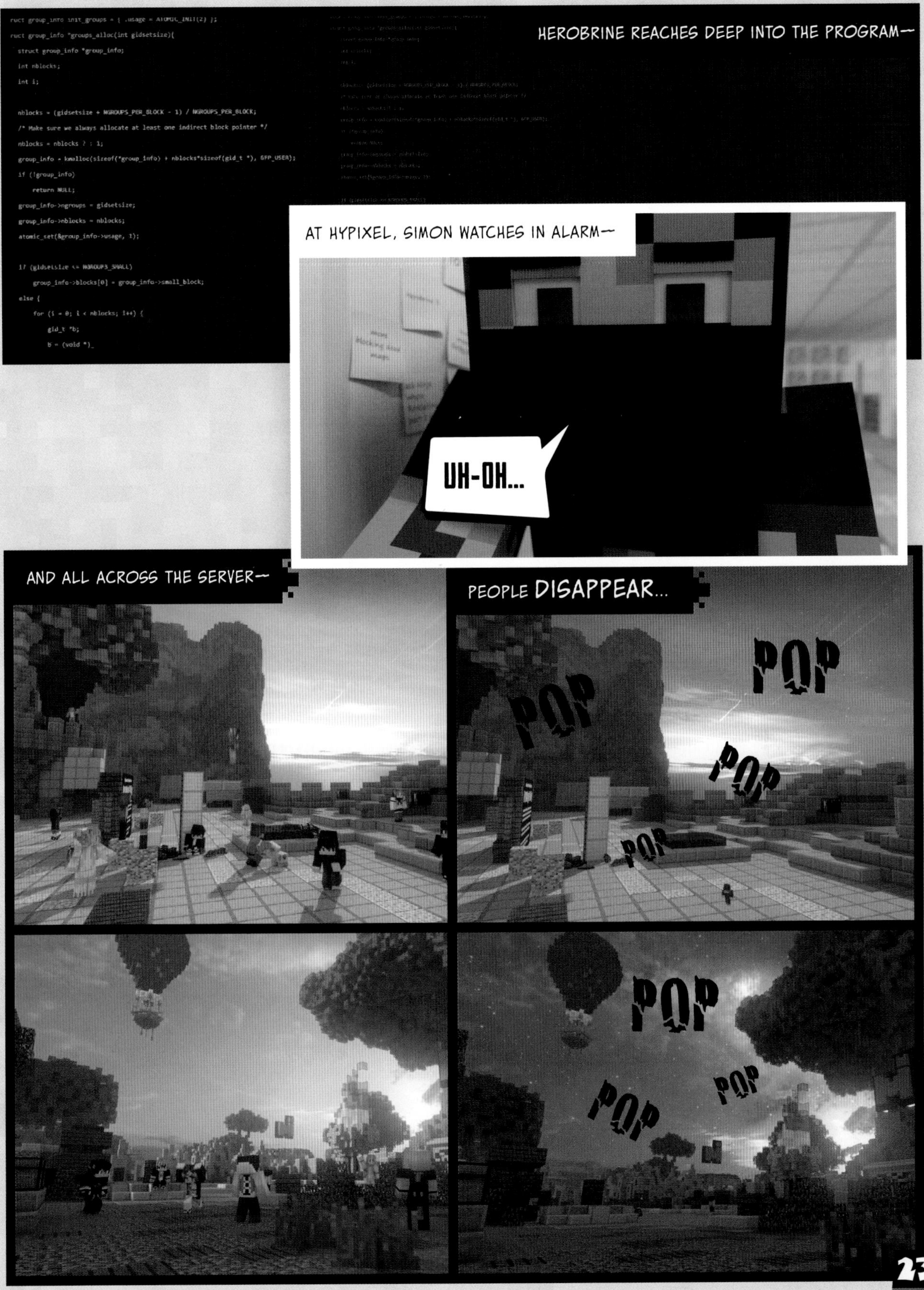

ruct group_info init_groups = { .usage = ATOMIC_INIT(2) };
ruct group_info *groups_alloc(int gidsetsize){
struct group_info *group_info;
int nblocks;
int i;
nblocks = (gidsetsize + NGROUPS_PER_BLOCK - 1) / NGROUPS_PER_BLOCK;
/* Make sure we always allocate at least one indirect block pointer */
nblocks = nblocks ? : 1;
group_info = kmalloc(sizeof(*group_info) + nblocks*sizeof(gid_t *), GFP_USER);
if (!group_info)
return NULL;
group_info->ngroups = gidsetsize;
group_info->nblocks = nblocks;
atomic_set(&group_info->usage, 1);
if (gidsetsize <= NGROUPS_SMALL)
group_info->blocks[0] = group_info->small_block;
else {
for (i = 0; i < nblocks; i++) {
gid_t *b;
b = (void *)_
HEROBRINE REACHES DEEP INTO THE PROGRAM—
AT HYPIXEL, SIMON WATCHES IN ALARM—
UH-OH...
AND ALL ACROSS THE SERVER—
PEOPLE DISAPPEAR...
POP
POP
POP
POP
POP
POP
POP

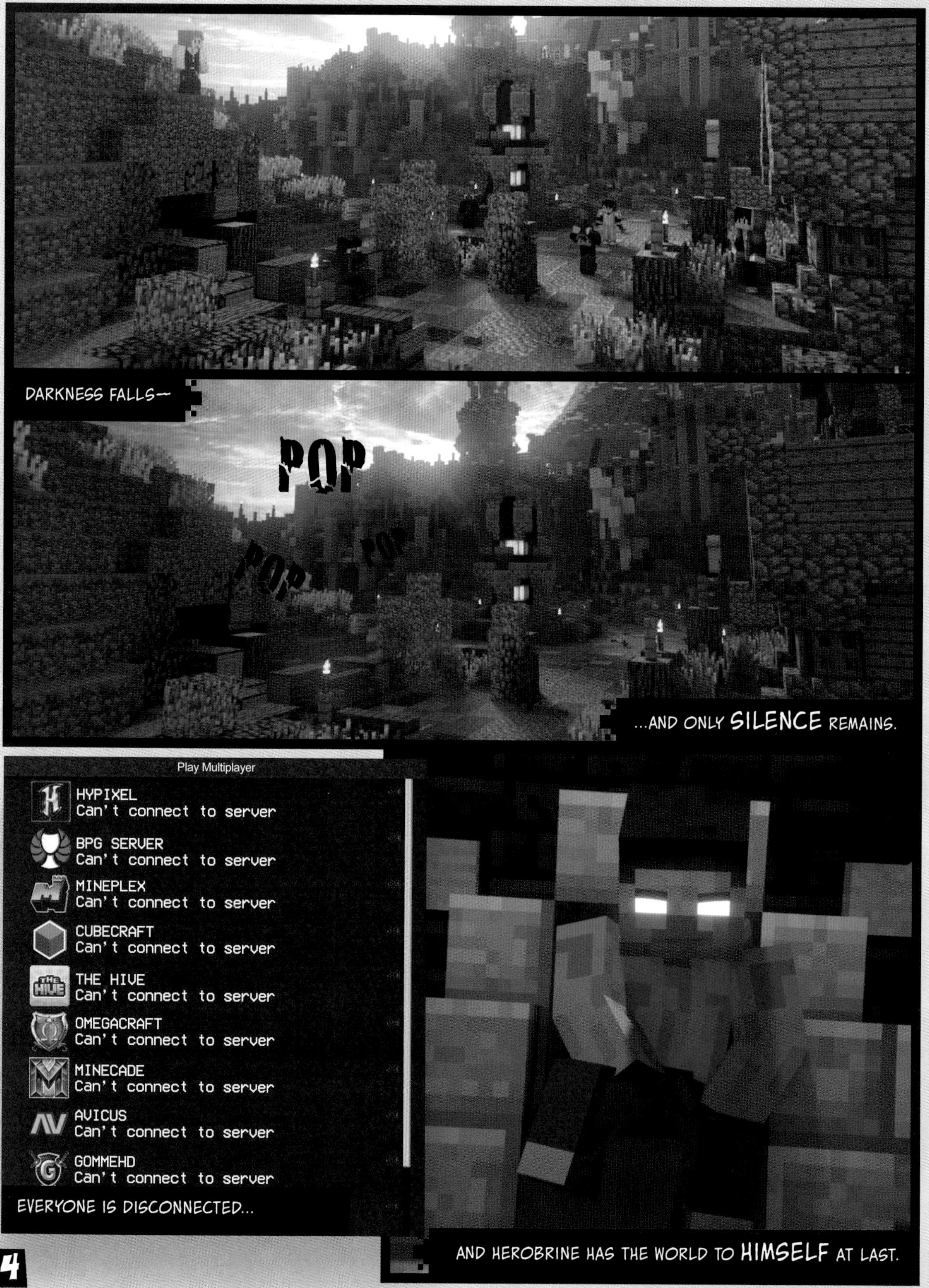

DARKNESS FALLS—
POP
POP
POP
...AND ONLY SILENCE REMAINS.
Play Multiplayer
HYPIXEL
Can't connect to server
BPG SERVER
Can't connect to server
MINEPLEX
Can't connect to server
CUBECRAFT
Can't connect to server
THE HIVE
Can't connect to server
OMEGACRAFT
Can't connect to server
MINECADE
Can't connect to server
AVICUS
Can't connect to server
GOMMEHD
Can't connect to server
EVERYONE IS DISCONNECTED...
AND HEROBRINE HAS THE WORLD TO HIMSELF AT LAST.

CHAPTER 6

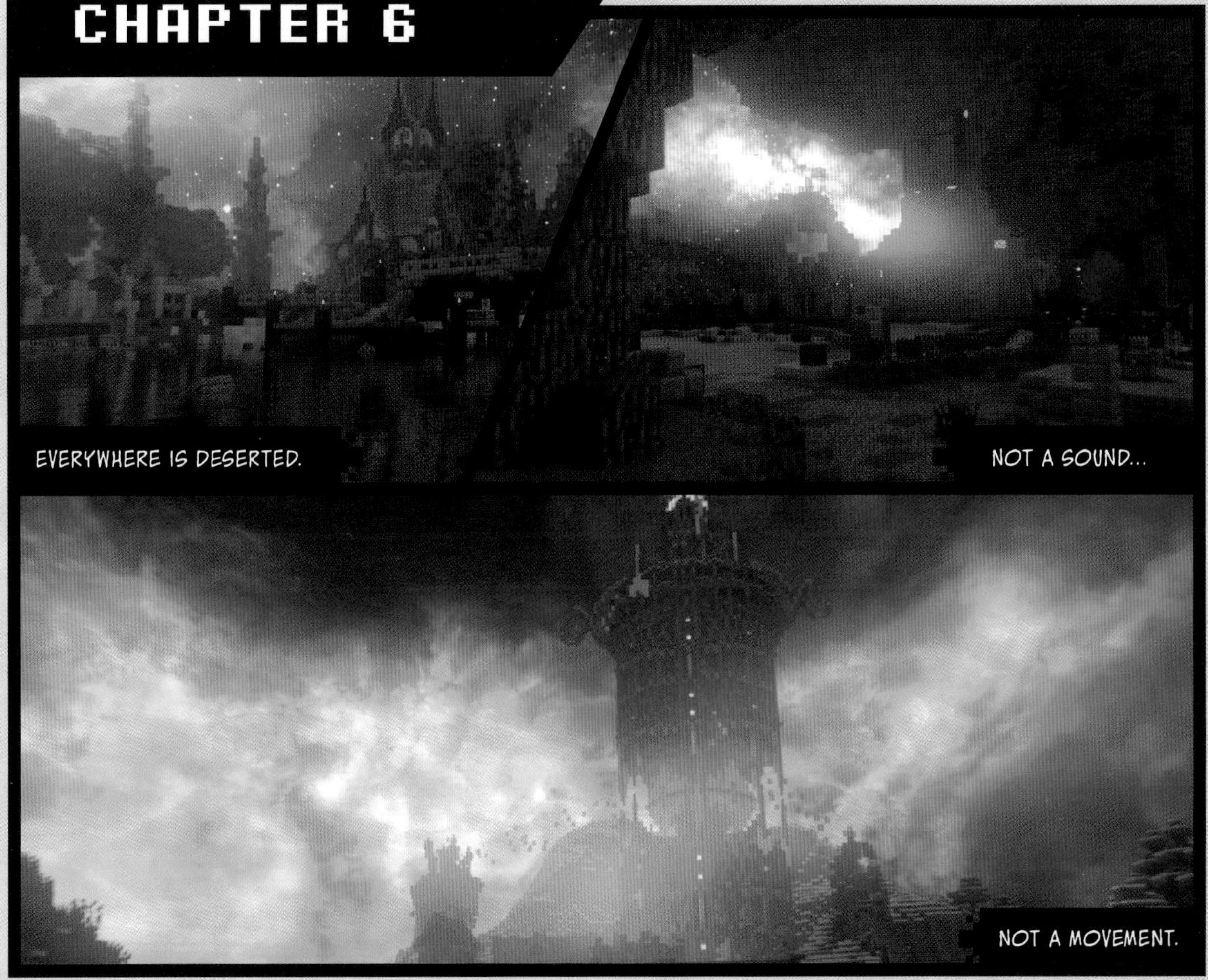
EVERYWHERE IS DESERTED.
NOT A SOUND...
NOT A MOVEMENT.

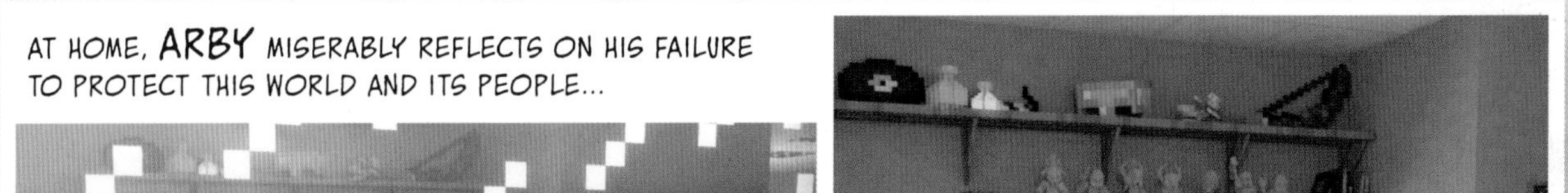
AT HOME, ARBY MISERABLY REFLECTS ON HIS FAILURE TO PROTECT THIS WORLD AND ITS PEOPLE...

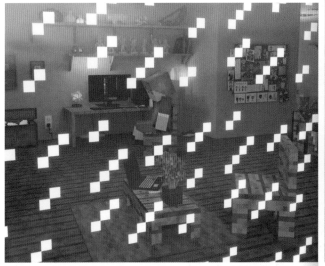

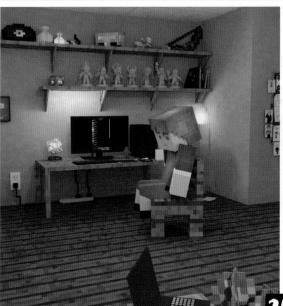

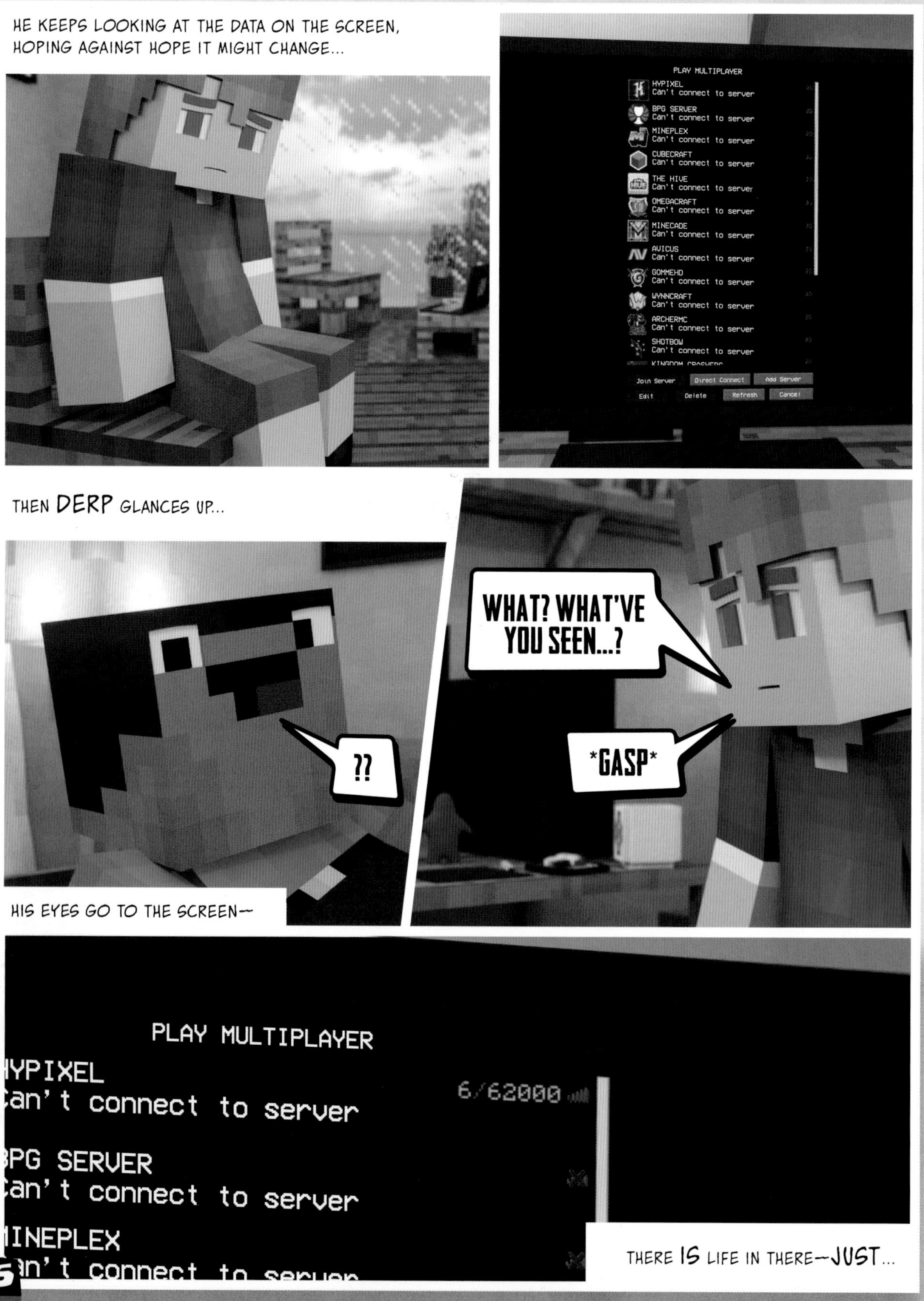
HE KEEPS LOOKING AT THE DATA ON THE SCREEN, HOPING AGAINST HOPE IT MIGHT CHANGE...
PLAY MULTIPLAYER
HYPIXEL
Can't connect to server
BPG SERVER
Can't connect to server
MINEPLEX
Can't connect to server
CUBECRAFT
Can't connect to server
THE HIVE
Can't connect to server
OMEGACRAFT
Can't connect to server
MINECADE
Can't connect to server
AVICUS
Can't connect to server
GOMMEHD
Can't connect to server
WYNNCRAFT
Can't connect to server
ARCHERMC
Can't connect to server
SHOTBOW
Can't connect to server
Join Server
Direct Connect
Add Server
Edit
Delete
Refresh
Cancel
THEN DERP GLANCES UP...
??
HIS EYES GO TO THE SCREEN—
WHAT? WHAT'VE YOU SEEN...?
GASP
PLAY MULTIPLAYER
HYPIXEL
Can't connect to server
6/62000
BPG SERVER
Can't connect to server
MINEPLEX
Can't connect to server
THERE IS LIFE IN THERE—JUST...

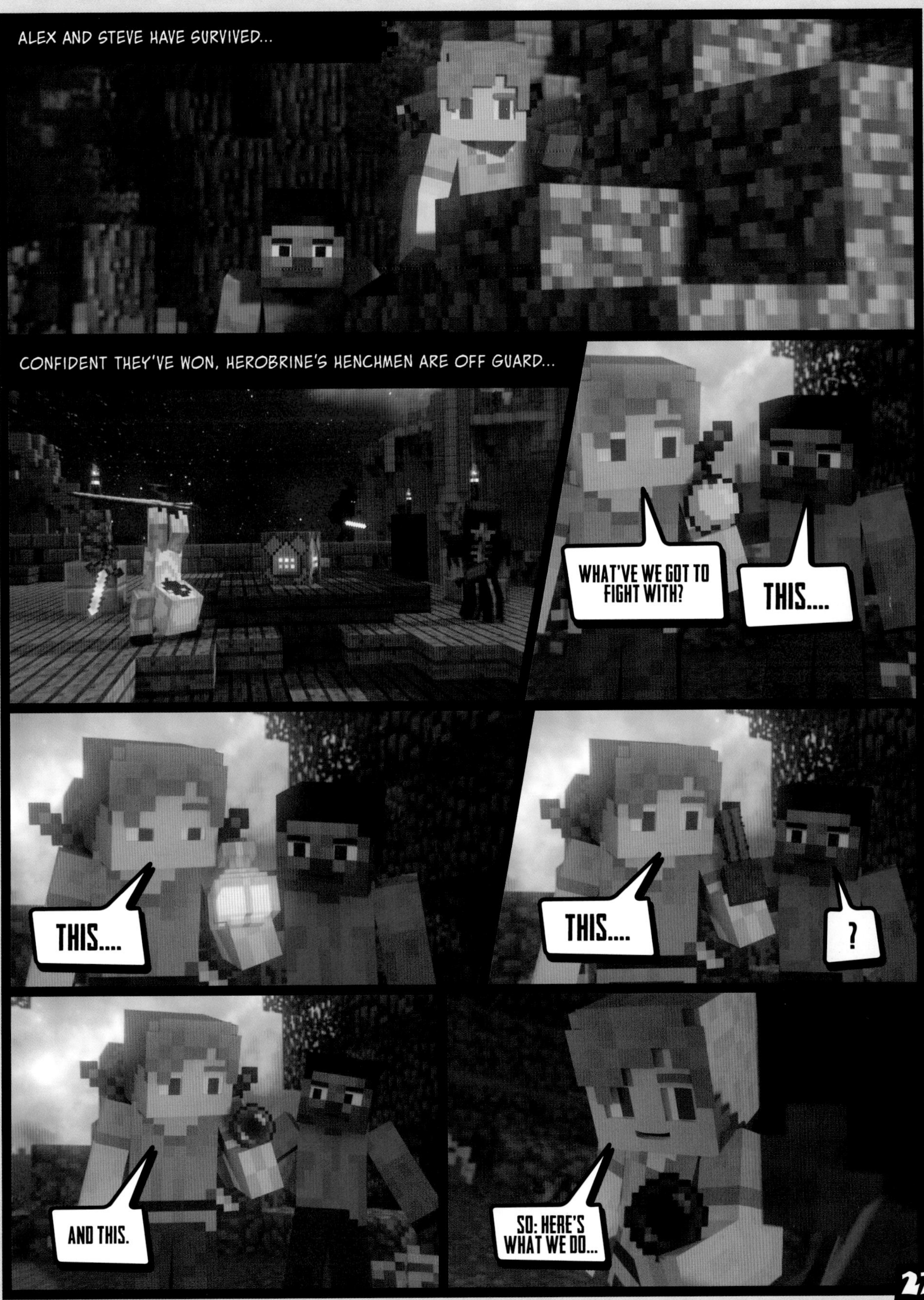
ALEX AND STEVE HAVE SURVIVED...
CONFIDENT THEY'VE WON, HEROBRINE'S HENCHMEN ARE OFF GUARD...
WHAT'VE WE GOT TO FIGHT WITH?
THIS....
THIS....
THIS....
?
AND THIS.
SO: HERE'S WHAT WE DO...

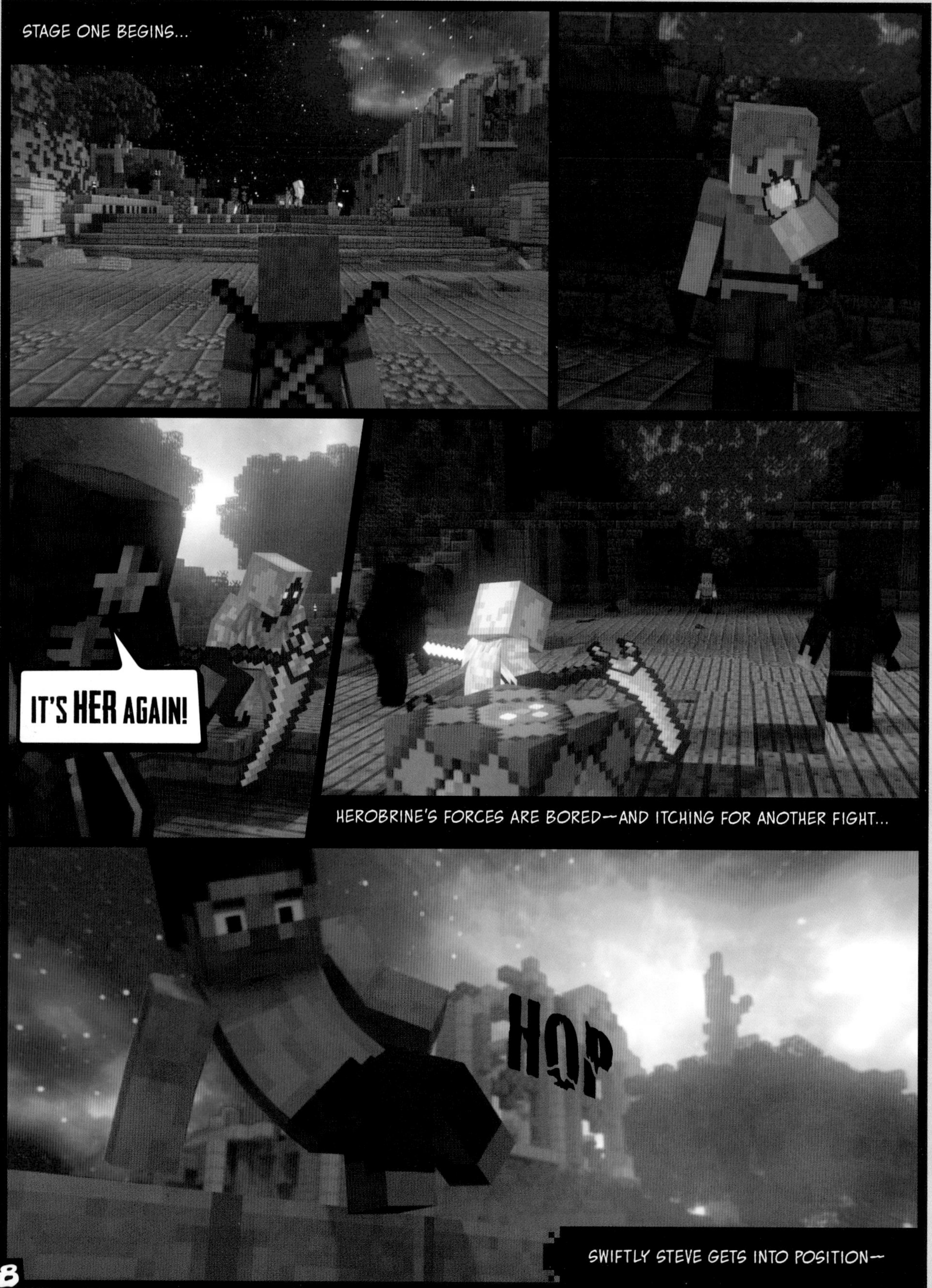
STAGE ONE BEGINS...
IT'S HER AGAIN!
HEROBRINE'S FORCES ARE BORED—AND ITCHING FOR ANOTHER FIGHT...
HOP
SWIFTLY STEVE GETS INTO POSITION—

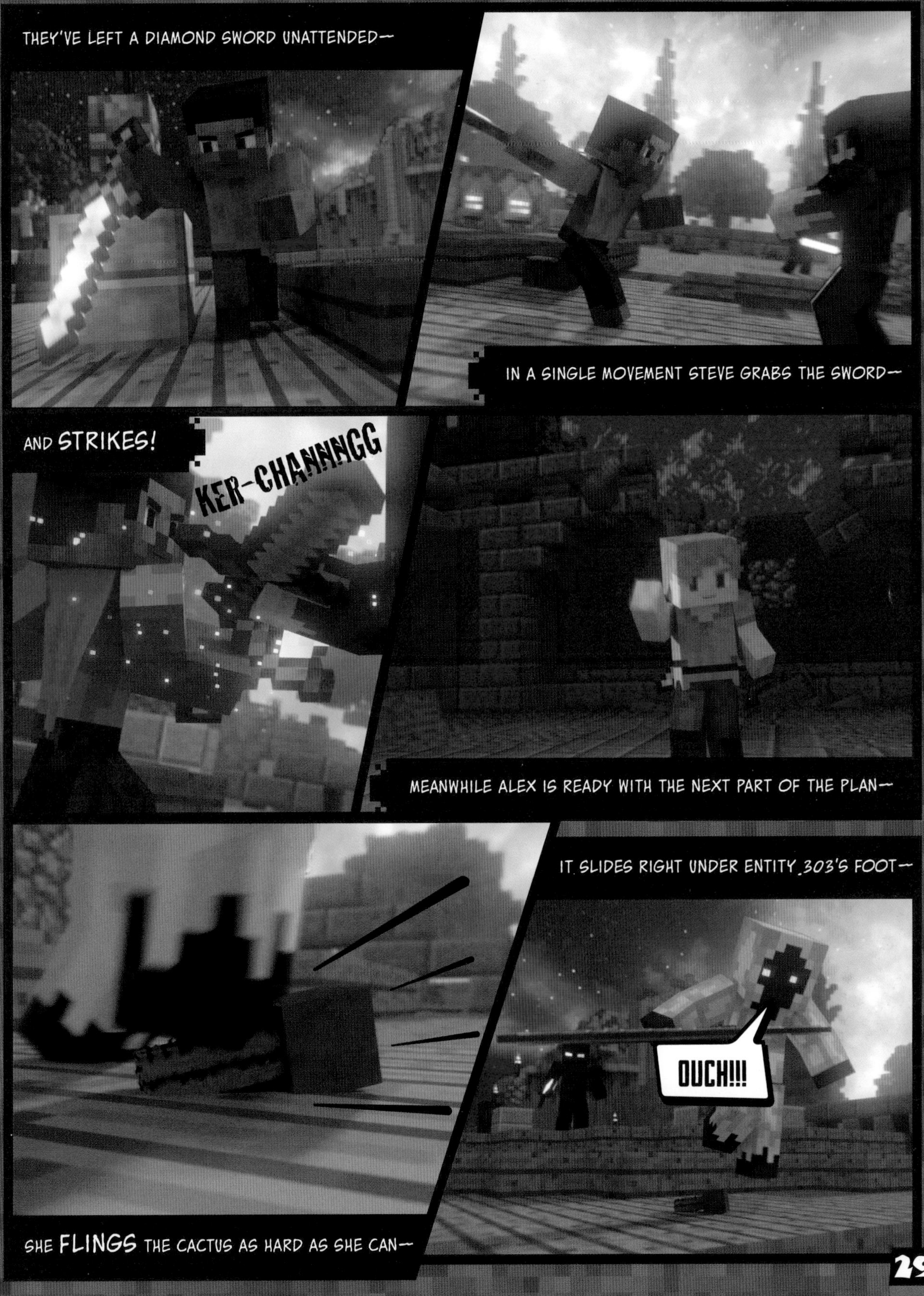

THEY'VE LEFT A DIAMOND SWORD UNATTENDED—
IN A SINGLE MOVEMENT STEVE GRABS THE SWORD—
AND STRIKES!
KER-CHANNNGG
MEANWHILE ALEX IS READY WITH THE NEXT PART OF THE PLAN—
SHE FLINGS THE CACTUS AS HARD AS SHE CAN—
IT SLIDES RIGHT UNDER ENTITY_303'S FOOT—
OUCH!!!

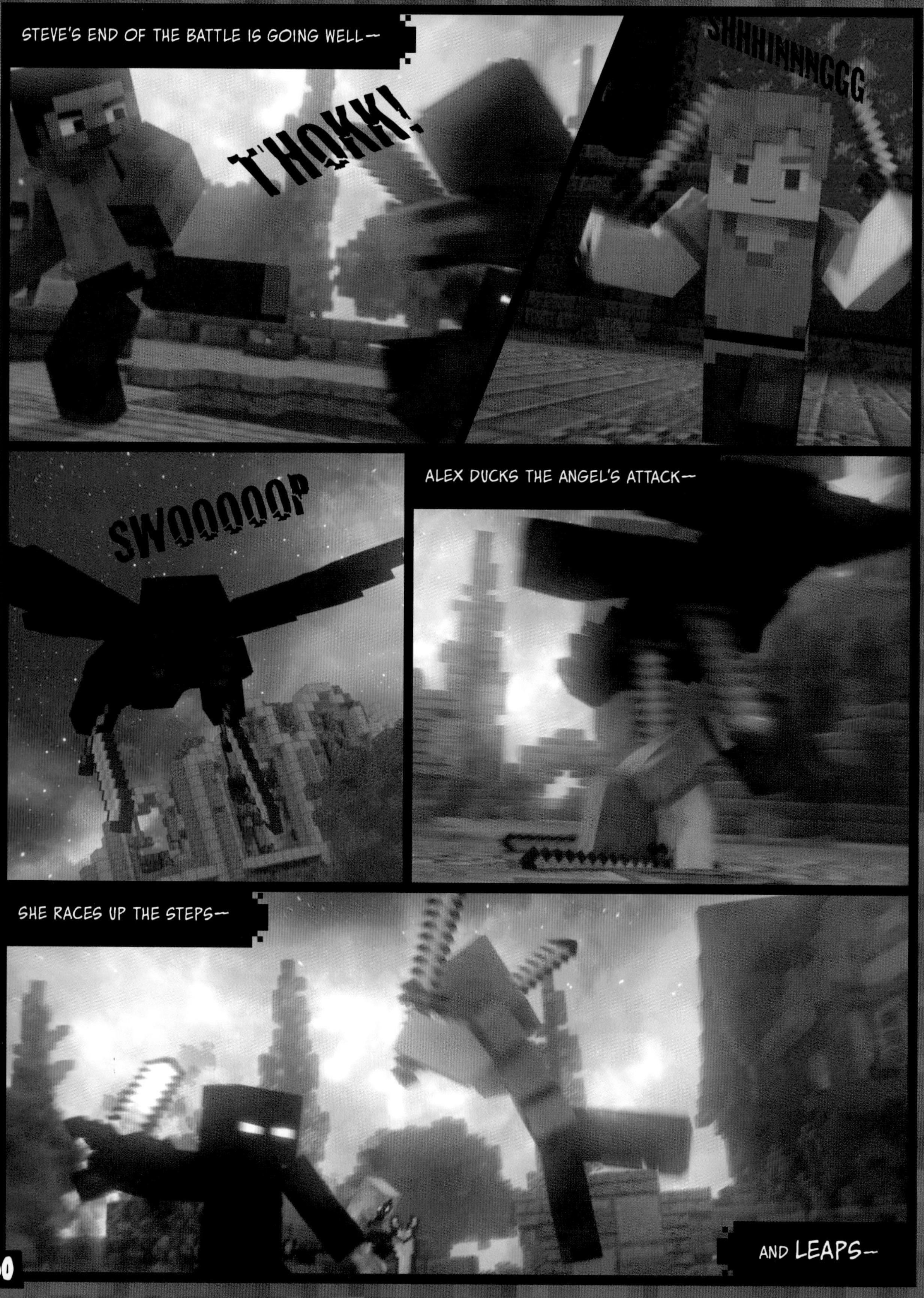
STEVE'S END OF THE BATTLE IS GOING WELL—
THOKK!
SHHHINNNNGGG
SWOOOOOP
ALEX DUCKS THE ANGEL'S ATTACK—
SHE RACES UP THE STEPS—
AND LEAPS—

ALEX AND STEVE HAVE GOT WHERE THEY NEED TO BE—BY THE COMMAND BLOCK!

HRRM.

IRRITATING.

READY?

READY.

HEROBRINE'S MINIONS CLOSE IN...

BUT ALEX REACHES FOR THE BLOCK—

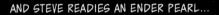

AND STEVE READIES AN ENDER PEARL...

AS THE FINAL ATTACK COMES—

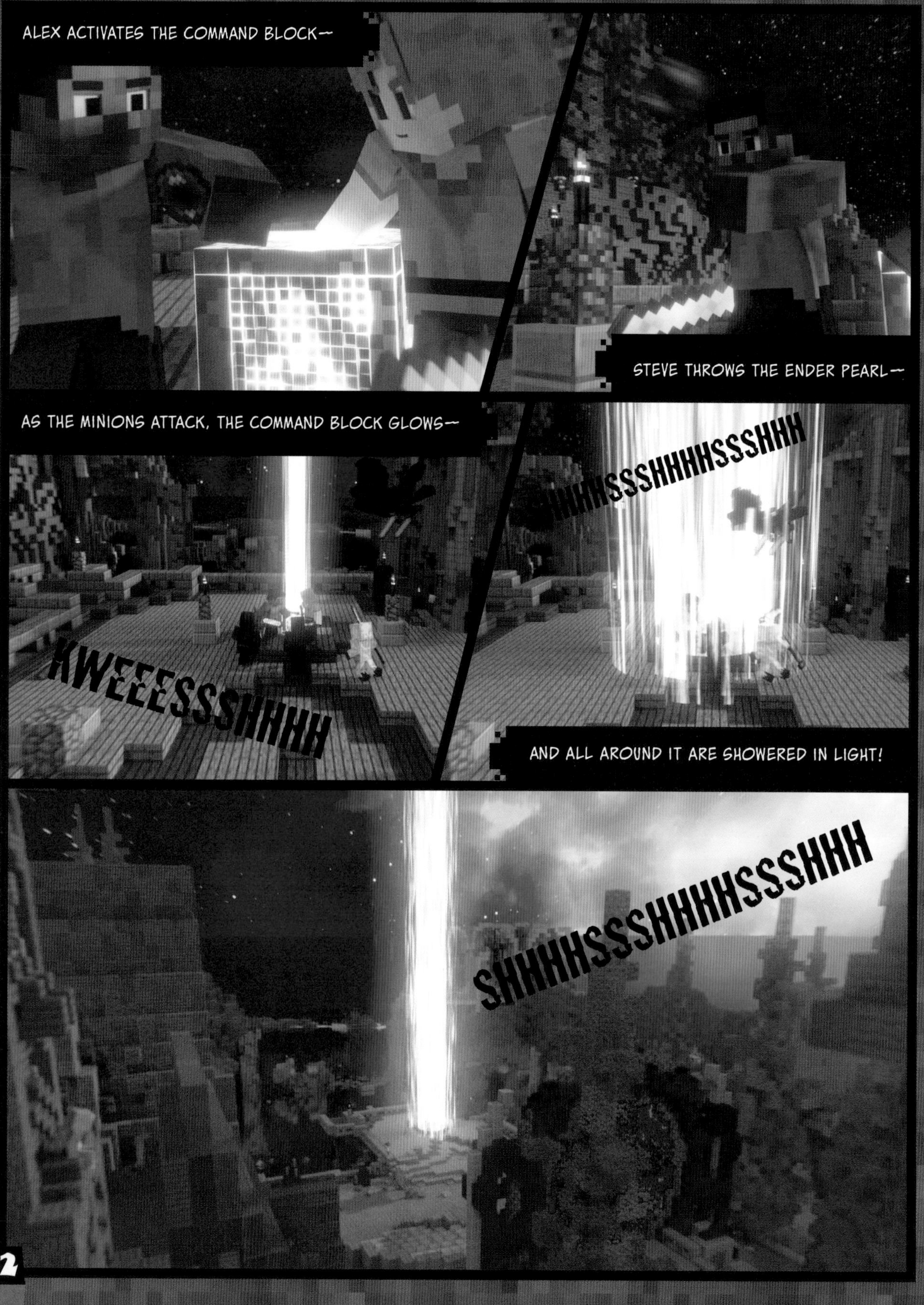
ALEX ACTIVATES THE COMMAND BLOCK—
STEVE THROWS THE ENDER PEARL—
AS THE MINIONS ATTACK, THE COMMAND BLOCK GLOWS—
KWEEEESSSHHHH
HHHSSSHHHHHSSSHHH
AND ALL AROUND IT ARE SHOWERED IN LIGHT!
SHHHHSSSHHHHHSSSHHH

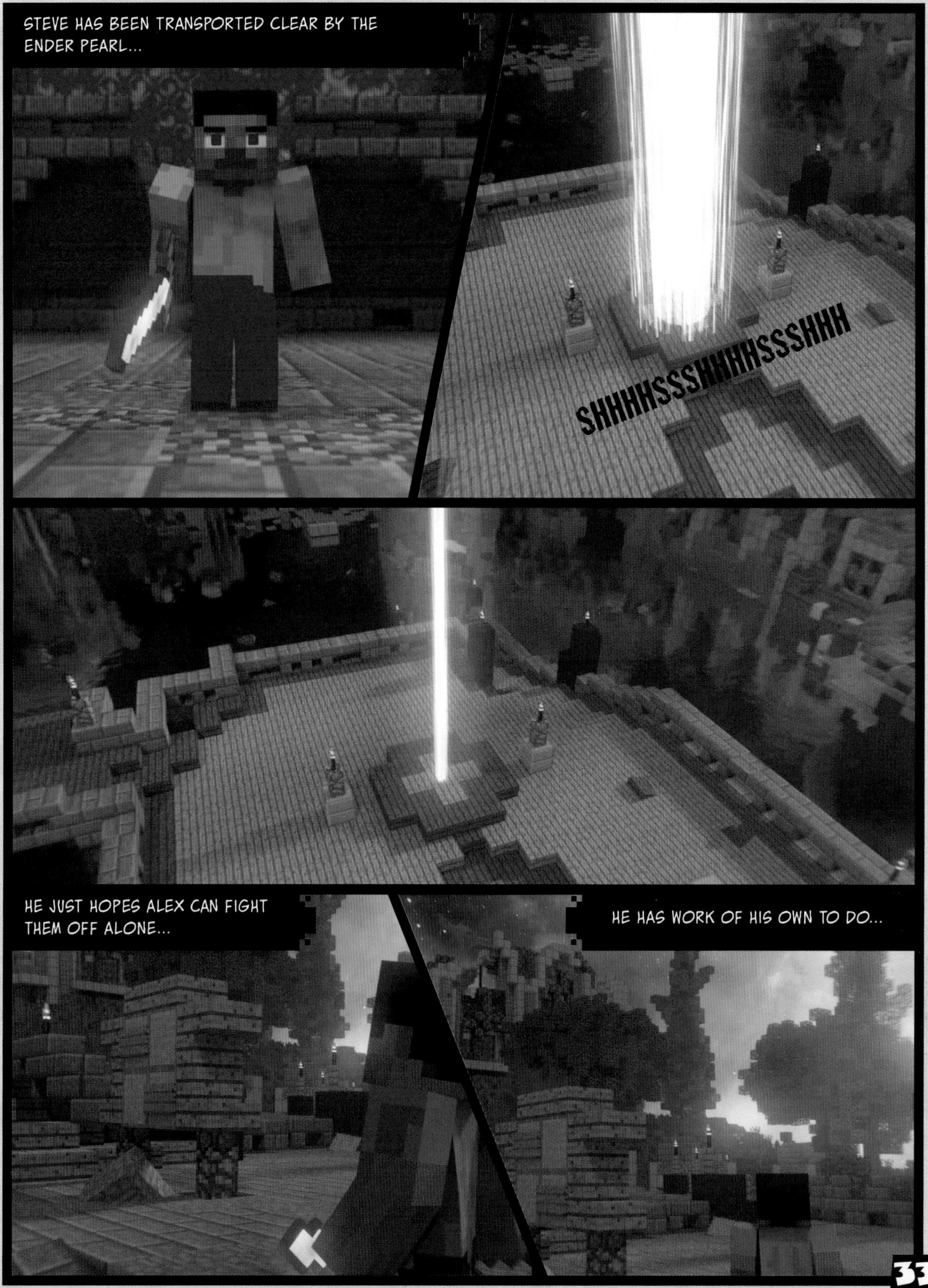
STEVE HAS BEEN TRANSPORTED CLEAR BY THE ENDER PEARL...
SHHHHSSSHHHHSSSHHH
HE JUST HOPES ALEX CAN FIGHT THEM OFF ALONE...
HE HAS WORK OF HIS OWN TO DO...

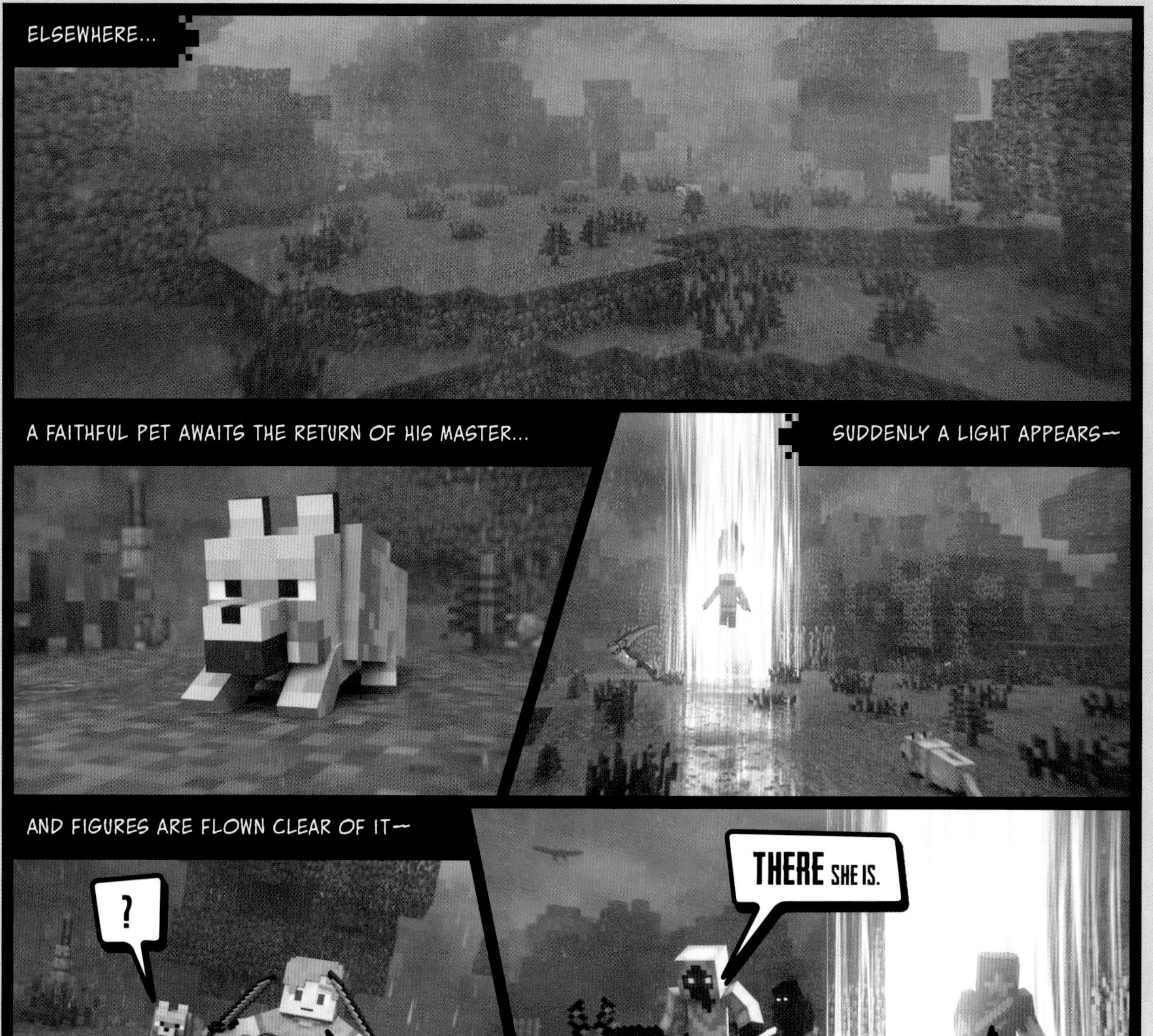
ELSEWHERE...
A FAITHFUL PET AWAITS THE RETURN OF HIS MASTER...
SUDDENLY A LIGHT APPEARS—
AND FIGURES ARE FLOWN CLEAR OF IT—
?
OOOF!
THERE SHE IS.
ALL TOO EASY...
IT'S JUST ALEX AND THE WOLF...

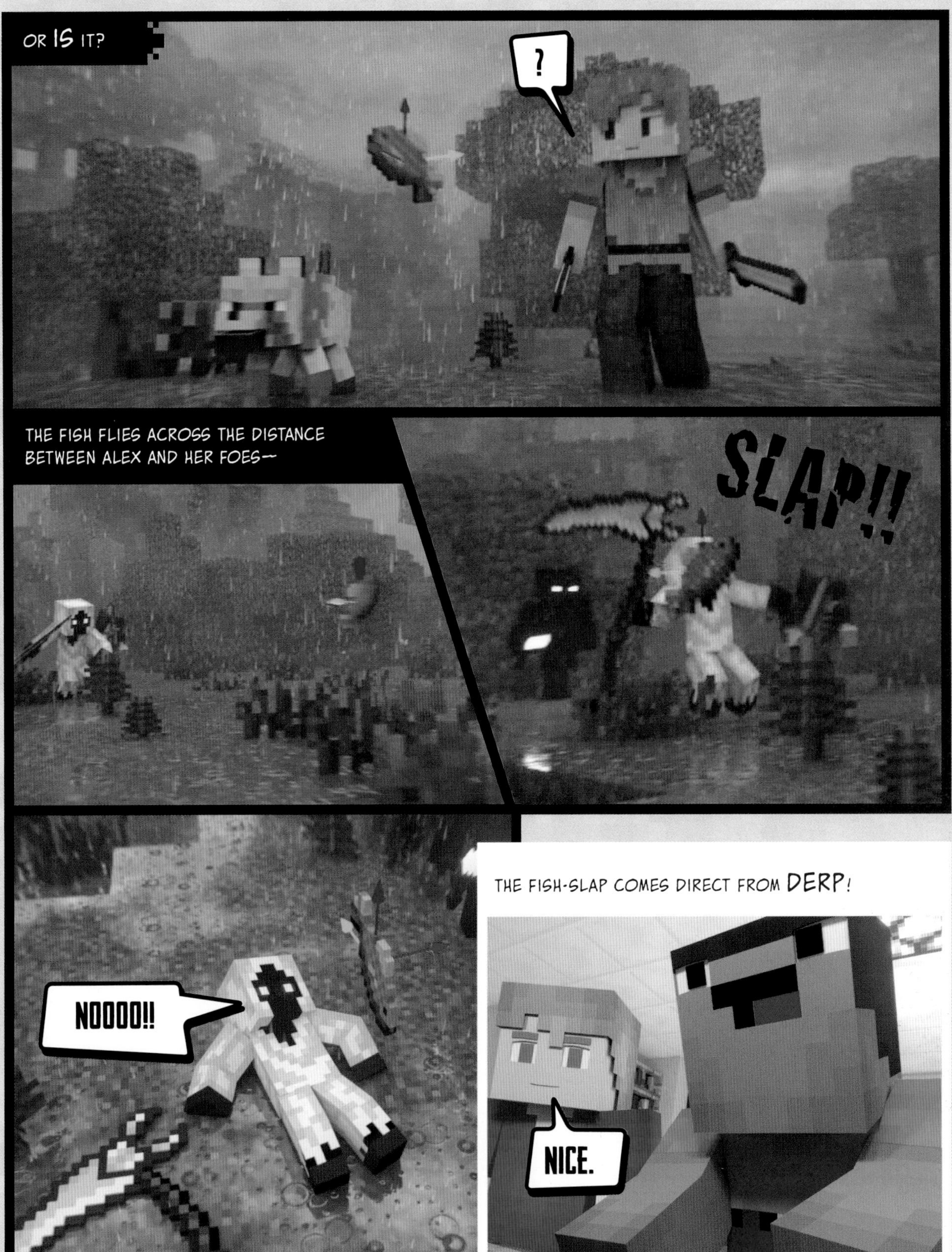

OR IS IT?
?
THE FISH FLIES ACROSS THE DISTANCE BETWEEN ALEX AND HER FOES—
SLAP!!
NOOOO!!
THE FISH-SLAP COMES DIRECT FROM DERP!
NICE.

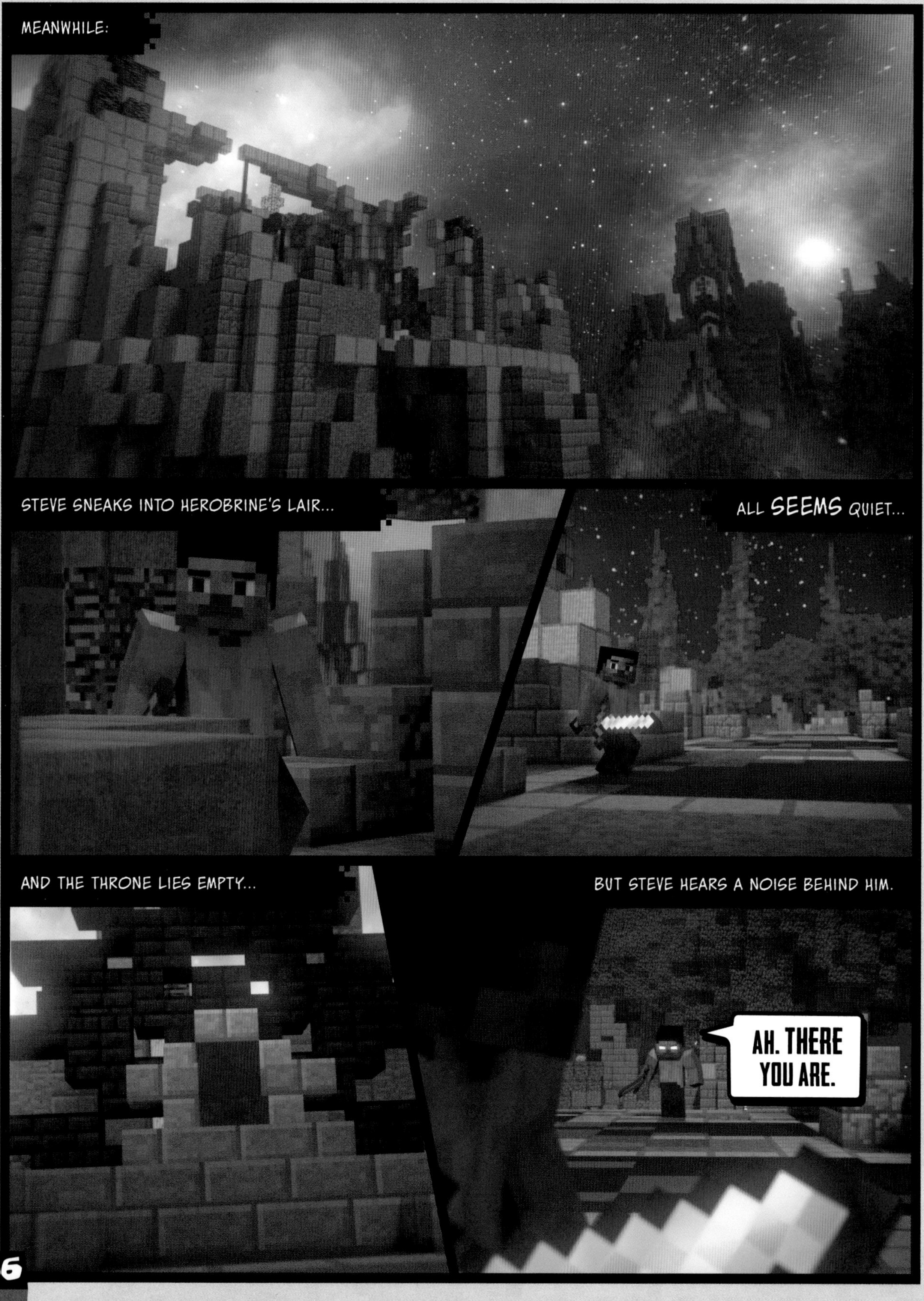
MEANWHILE:
STEVE SNEAKS INTO HEROBRINE'S LAIR...
ALL SEEMS QUIET...
AND THE THRONE LIES EMPTY...
BUT STEVE HEARS A NOISE BEHIND HIM.
AH. THERE YOU ARE.

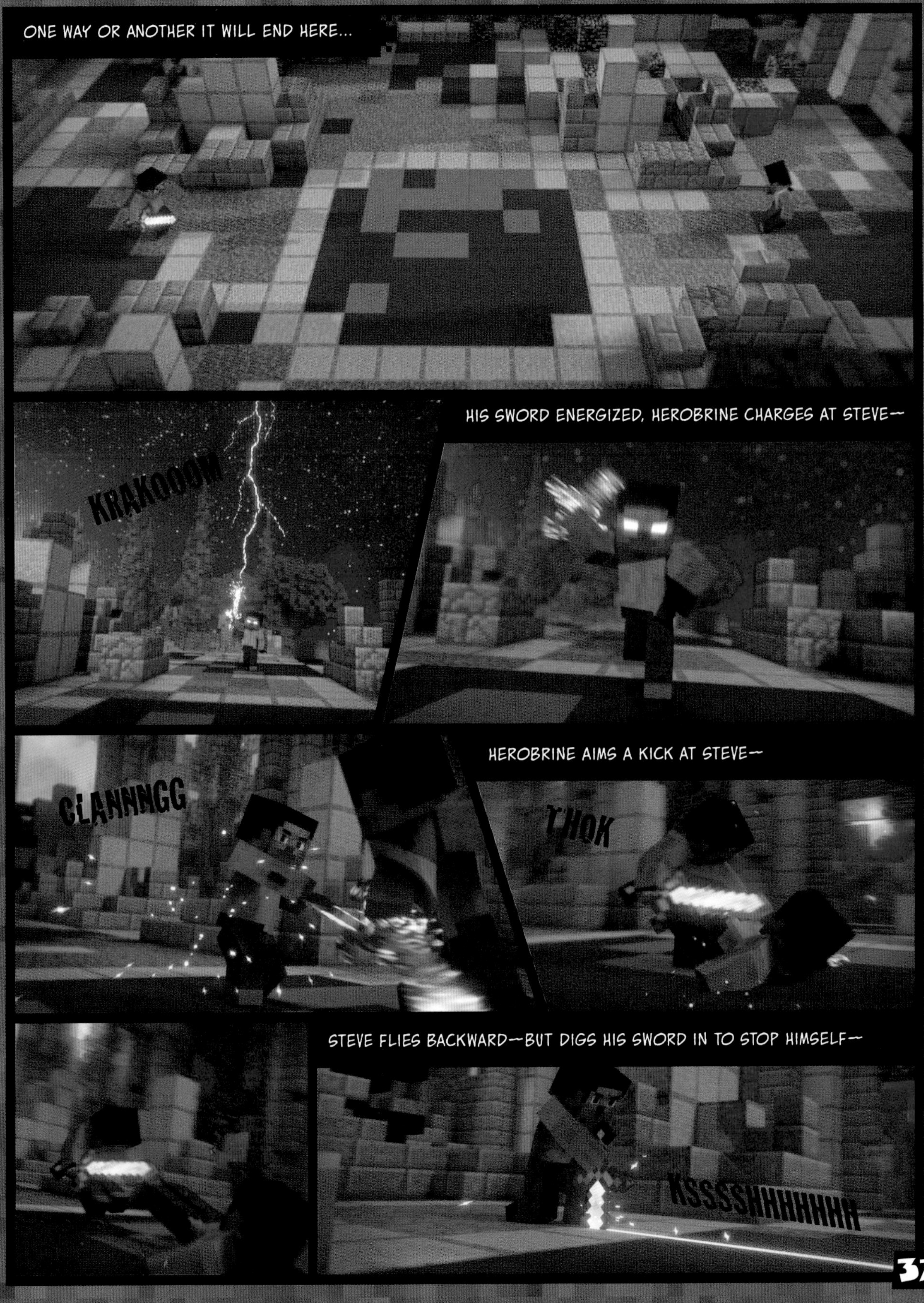
ONE WAY OR ANOTHER IT WILL END HERE...
HIS SWORD ENERGIZED, HEROBRINE CHARGES AT STEVE—
KRAKOOOM
HEROBRINE AIMS A KICK AT STEVE—
CLANNNGG
THOK
STEVE FLIES BACKWARD—BUT DIGS HIS SWORD IN TO STOP HIMSELF—
KSSSSHHHHHHH

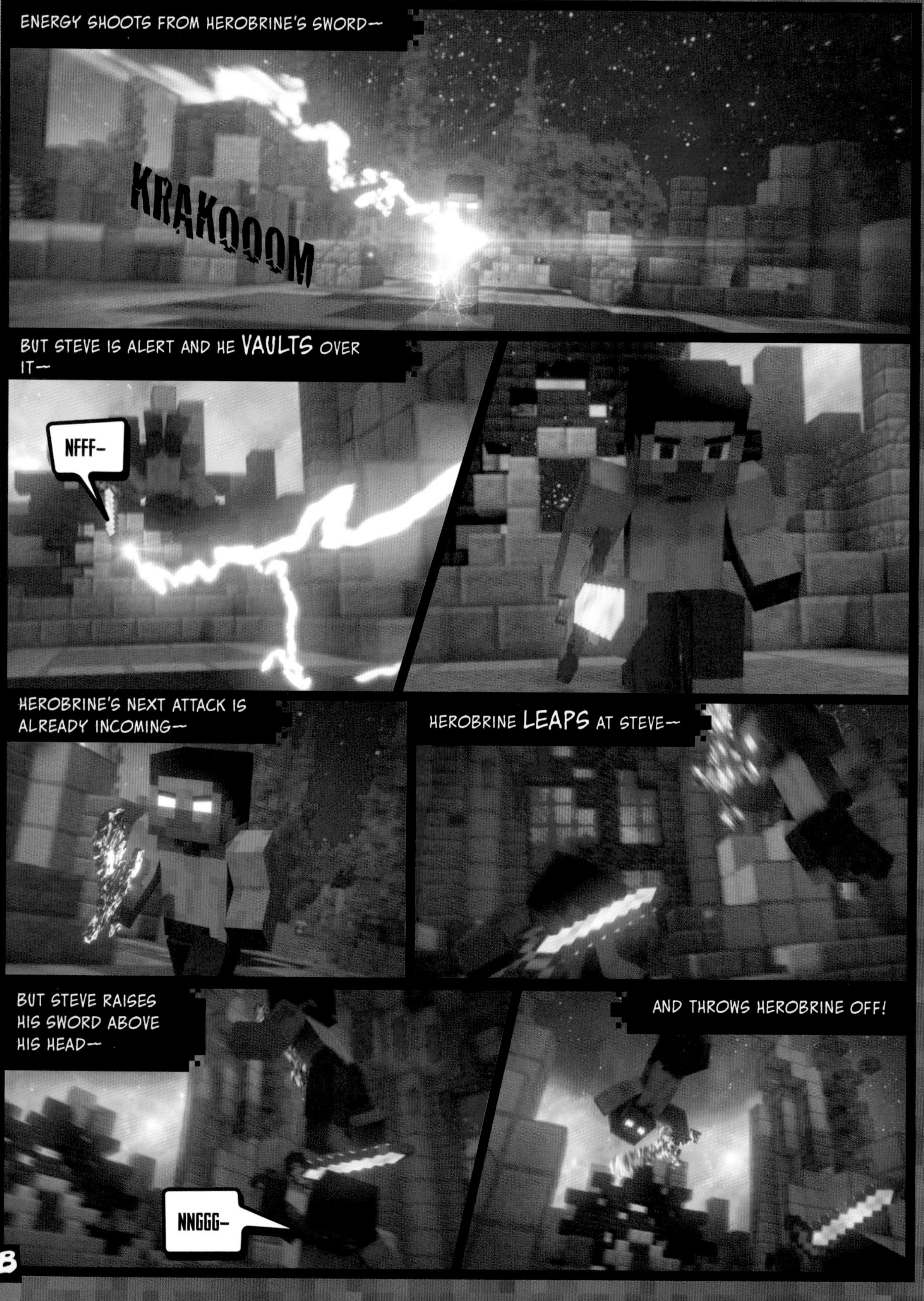

ENERGY SHOOTS FROM HEROBRINE'S SWORD—
KRAKOOOM
BUT STEVE IS ALERT AND HE VAULTS OVER IT—
NFFF-
HEROBRINE'S NEXT ATTACK IS ALREADY INCOMING—
HEROBRINE LEAPS AT STEVE—
BUT STEVE RAISES HIS SWORD ABOVE HIS HEAD—
NNGGG-
AND THROWS HEROBRINE OFF!

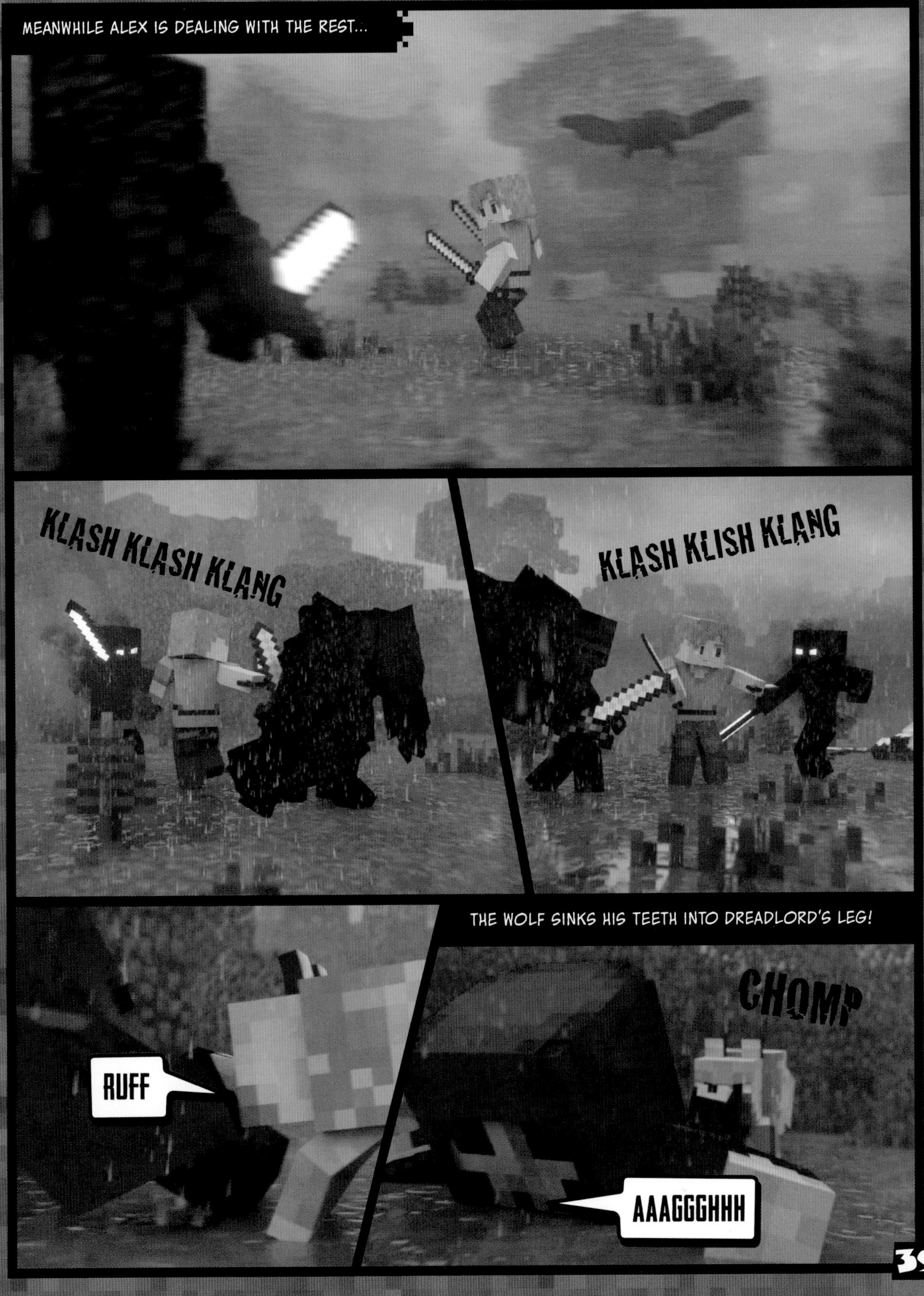
MEANWHILE ALEX IS DEALING WITH THE REST...
KLASH KLASH KLANG
KLASH KLISH KLANG
RUFF
THE WOLF SINKS HIS TEETH INTO DREADLORD'S LEG!
CHOMP
AAAGGGHHH

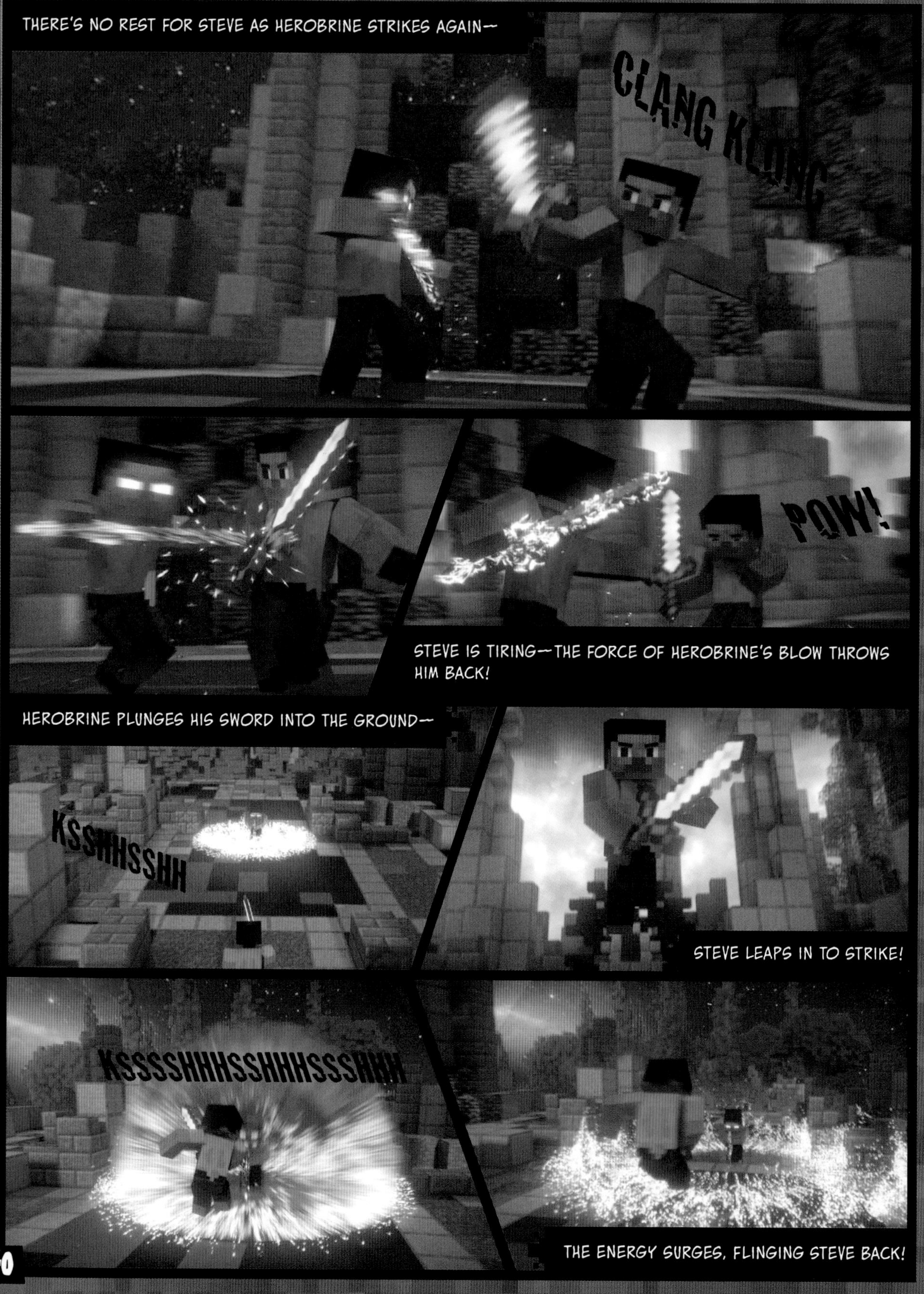
THERE'S NO REST FOR STEVE AS HEROBRINE STRIKES AGAIN—
CLANG KLONG
POW!
STEVE IS TIRING—THE FORCE OF HEROBRINE'S BLOW THROWS HIM BACK!
HEROBRINE PLUNGES HIS SWORD INTO THE GROUND—
KSSHHSSHH
STEVE LEAPS IN TO STRIKE!
KSSSSHHHSSHHHSSSHHH
THE ENERGY SURGES, FLINGING STEVE BACK!

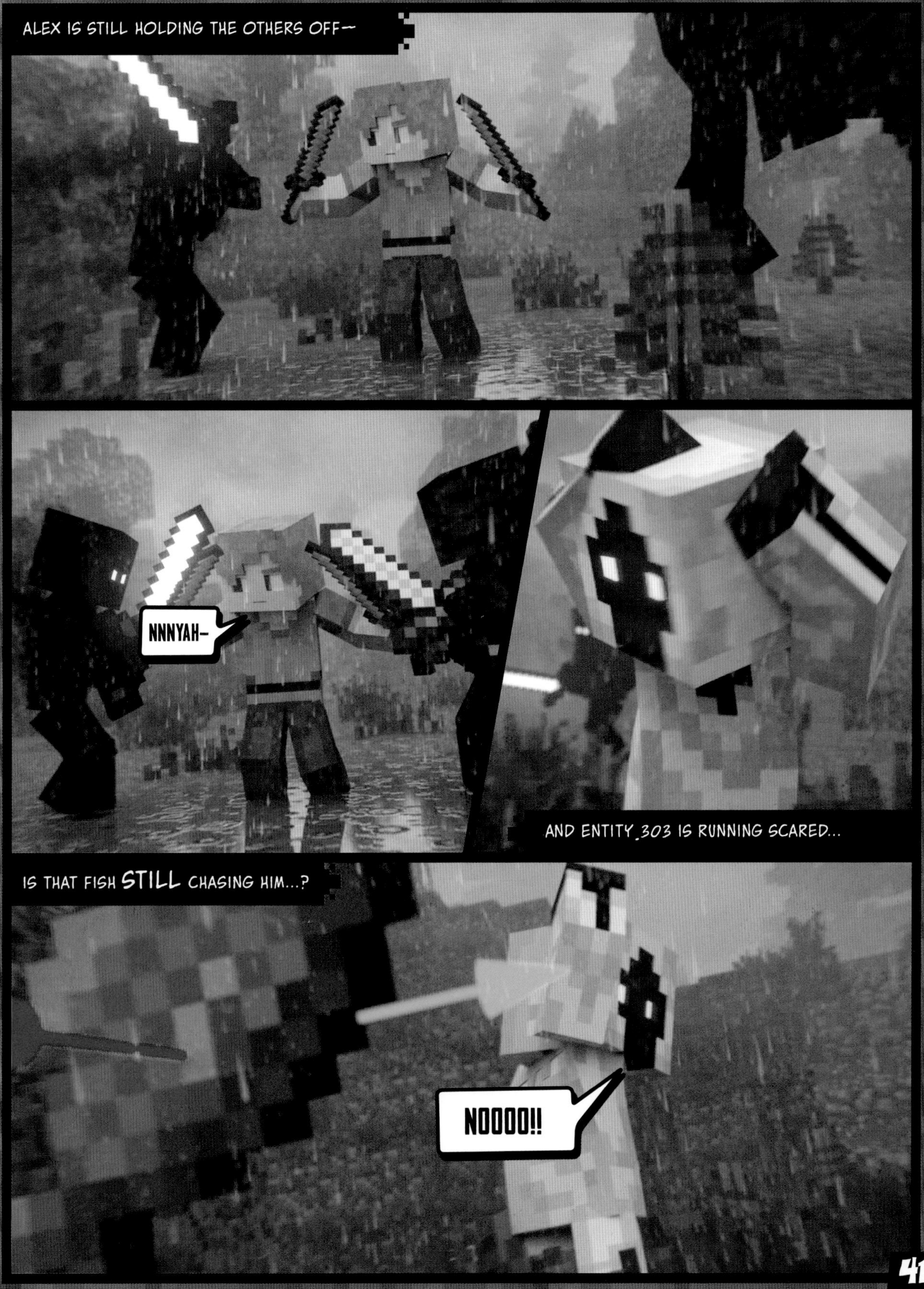

ALEX IS STILL HOLDING THE OTHERS OFF—
NNNYAH—
AND ENTITY_303 IS RUNNING SCARED...
IS THAT FISH STILL CHASING HIM...?
NOOOO!!

BUT HEROBRINE IS WINNING—

KKRRRSSSSHHKKRRRSSSSHH

KKRRRSSSHHKKRRRSSSSHH

THE BOLT STRIKES THE STONE ARCH ABOVE HEROBRINE'S HEAD—

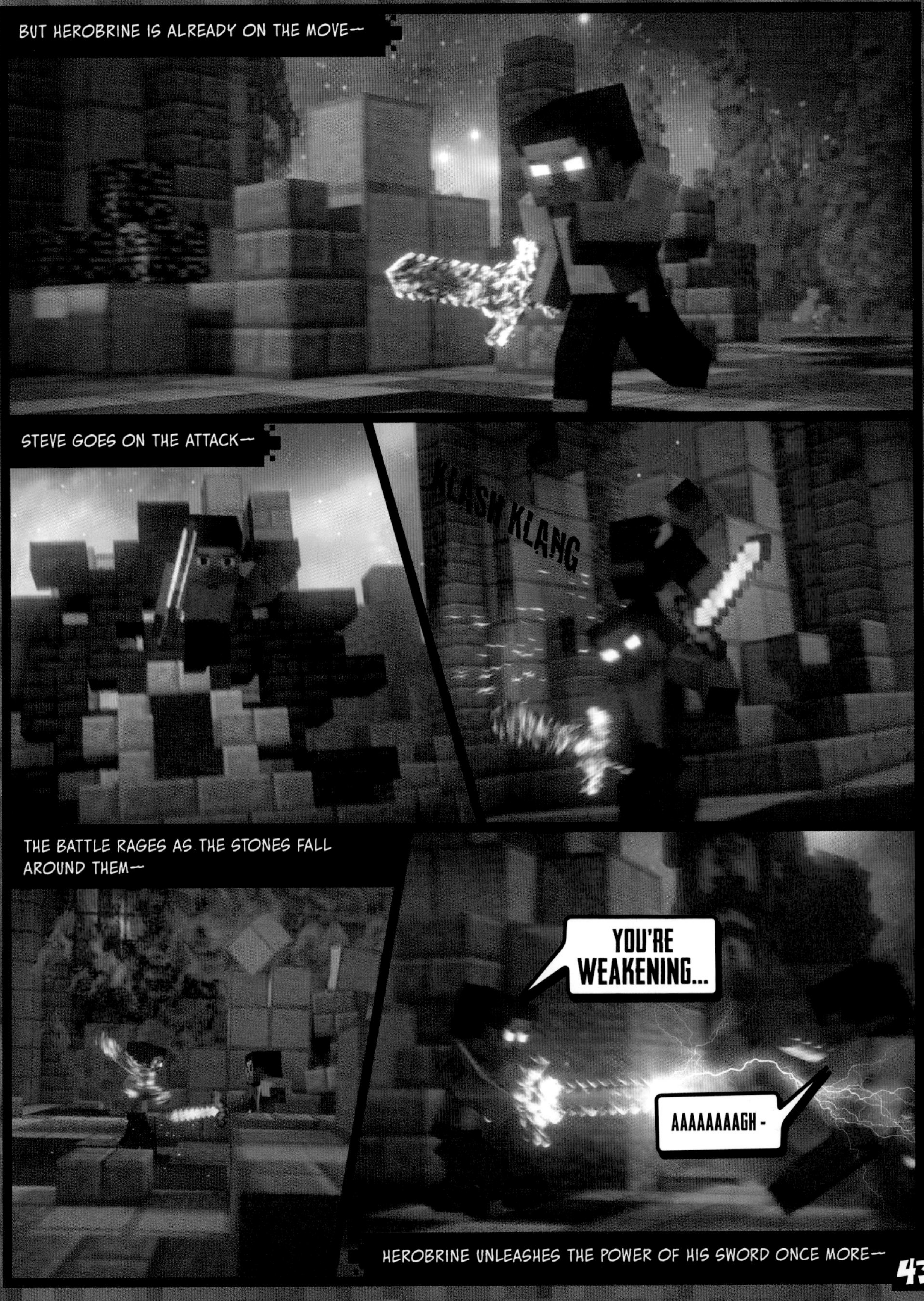
BUT HEROBRINE IS ALREADY ON THE MOVE—
STEVE GOES ON THE ATTACK—
KLASH KLANG
THE BATTLE RAGES AS THE STONES FALL AROUND THEM—
YOU'RE WEAKENING...
AAAAAAAAGH -
HEROBRINE UNLEASHES THE POWER OF HIS SWORD ONCE MORE—

AAAAAAAA...

STEVE FALLS, AND DESPAIRS...

HE REALIZES HE CAN'T WIN.

HIS OPPONENT IS TOO STRONG...

STEVE DRAGS HIMSELF SLOWLY, PAINFULLY, TO THE WATER...

AND HE SEES WHAT HE SAW ONCE BEFORE...

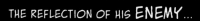

THE REFLECTION OF HIS ENEMY...

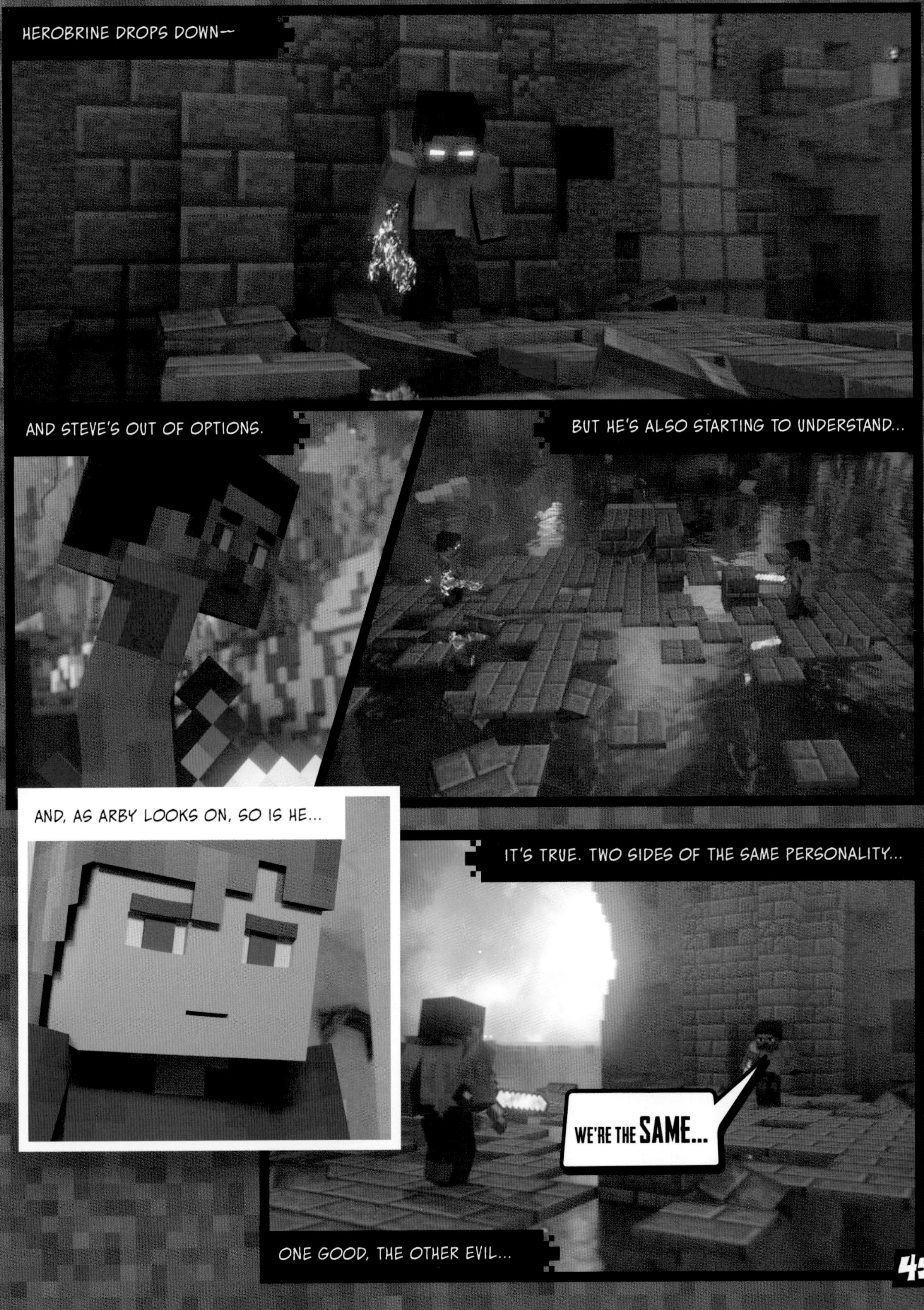
HEROBRINE DROPS DOWN—
AND STEVE'S OUT OF OPTIONS.
BUT HE'S ALSO STARTING TO UNDERSTAND...
AND, AS ARBY LOOKS ON, SO IS HE...
IT'S TRUE. TWO SIDES OF THE SAME PERSONALITY...
WE'RE THE SAME...
ONE GOOD, THE OTHER EVIL...

HYPIXEL
Can't connect to server

1/62000

BPG SERVER
Can't connect to server

MINEPLEX
Can't connect to server

CUBECRAFT
Can't connect to server

THE HIVE
Can't connect to server

OMEGACRAFT

THERE'S ONLY ONE PERSON IN HYPIXEL—BECAUSE STEVE AND HEROBRINE ARE THE **SAME PERSON!**

WOAH...

STEVE THINKS BACK THROUGH THE MOMENTS OF HIS LIFE SO FAR...

SOMETHING HE FELT THE MOMENT HE WOKE UP~

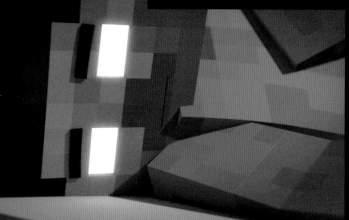

THOUGH IT ONLY LASTED A SECOND ... THE REFLECTION HE SAW AT THE LAKE~

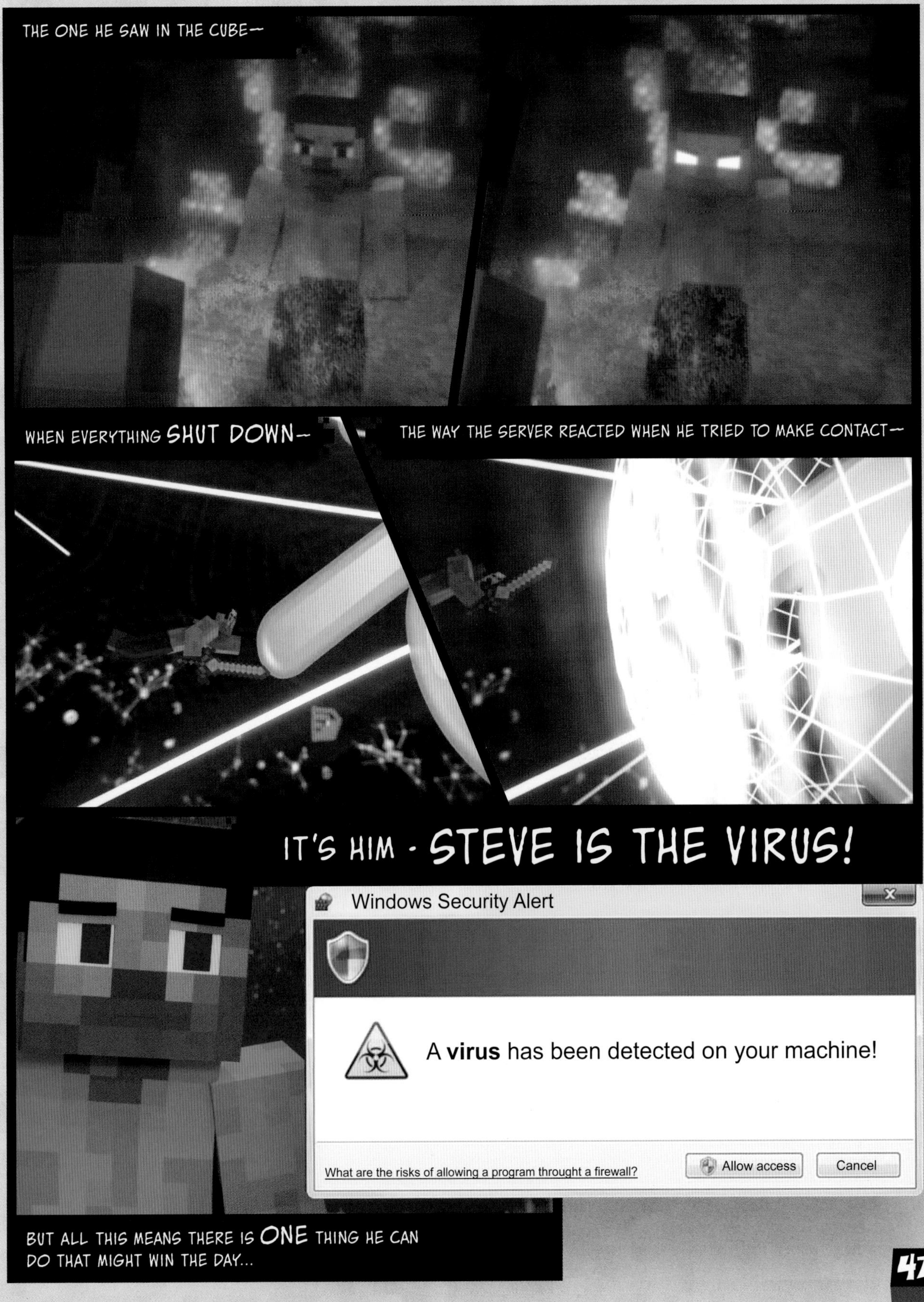
THE ONE HE SAW IN THE CUBE—
WHEN EVERYTHING SHUT DOWN—
THE WAY THE SERVER REACTED WHEN HE TRIED TO MAKE CONTACT—
IT'S HIM - STEVE IS THE VIRUS!
Windows Security Alert
A **virus** has been detected on your machine!
What are the risks of allowing a program throught a firewall?
Allow access
Cancel
BUT ALL THIS MEANS THERE IS ONE THING HE CAN DO THAT MIGHT WIN THE DAY...

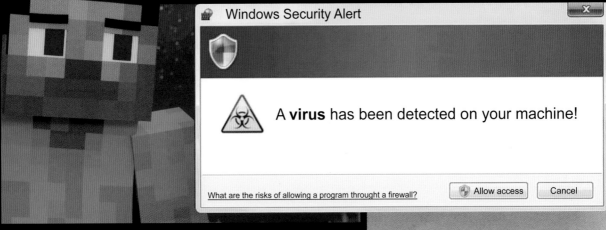

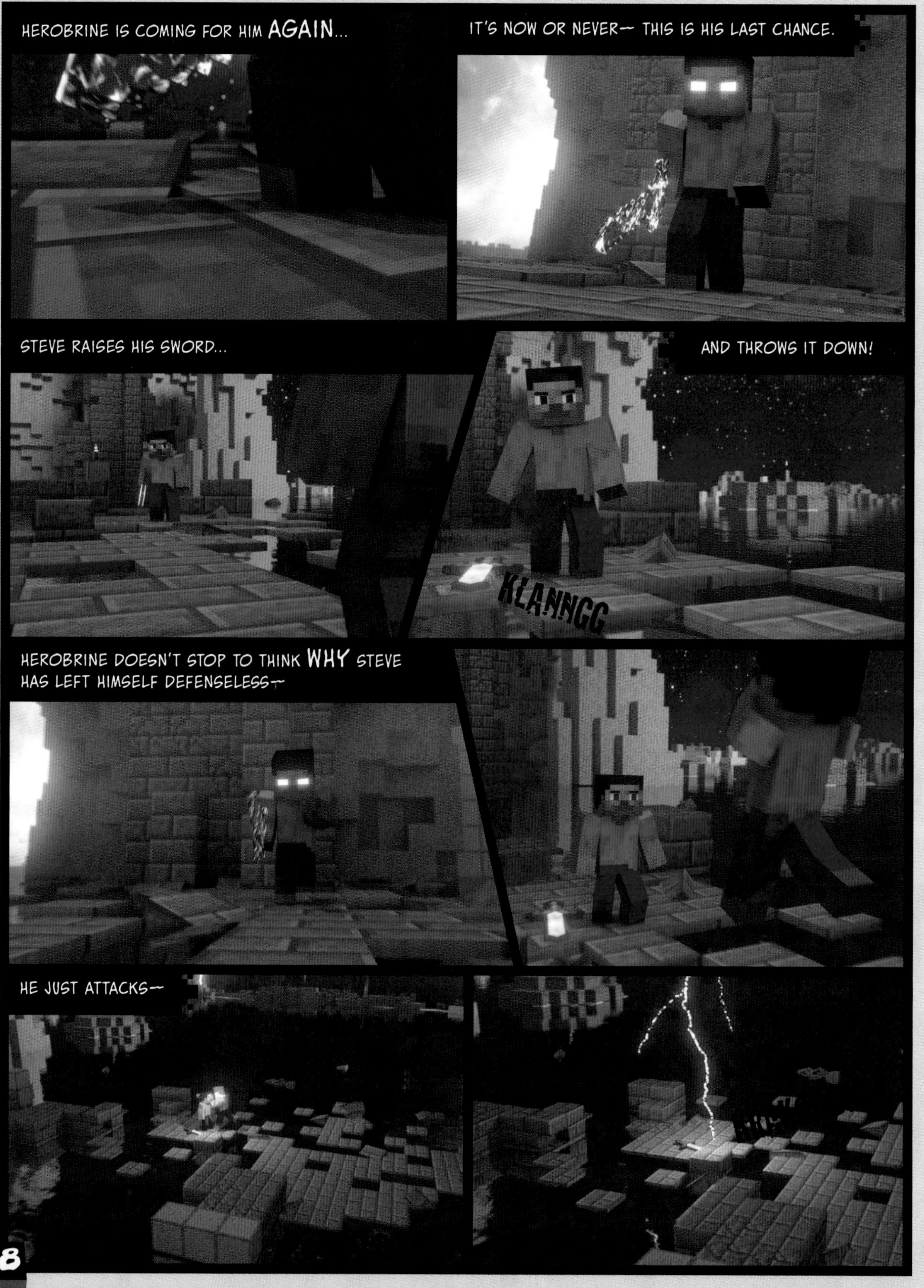
HEROBRINE IS COMING FOR HIM AGAIN...
IT'S NOW OR NEVER— THIS IS HIS LAST CHANCE.
STEVE RAISES HIS SWORD...
AND THROWS IT DOWN!
KLANNGG
HEROBRINE DOESN'T STOP TO THINK WHY STEVE HAS LEFT HIMSELF DEFENSELESS—
HE JUST ATTACKS—

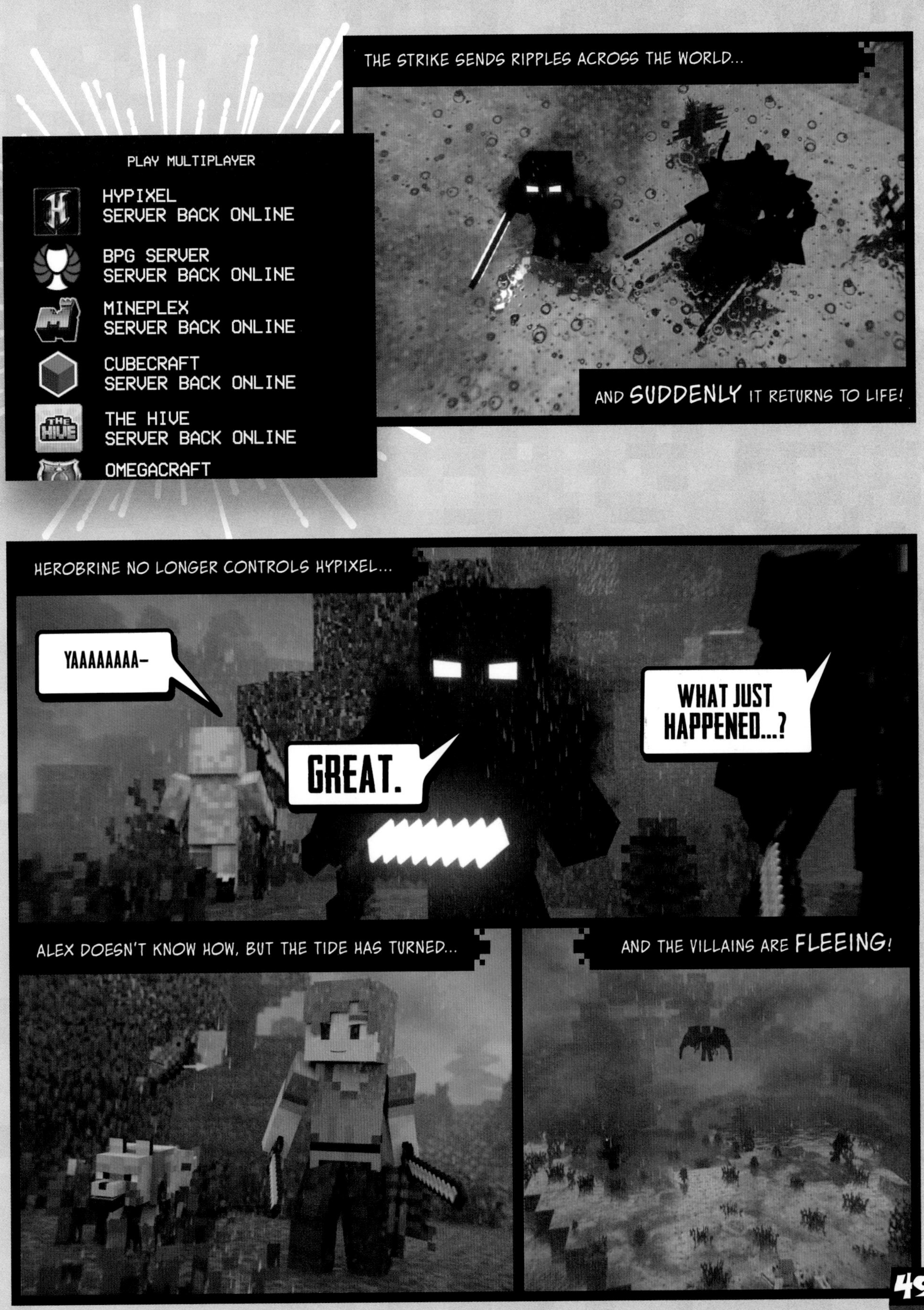
THE STRIKE SENDS RIPPLES ACROSS THE WORLD...
PLAY MULTIPLAYER
HYPIXEL
SERVER BACK ONLINE
BPG SERVER
SERVER BACK ONLINE
MINEPLEX
SERVER BACK ONLINE
CUBECRAFT
SERVER BACK ONLINE
THE HIVE
SERVER BACK ONLINE
OMEGACRAFT
AND SUDDENLY IT RETURNS TO LIFE!
HEROBRINE NO LONGER CONTROLS HYPIXEL...
YAAAAAAAA–
GREAT.
WHAT JUST HAPPENED...?
ALEX DOESN'T KNOW HOW, BUT THE TIDE HAS TURNED...
AND THE VILLAINS ARE FLEEING!

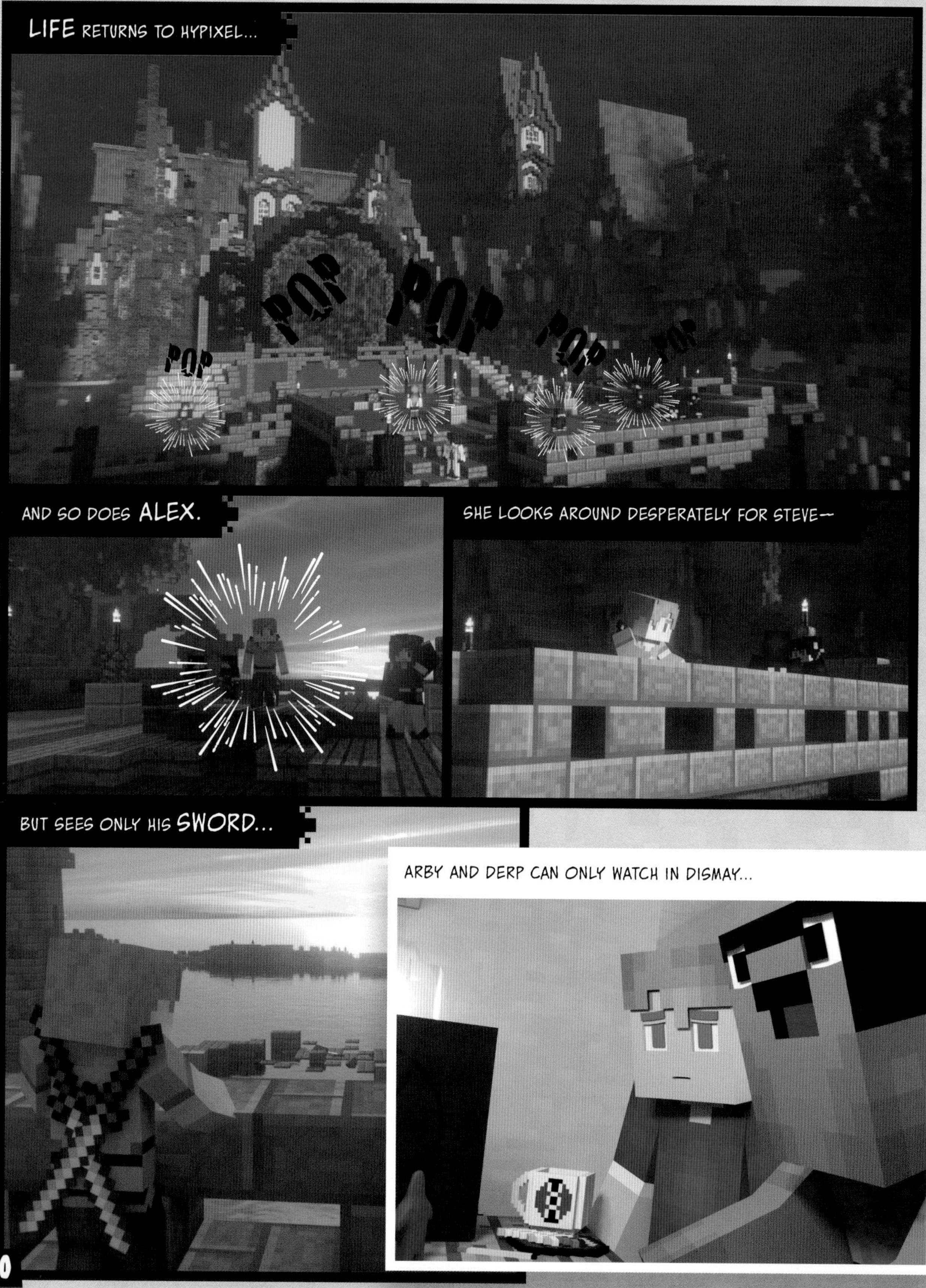
LIFE RETURNS TO HYPIXEL...
POP
POP
POP
POP
POP
AND SO DOES ALEX.
SHE LOOKS AROUND DESPERATELY FOR STEVE—
BUT SEES ONLY HIS SWORD...
ARBY AND DERP CAN ONLY WATCH IN DISMAY...

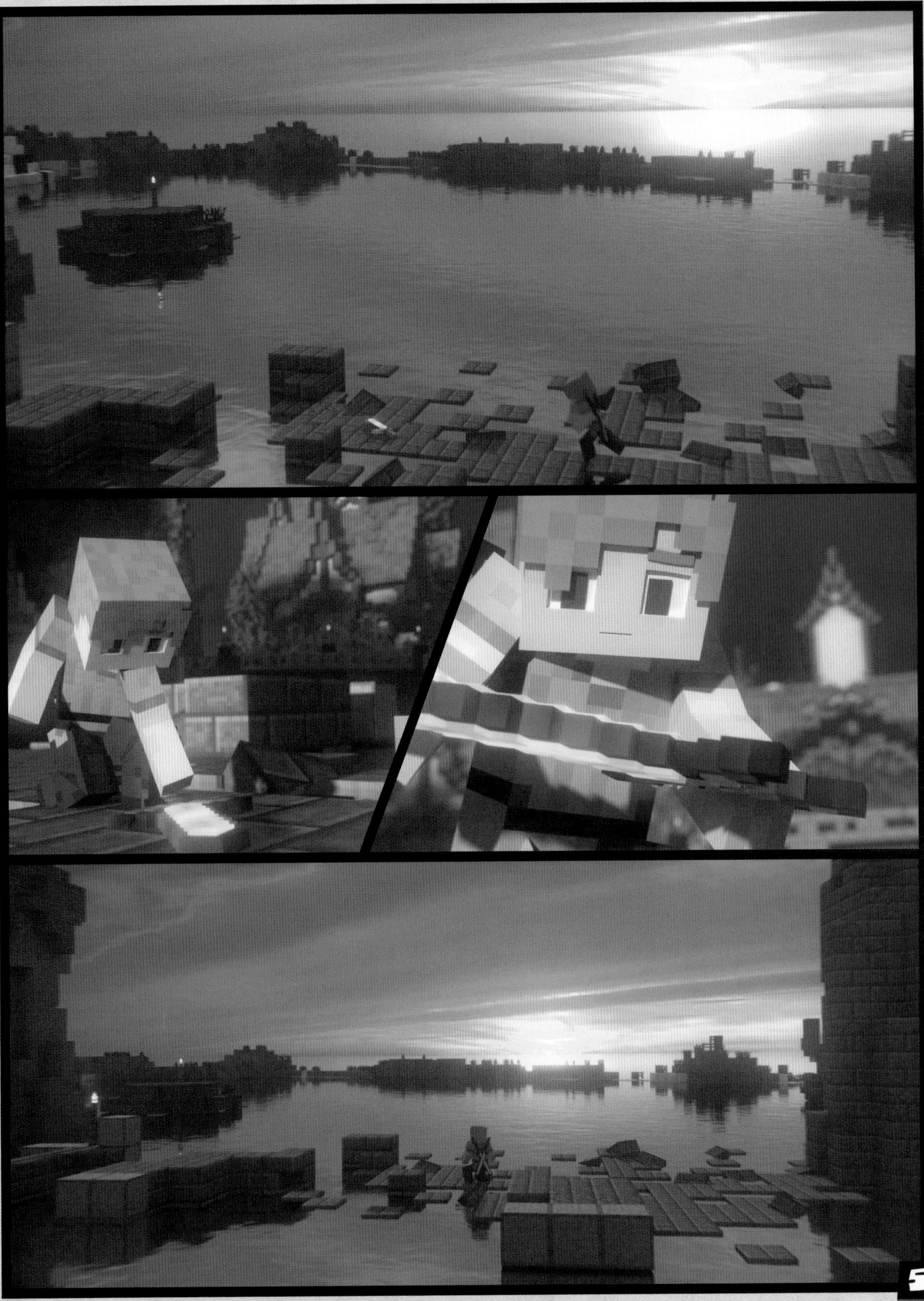

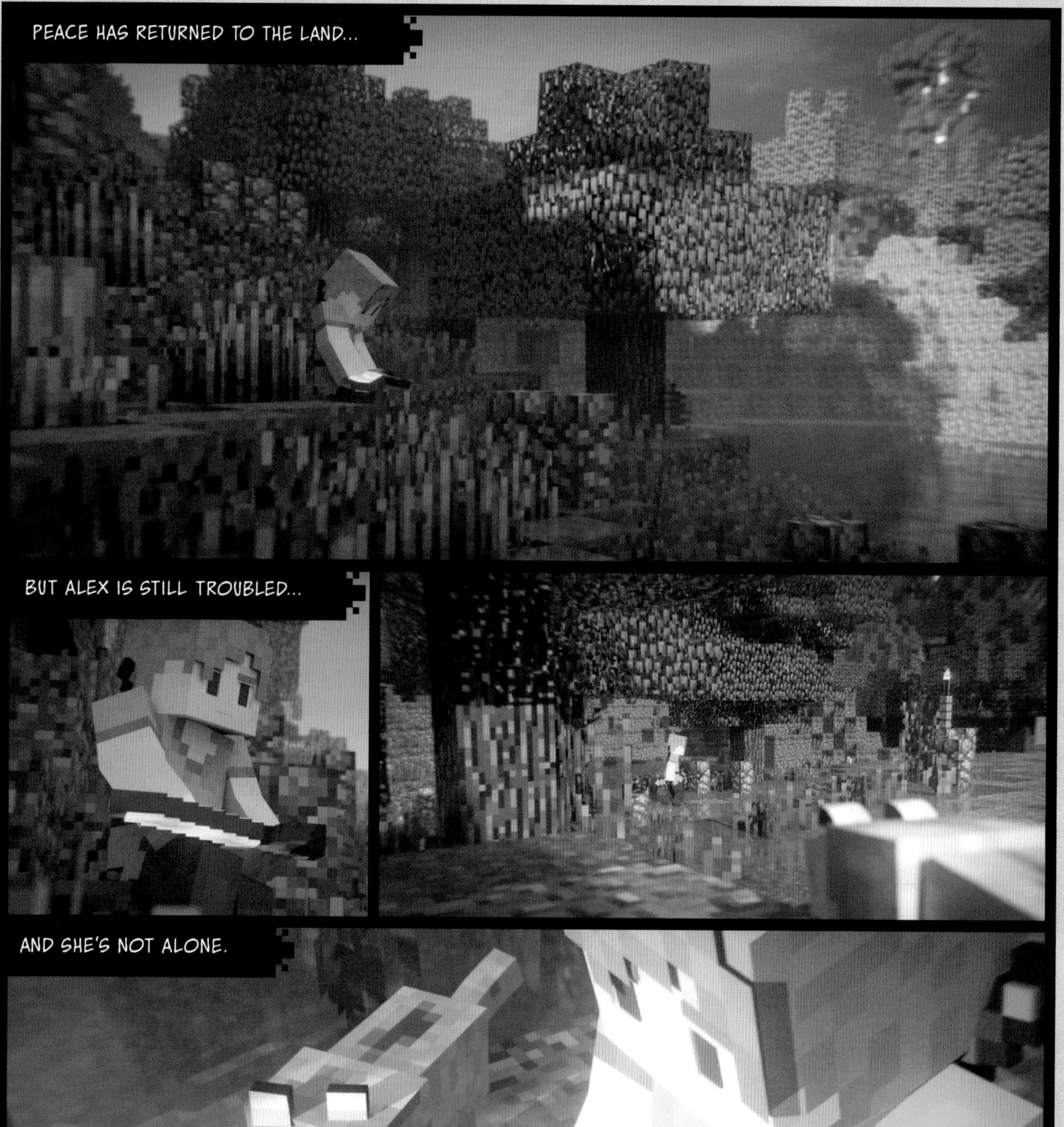
PEACE HAS RETURNED TO THE LAND...
BUT ALEX IS STILL TROUBLED...
AND SHE'S NOT ALONE.
LET'S GO GET HIM BACK.

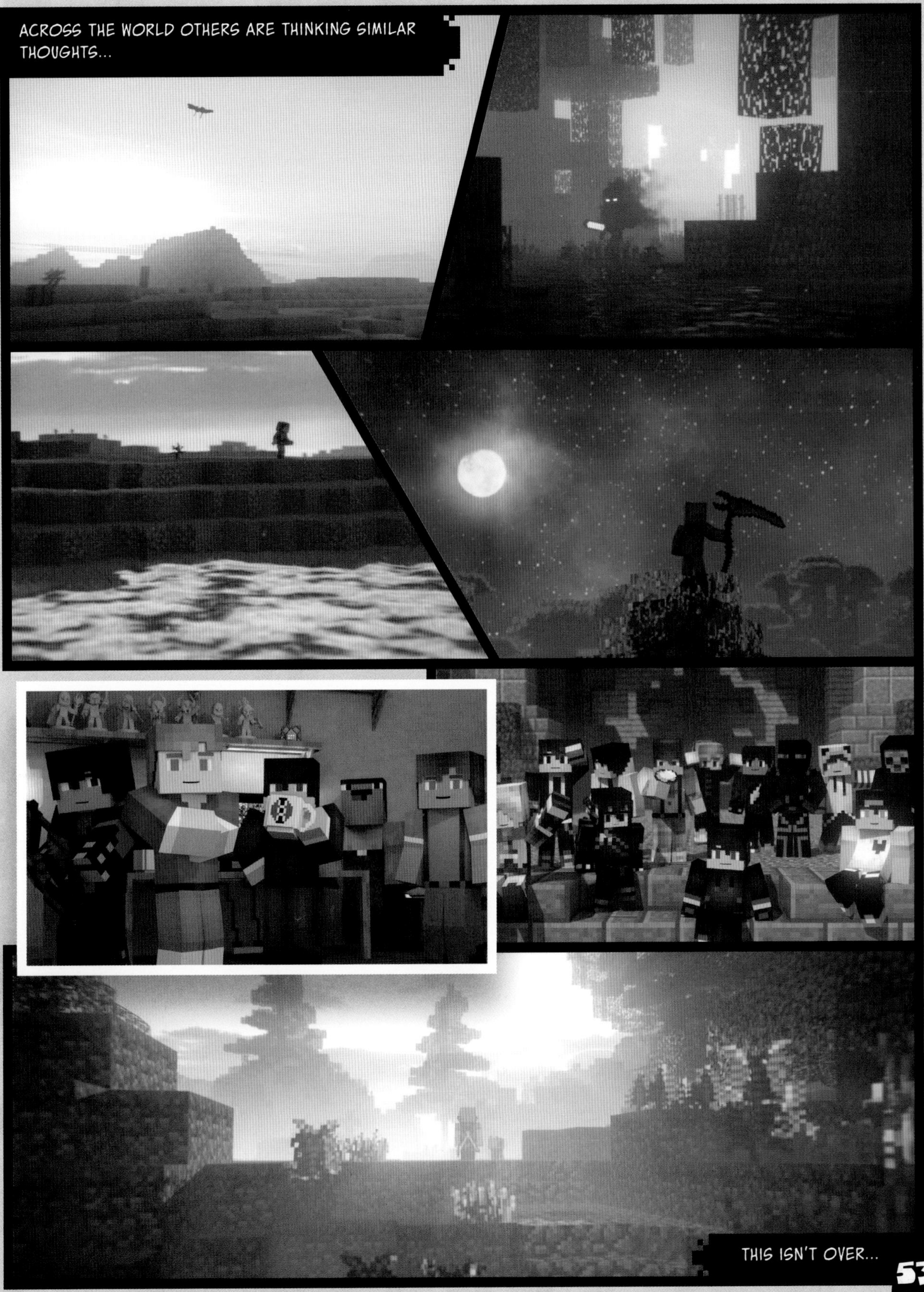
ACROSS THE WORLD OTHERS ARE THINKING SIMILAR THOUGHTS...
THIS ISN'T OVER...

CHAPTER 7

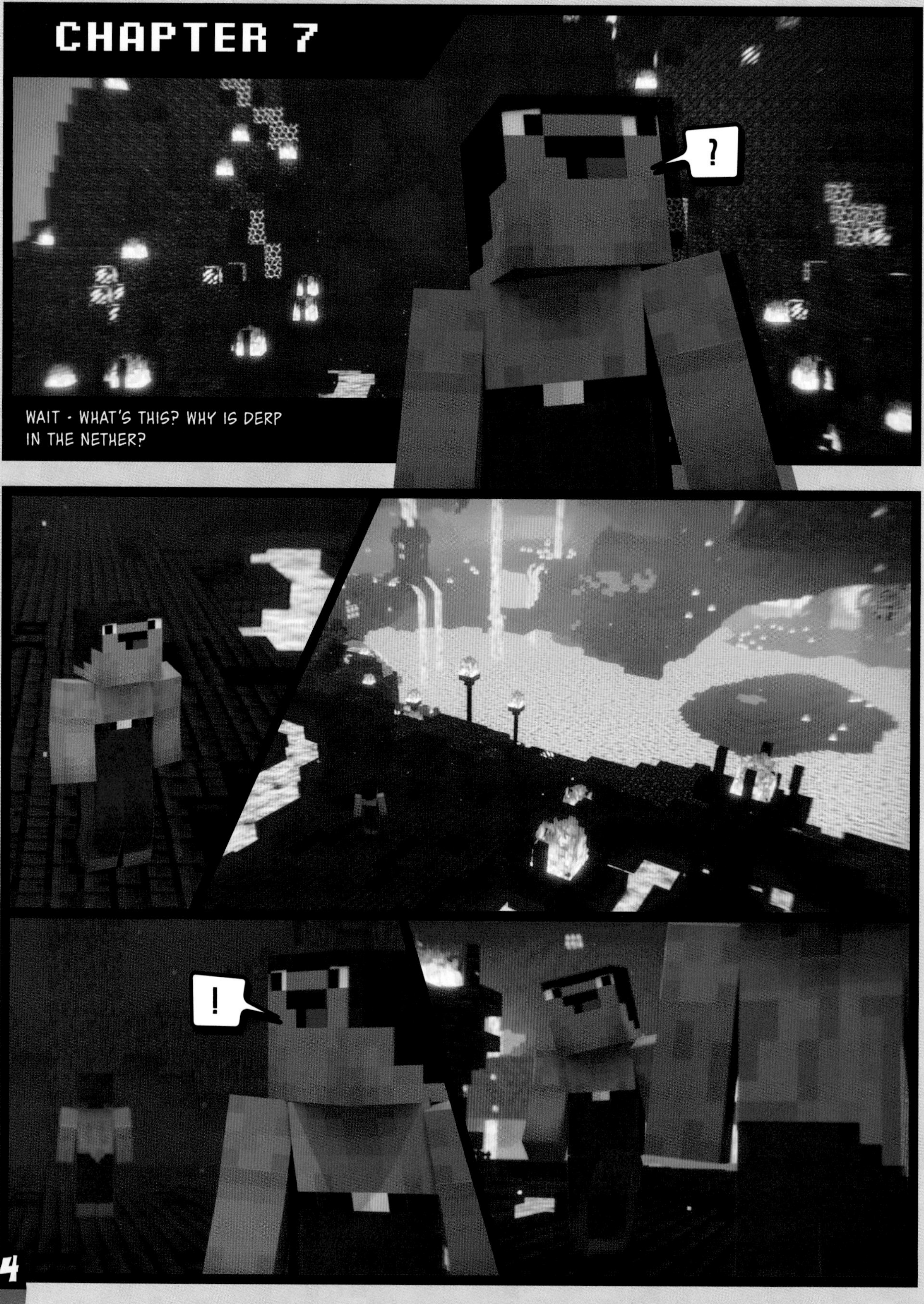
?
WAIT - WHAT'S THIS? WHY IS DERP IN THE NETHER?
!

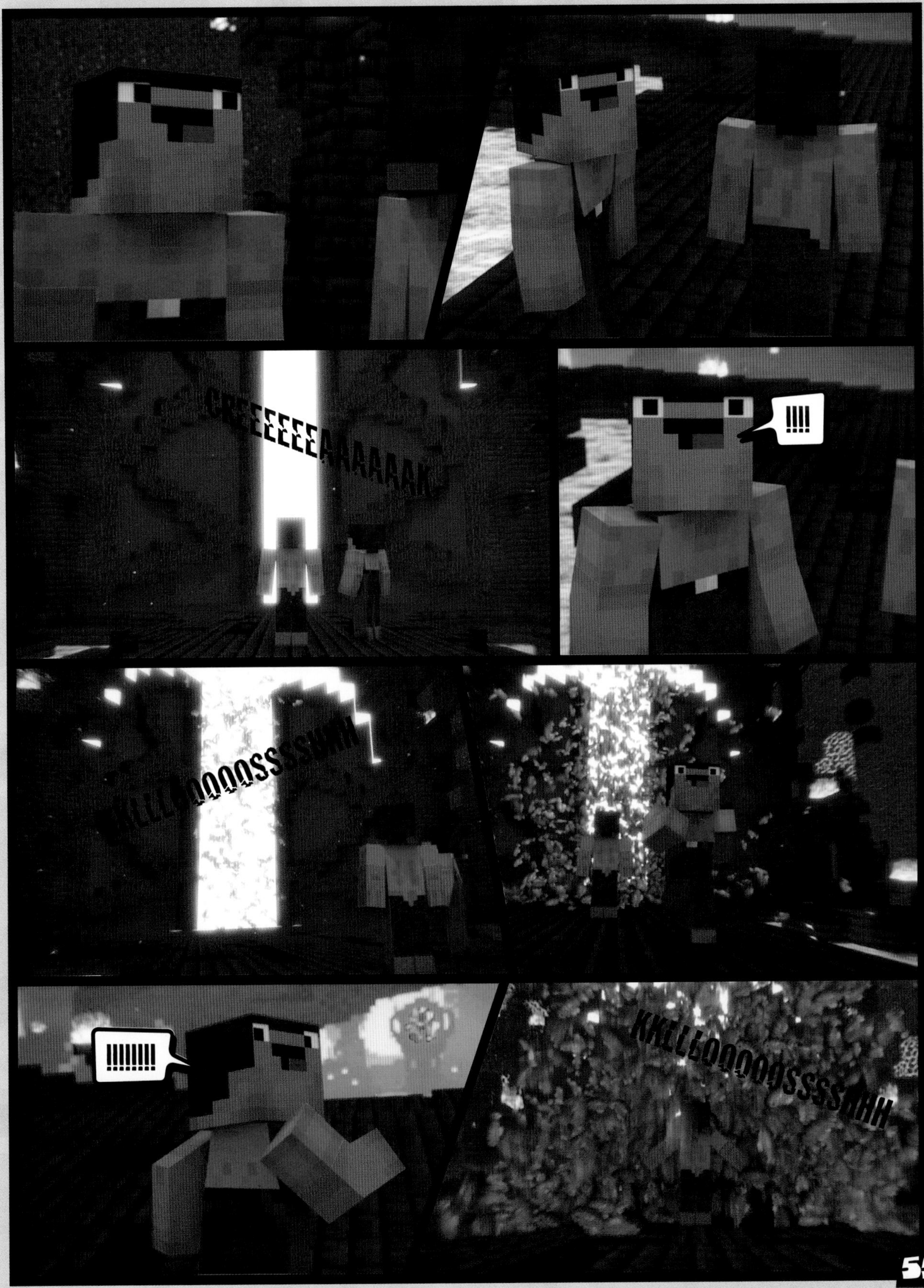
CREEEEEEAAAAAAK
!!!!
KKLLLOOOOOSSSSSHHH
!!!!!!!!
KKLLLOOOOOOSSSSHHH

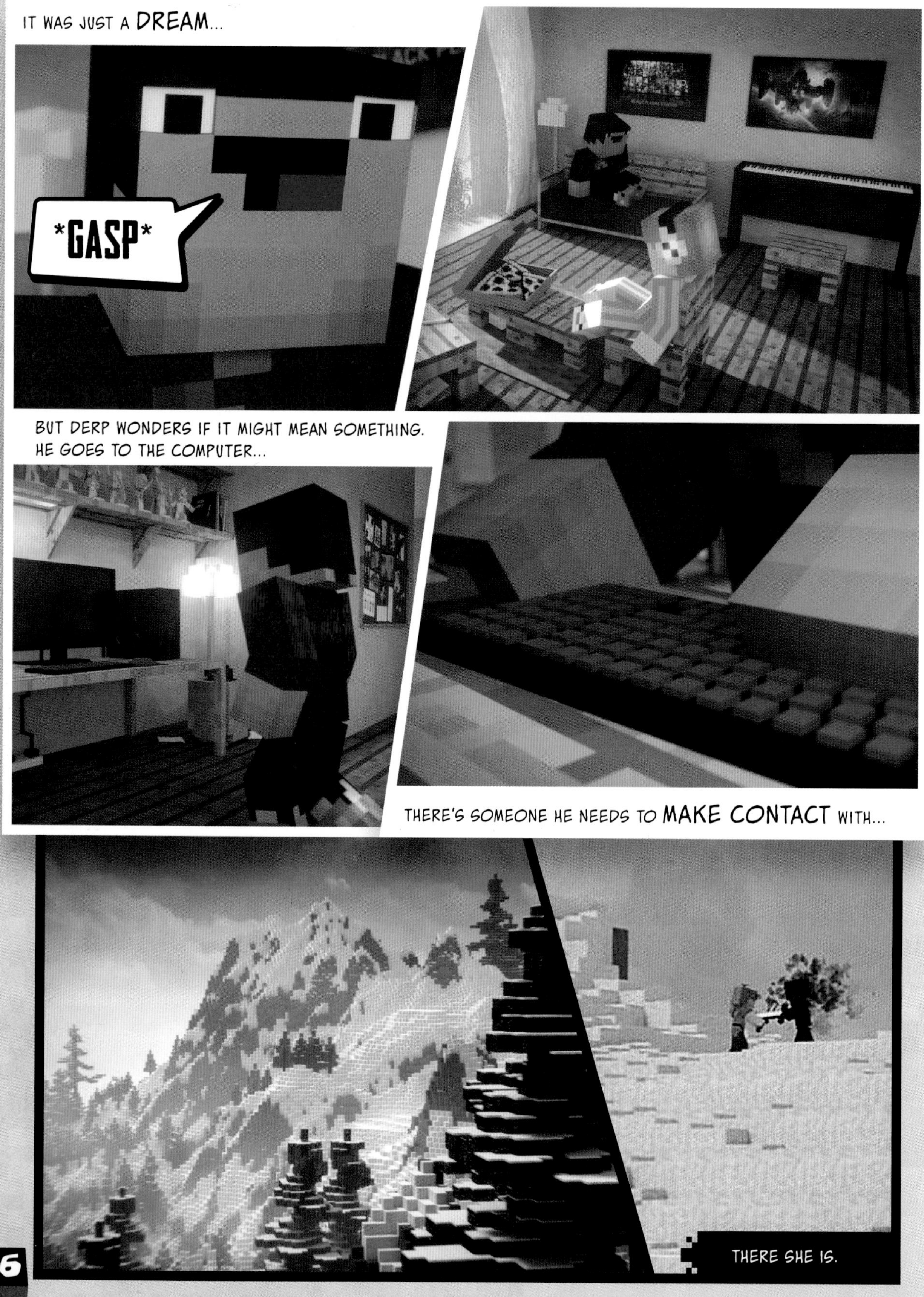
IT WAS JUST A DREAM...
GASP
BUT DERP WONDERS IF IT MIGHT MEAN SOMETHING. HE GOES TO THE COMPUTER...
THERE'S SOMEONE HE NEEDS TO MAKE CONTACT WITH...
THERE SHE IS.

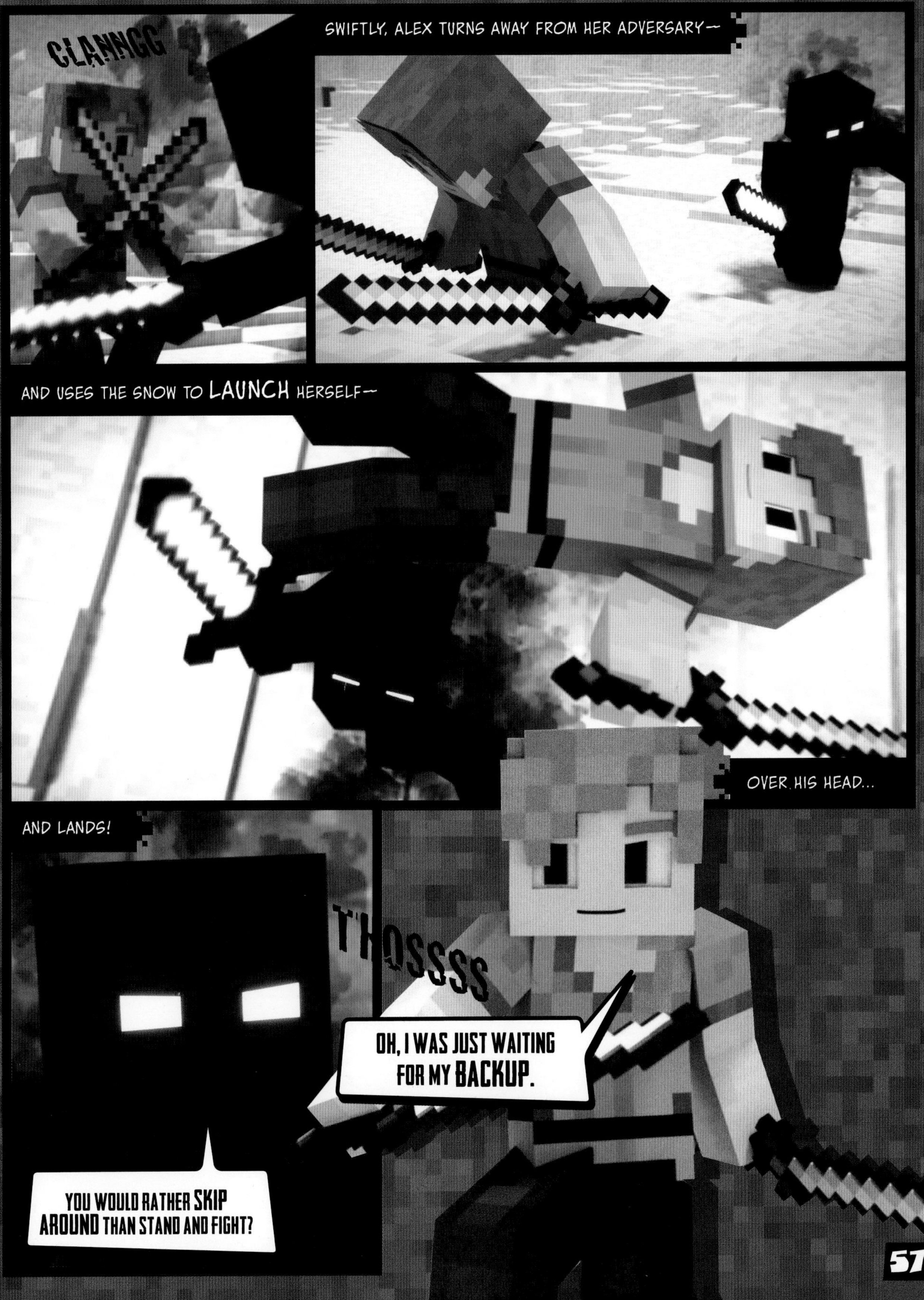
CLANNGG
SWIFTLY, ALEX TURNS AWAY FROM HER ADVERSARY—
AND USES THE SNOW TO LAUNCH HERSELF—
OVER HIS HEAD...
AND LANDS!
T'HOSSSS
OH, I WAS JUST WAITING FOR MY BACKUP.
YOU WOULD RATHER SKIP AROUND THAN STAND AND FIGHT?

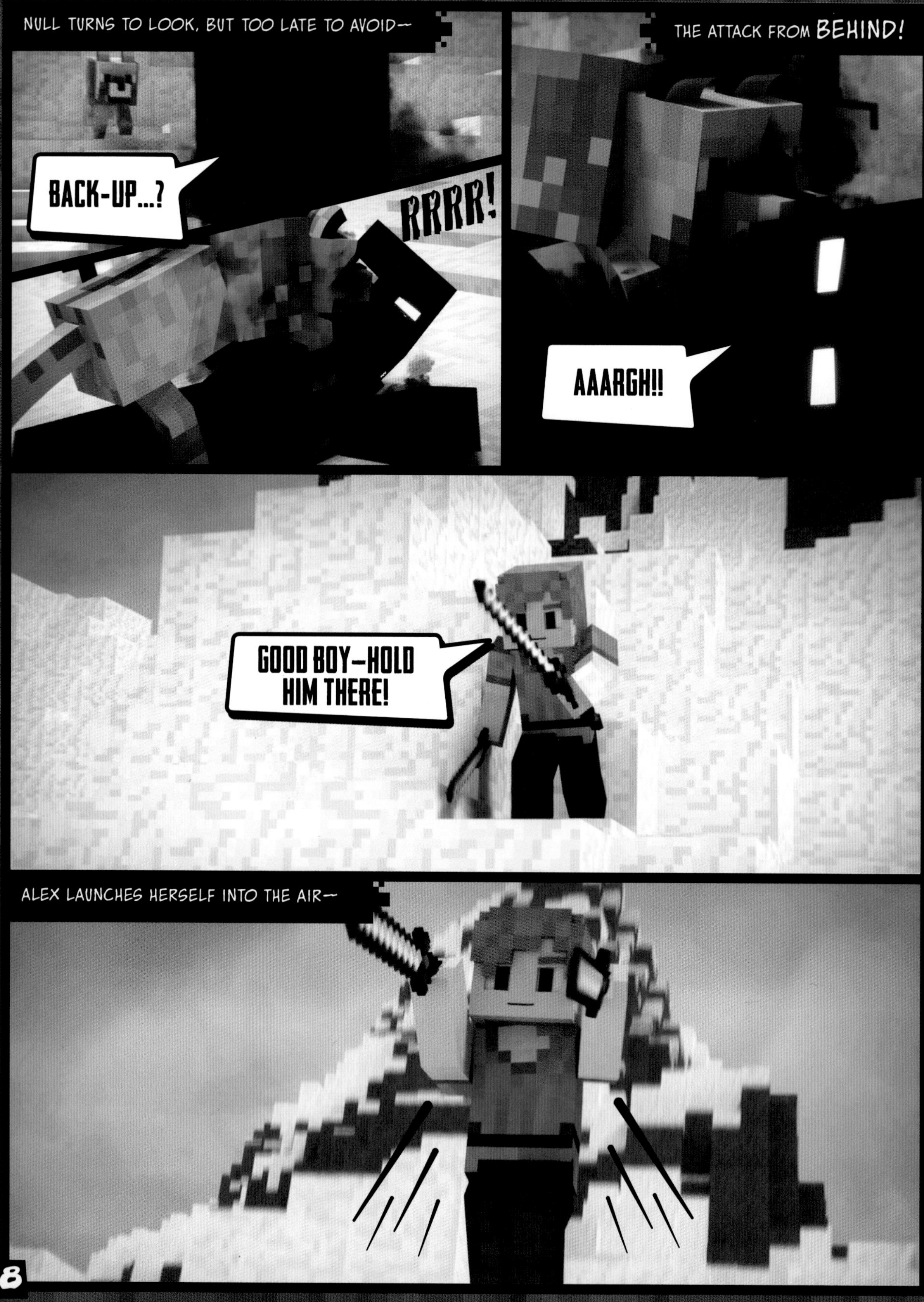
NULL TURNS TO LOOK, BUT TOO LATE TO AVOID—
BACK-UP...?
RRRR!
THE ATTACK FROM BEHIND!
AAARGH!!
GOOD BOY—HOLD HIM THERE!
ALEX LAUNCHES HERSELF INTO THE AIR—

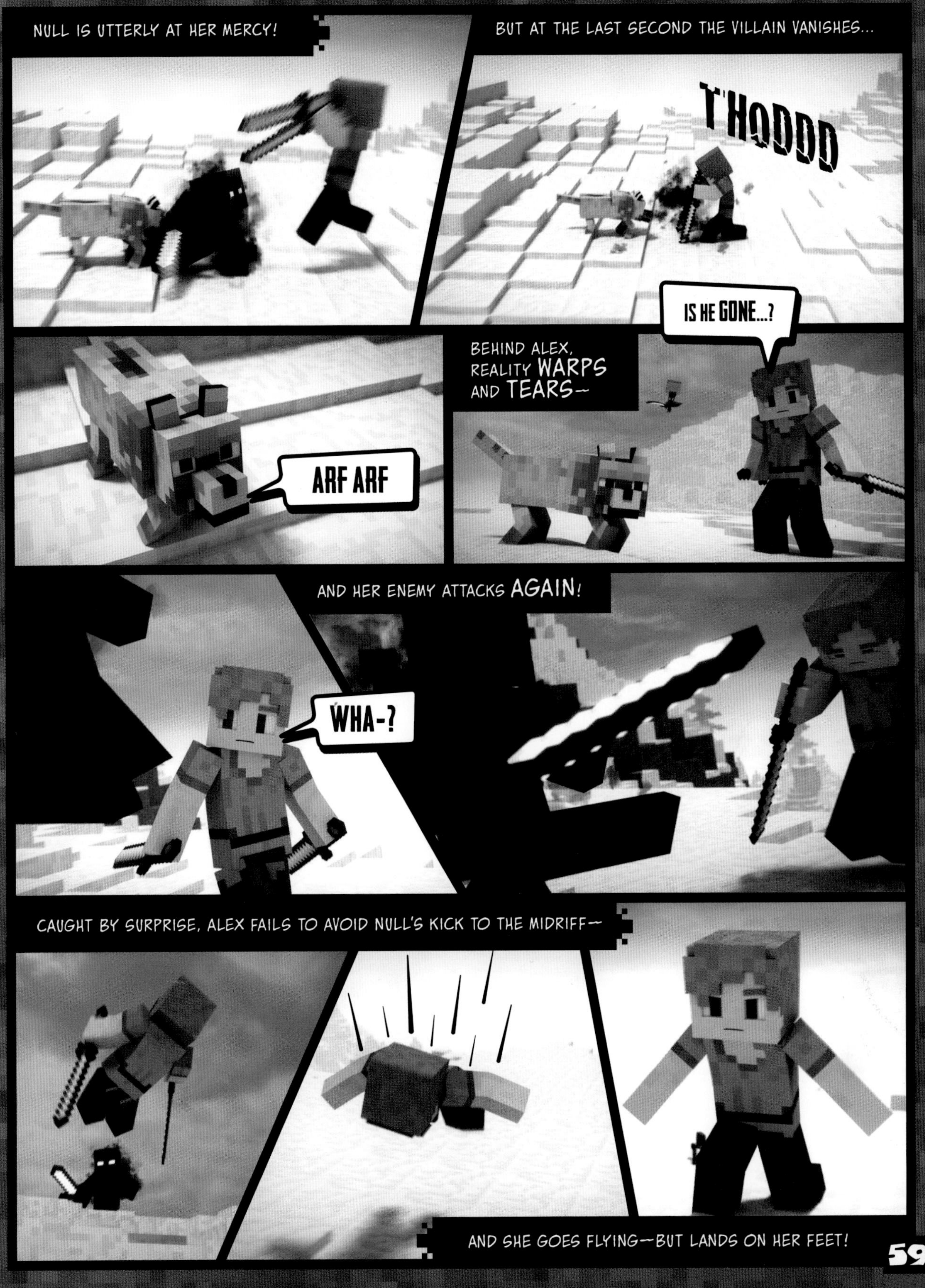
NULL IS UTTERLY AT HER MERCY!
BUT AT THE LAST SECOND THE VILLAIN VANISHES...
T'HODDD
IS HE GONE...?
ARF ARF
BEHIND ALEX, REALITY WARPS AND TEARS—
AND HER ENEMY ATTACKS AGAIN!
WHA-?
CAUGHT BY SURPRISE, ALEX FAILS TO AVOID NULL'S KICK TO THE MIDRIFF—
AND SHE GOES FLYING—BUT LANDS ON HER FEET!

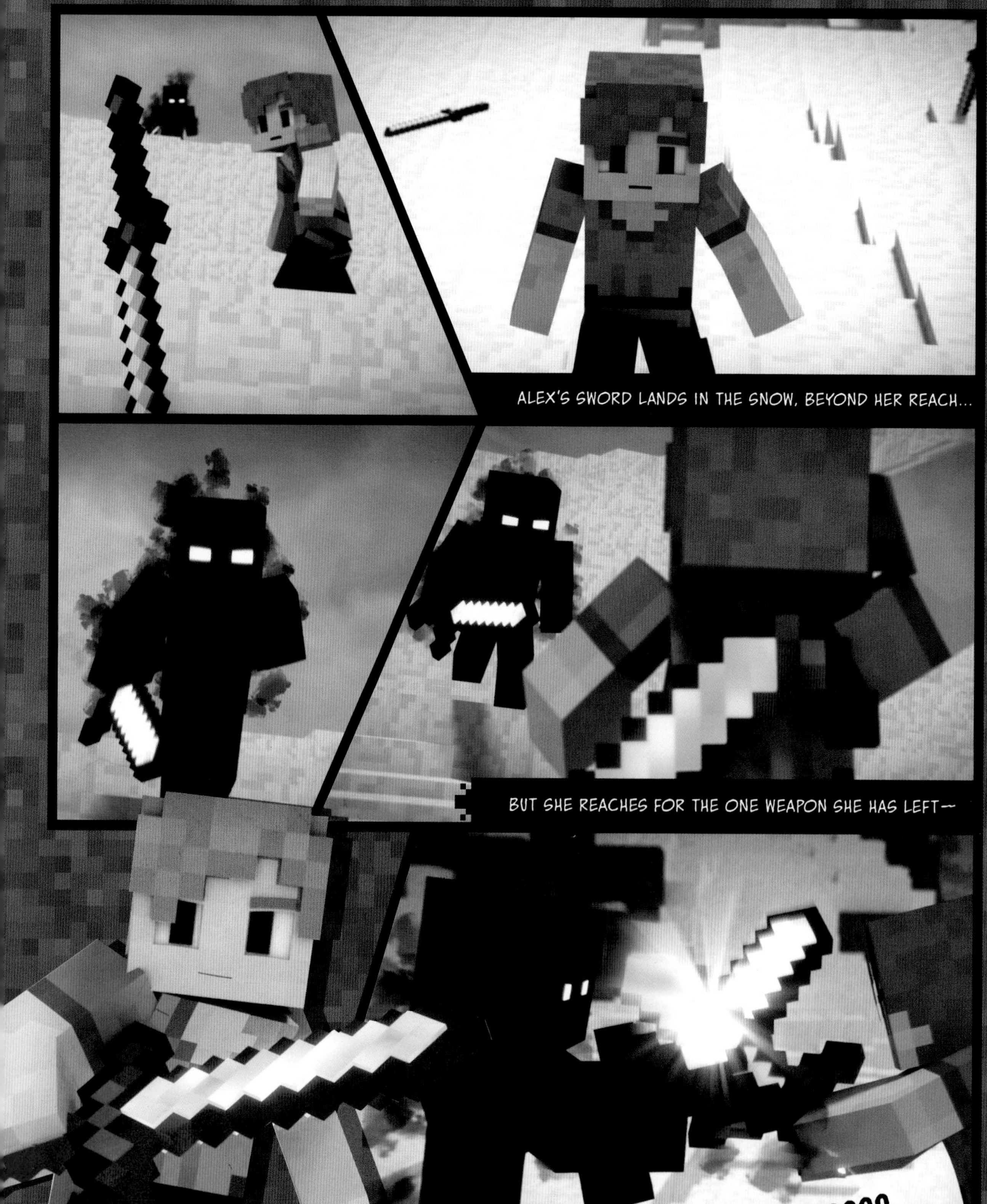
ALEX'S SWORD LANDS IN THE SNOW, BEYOND HER REACH...
BUT SHE REACHES FOR THE ONE WEAPON SHE HAS LEFT—
KLANNNNNGGGGGG

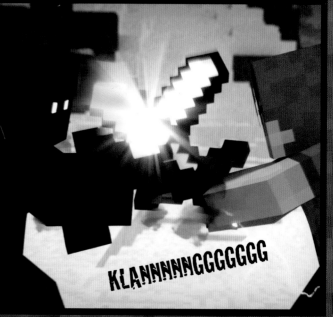

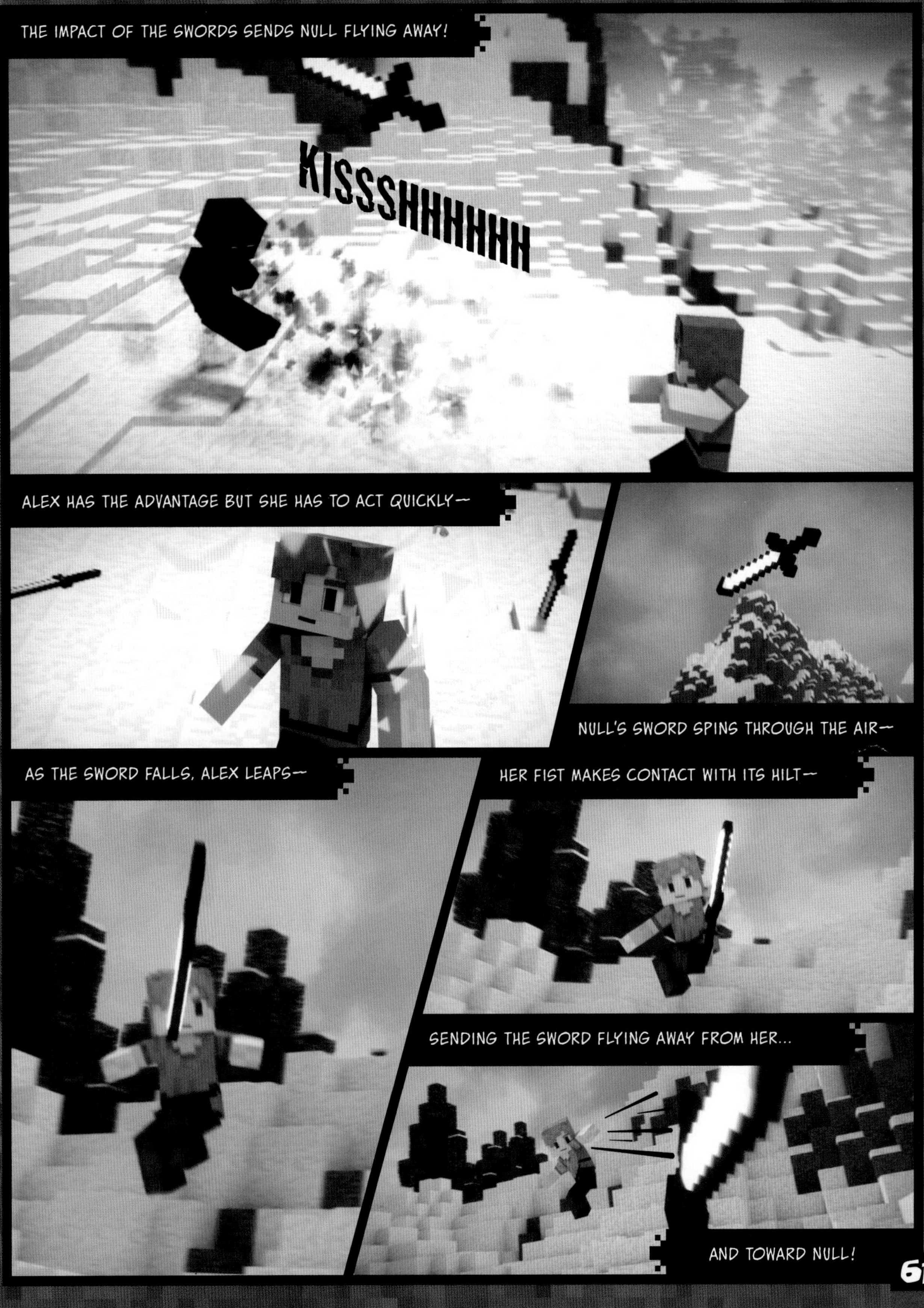

THE IMPACT OF THE SWORDS SENDS NULL FLYING AWAY!
KISSSHHHHHH
ALEX HAS THE ADVANTAGE BUT SHE HAS TO ACT QUICKLY—
NULL'S SWORD SPINS THROUGH THE AIR—
AS THE SWORD FALLS, ALEX LEAPS—
HER FIST MAKES CONTACT WITH ITS HILT—
SENDING THE SWORD FLYING AWAY FROM HER...
AND TOWARD NULL!

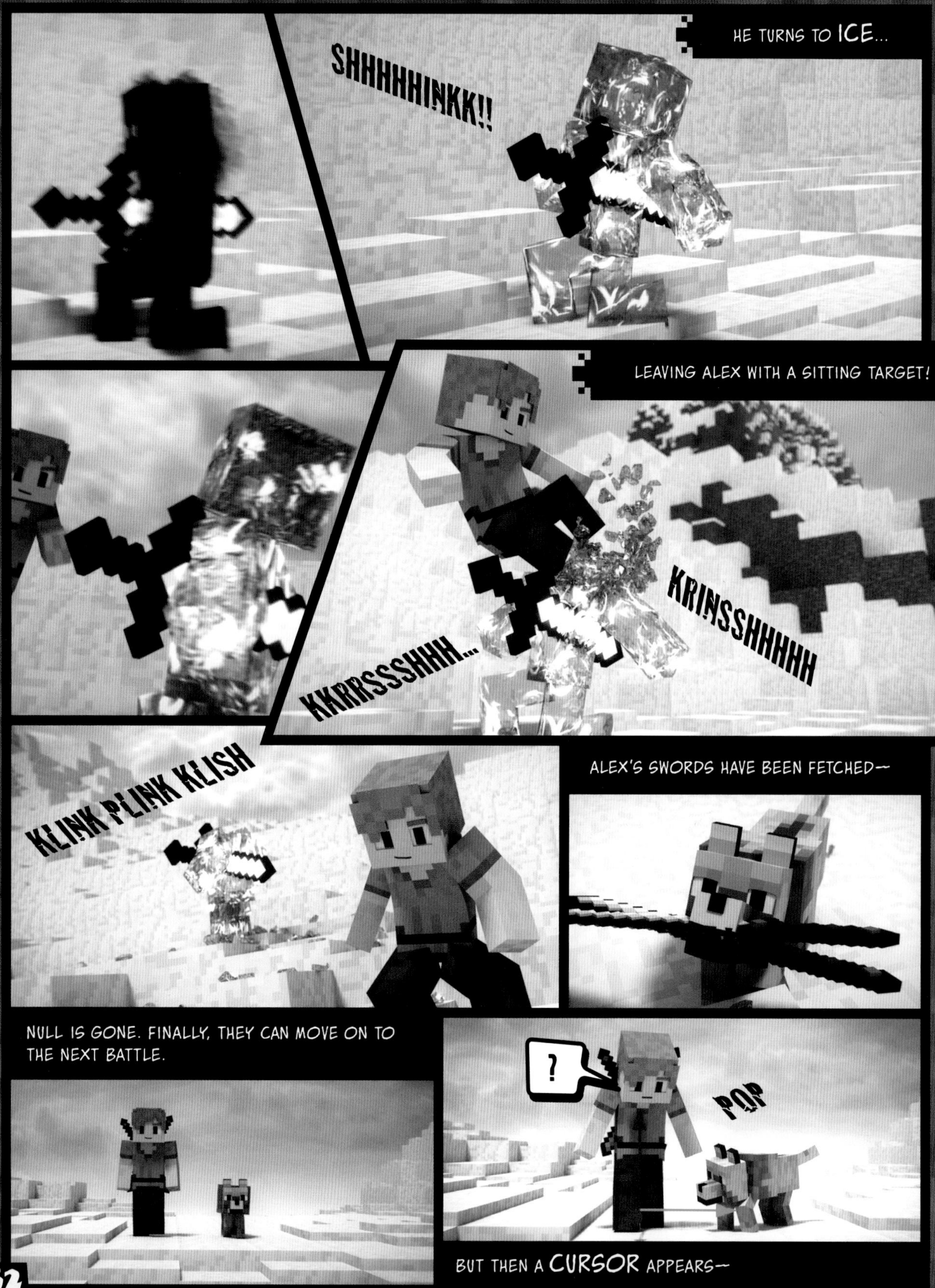

HE TURNS TO ICE...
SHHHHHINKK!!
LEAVING ALEX WITH A SITTING TARGET!
KRINSSHHHHH
KKRRSSSHHH...
KLINK PLINK KLISH
ALEX'S SWORDS HAVE BEEN FETCHED—
NULL IS GONE. FINALLY, THEY CAN MOVE ON TO THE NEXT BATTLE.
?
POP
BUT THEN A CURSOR APPEARS—

AND IT STARTS TO PULL ALEX AWAY!

WAAAH!

ARF! ARF ARF!

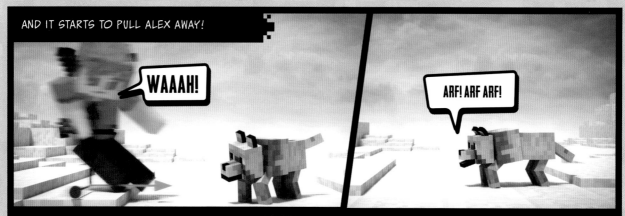

ALEX FINDS HERSELF DRAGGED **HERE**—

AND HER COMPANION IS BROUGHT TO JOIN HER!

WHINE

POP

A FAMILIAR FIGURE APPEARS—

STEVE...?

YES, IT **LOOKS** LIKE STEVE...

BUT THEN THE FACE STARTS TO **CHANGE**...

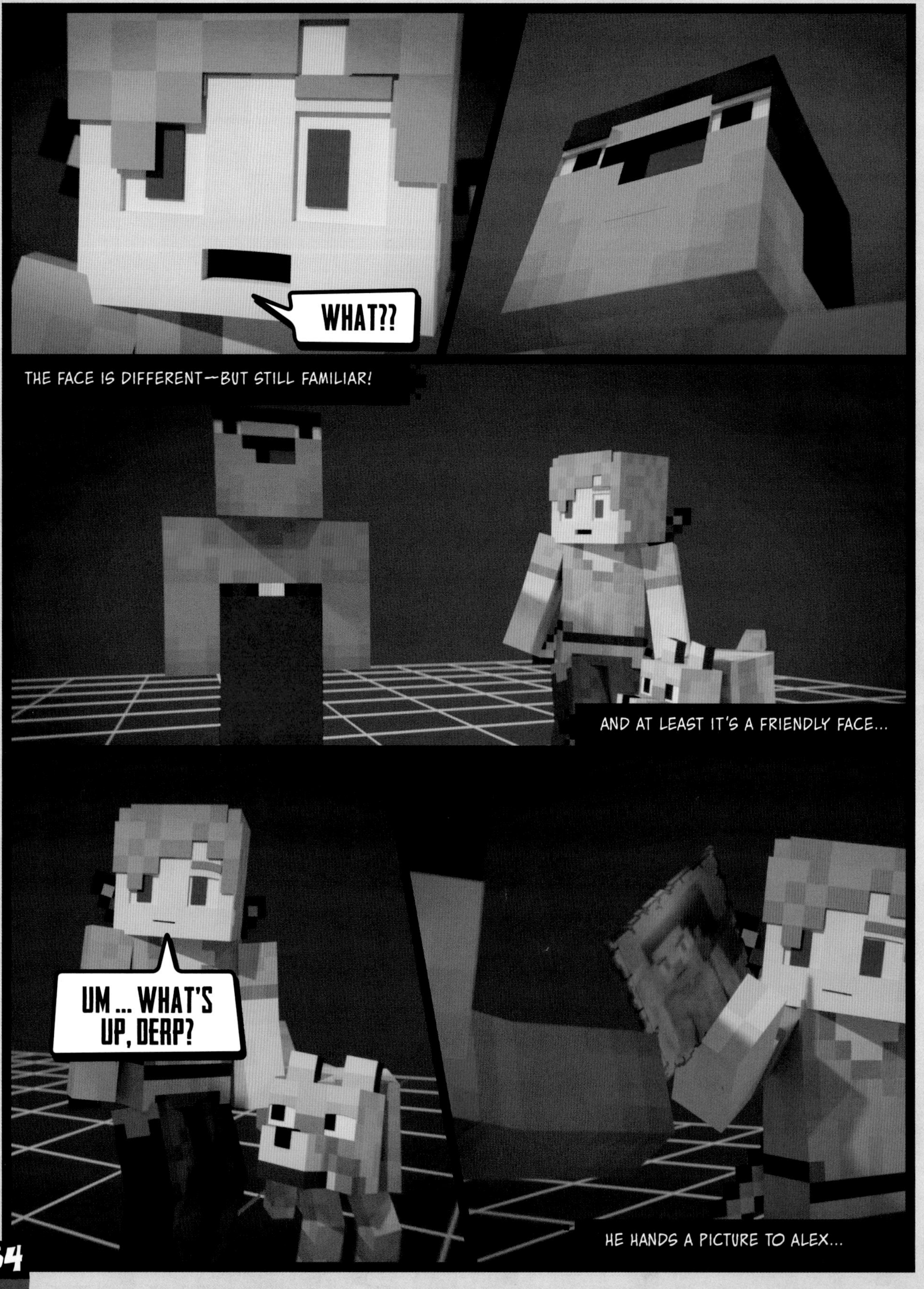
WHAT??
THE FACE IS DIFFERENT—BUT STILL FAMILIAR!
AND AT LEAST IT'S A FRIENDLY FACE...
UM ... WHAT'S UP, DERP?
HE HANDS A PICTURE TO ALEX...

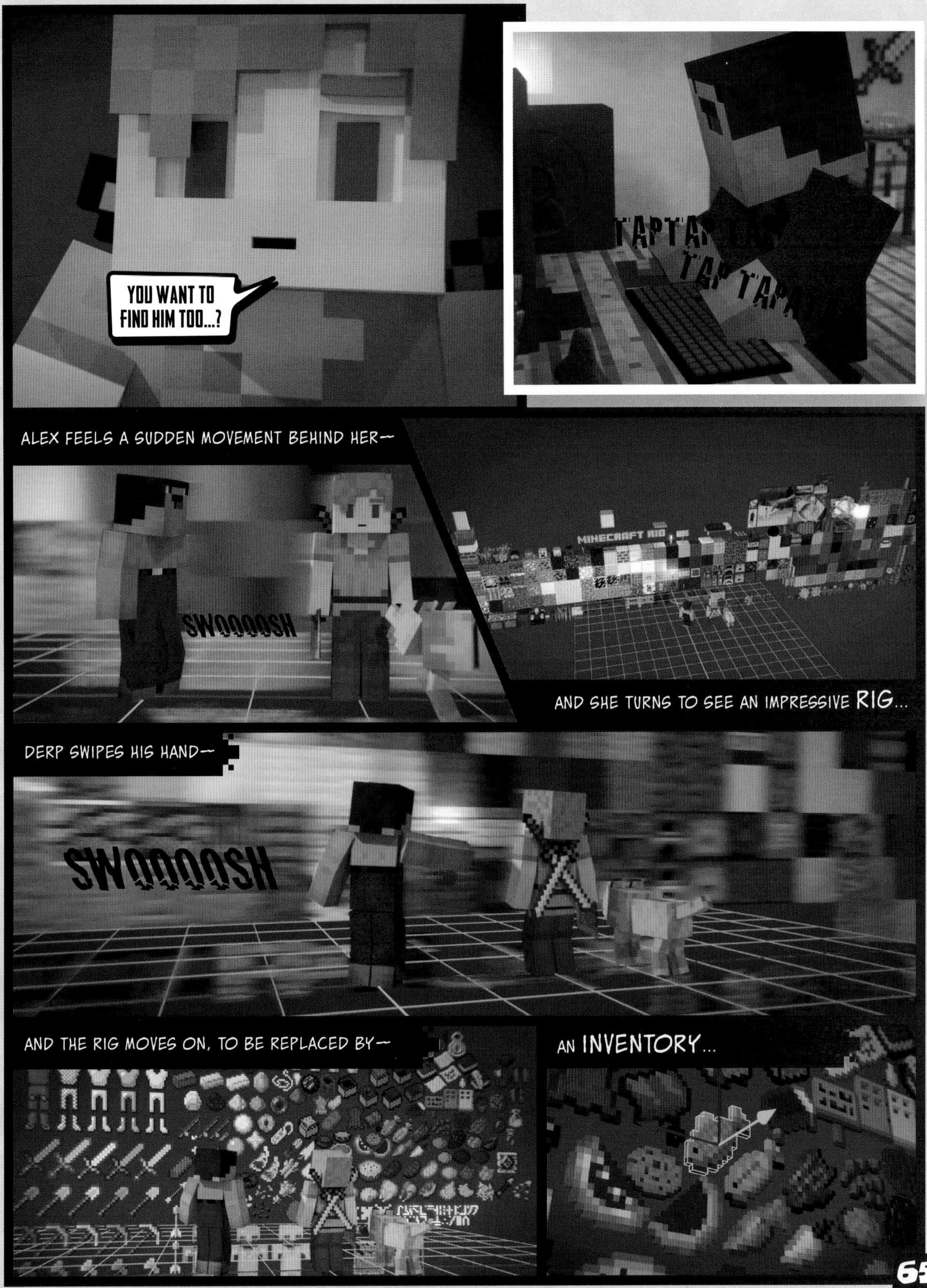
YOU WANT TO FIND HIM TOO...?
TAPTAP TAP TAP TAPTAP
ALEX FEELS A SUDDEN MOVEMENT BEHIND HER—
SWOOOOSH
MINECRAFT RIG
AND SHE TURNS TO SEE AN IMPRESSIVE RIG...
DERP SWIPES HIS HAND—
SWOOOOSH
AND THE RIG MOVES ON, TO BE REPLACED BY—
AN INVENTORY...

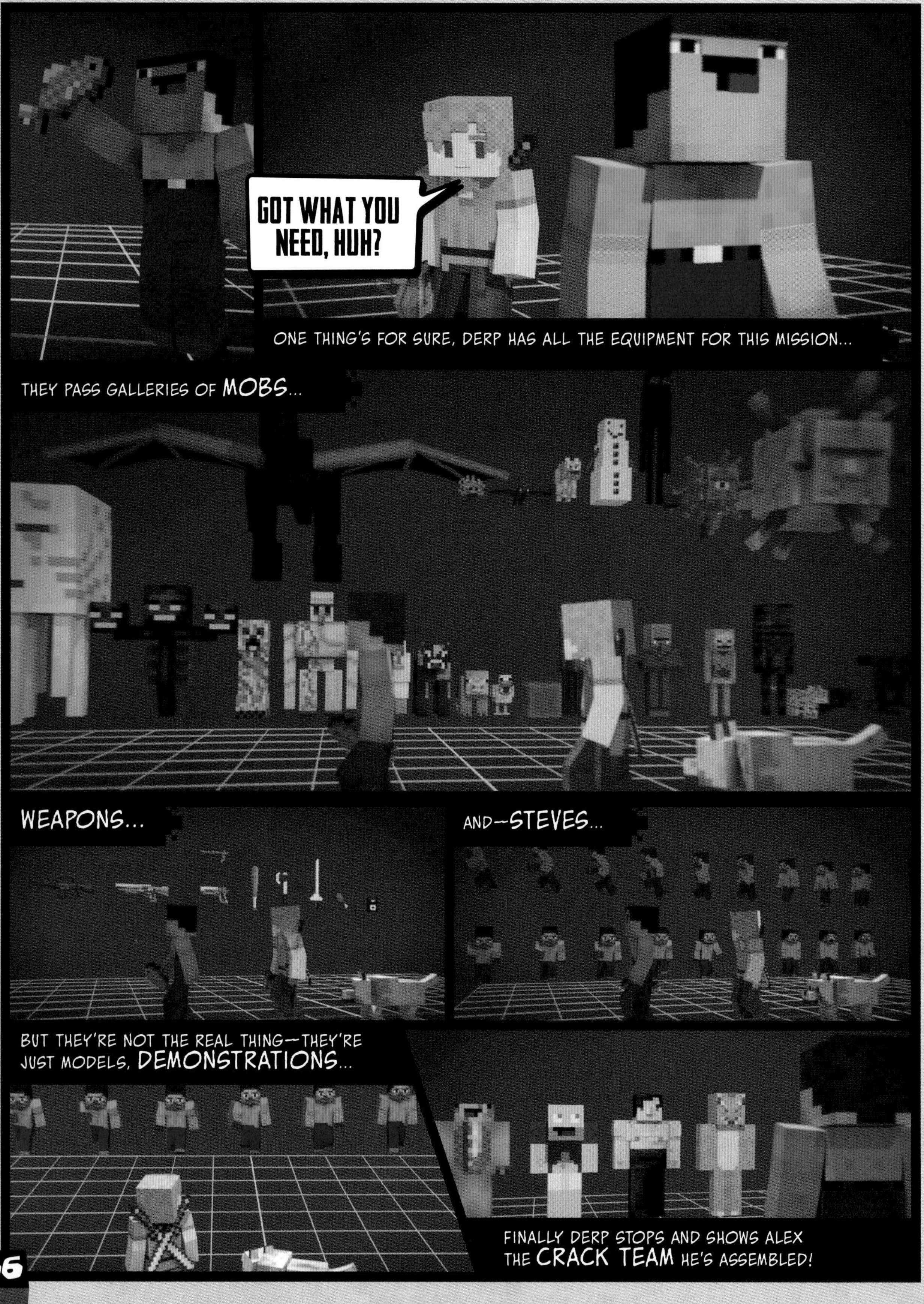

GOT WHAT YOU NEED, HUH?
ONE THING'S FOR SURE, DERP HAS ALL THE EQUIPMENT FOR THIS MISSION...
THEY PASS GALLERIES OF MOBS...
WEAPONS...
AND—STEVES...
BUT THEY'RE NOT THE REAL THING—THEY'RE JUST MODELS, DEMONSTRATIONS...
FINALLY DERP STOPS AND SHOWS ALEX THE CRACK TEAM HE'S ASSEMBLED!

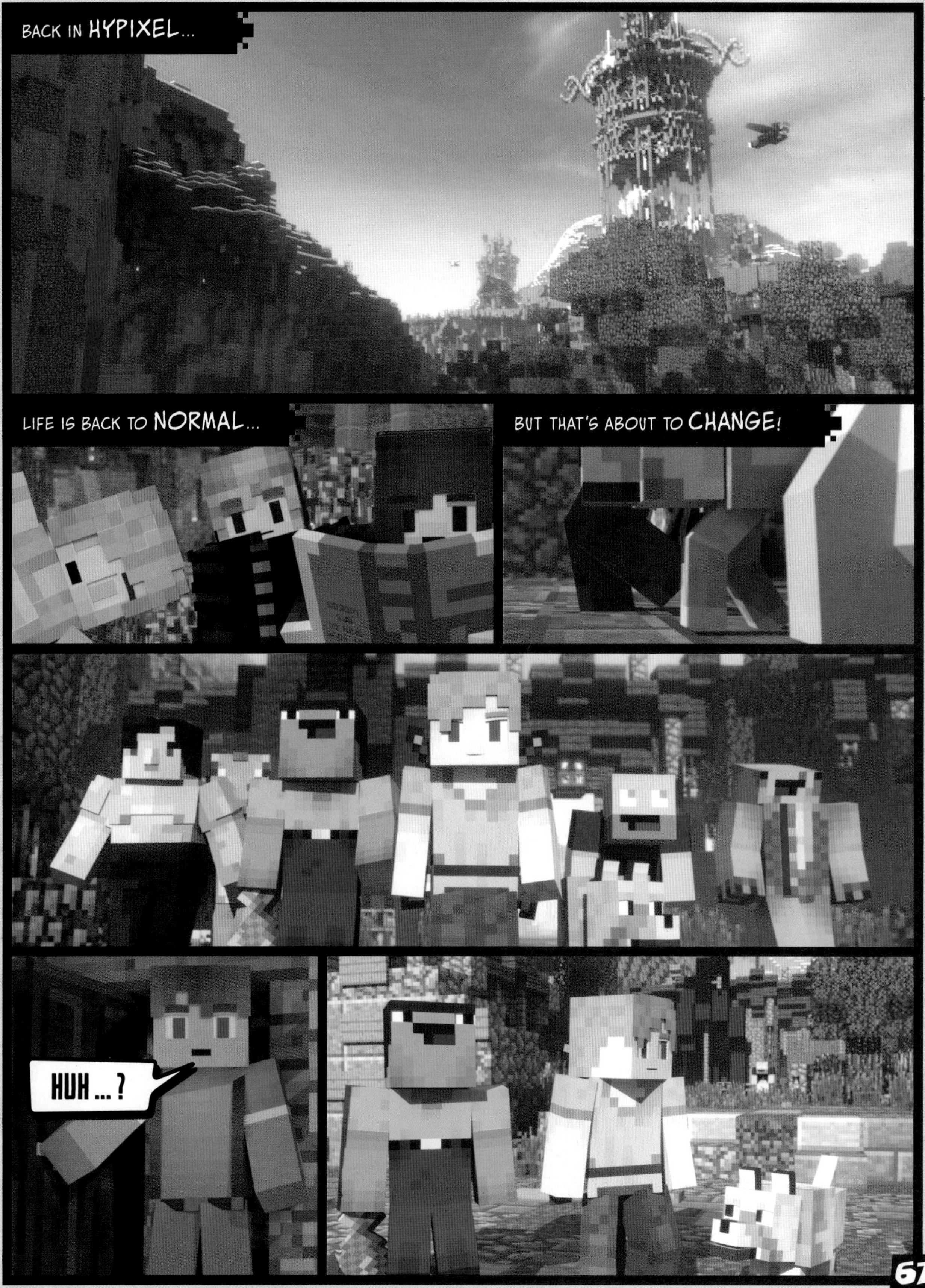
BACK IN HYPIXEL...
LIFE IS BACK TO NORMAL...
BUT THAT'S ABOUT TO CHANGE!
HUH...?

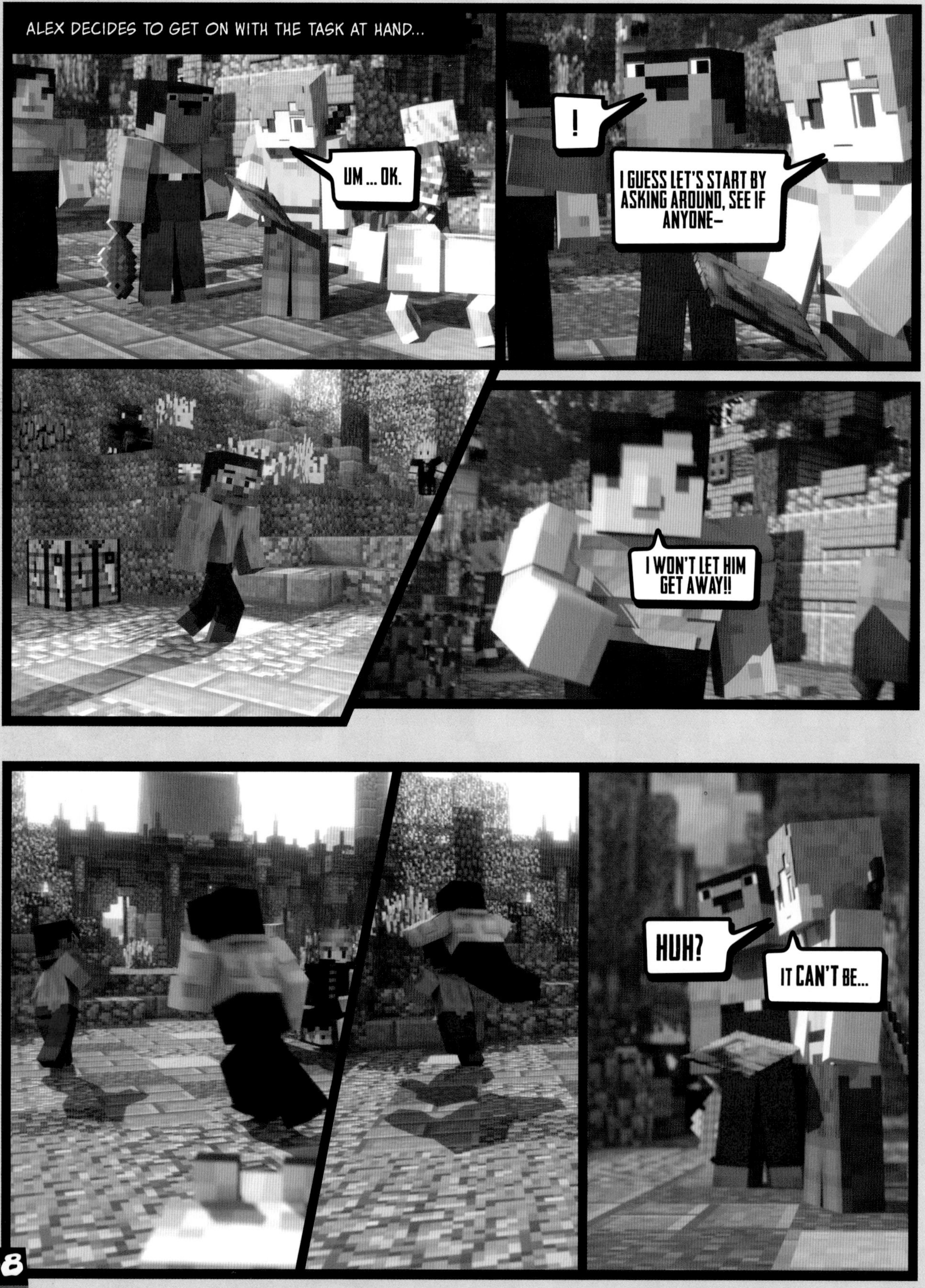
ALEX DECIDES TO GET ON WITH THE TASK AT HAND...
UM ... OK.
!
I GUESS LET'S START BY ASKING AROUND, SEE IF ANYONE–
I WON'T LET HIM GET AWAY!!
HUH?
IT CAN'T BE...

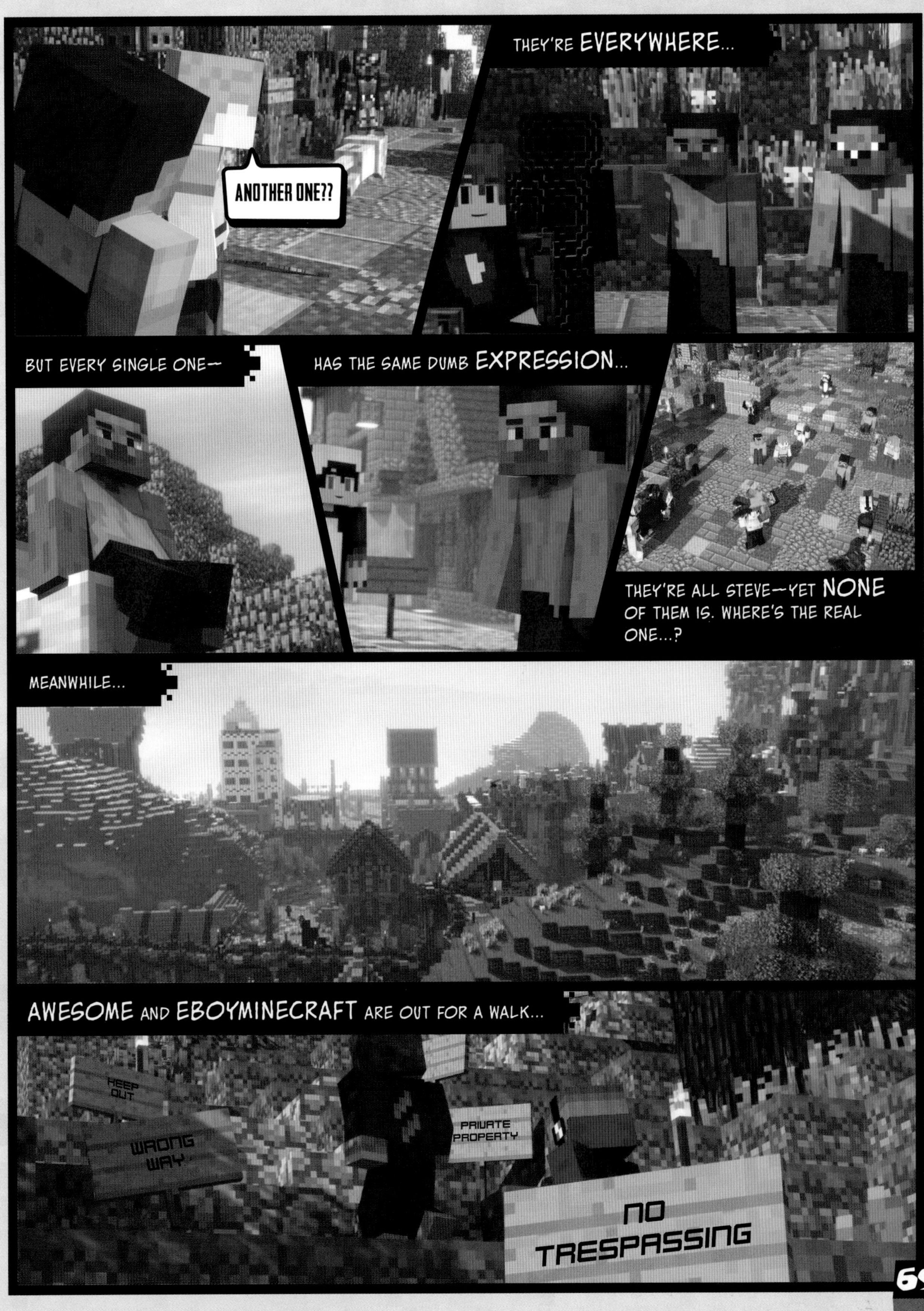
ANOTHER ONE??
THEY'RE EVERYWHERE...
BUT EVERY SINGLE ONE—
HAS THE SAME DUMB EXPRESSION...
THEY'RE ALL STEVE—YET NONE OF THEM IS. WHERE'S THE REAL ONE...?
MEANWHILE...
AWESOME AND EBOYMINECRAFT ARE OUT FOR A WALK...
KEEP OUT
WRONG WAY
PRIVATE PROPERTY
NO TRESPASSING

I WONDER WHY NO ONE COMES UP HERE...

THIS PLACE IS COOL...

WOAH—WAIT...

THE FIGURE TURNS TO FACE THEM~

AND THEY BOTH FLEE!

YAAAAAA

BUT IF THEY'D STUCK AROUND, THEY MIGHT HAVE NOTICED THE FIGURE'S **OTHER** EYE...

STEVE IS TORMENTED BY VISIONS OF HIS LIFE BEFORE~

A BATTLE IS GOING ON INSIDE HIM~

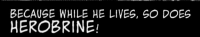

BECAUSE WHILE HE LIVES, SO DOES **HEROBRINE**!

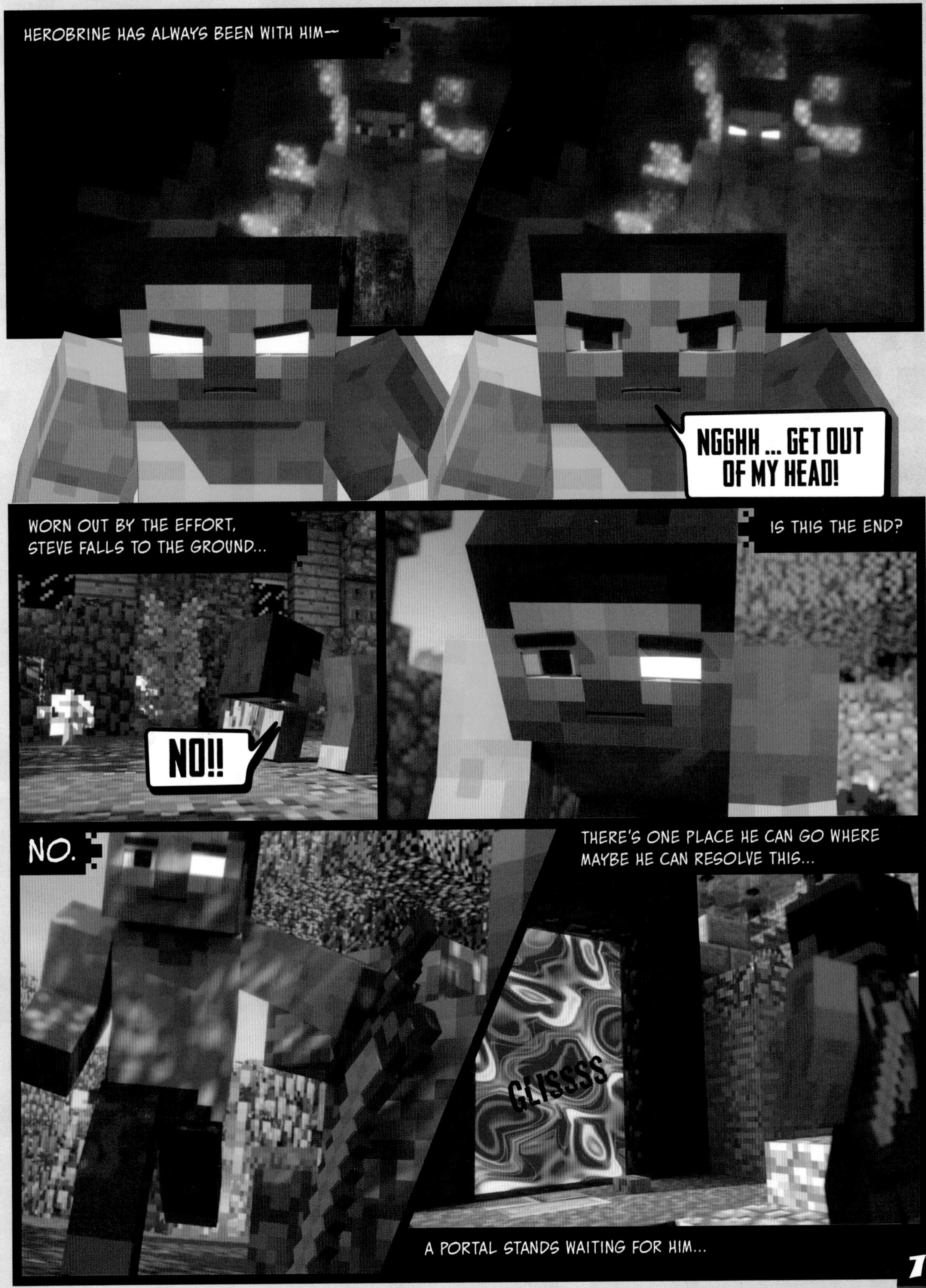

HEROBRINE HAS ALWAYS BEEN WITH HIM—
NGGHH ... GET OUT OF MY HEAD!
WORN OUT BY THE EFFORT, STEVE FALLS TO THE GROUND...
NO!!
IS THIS THE END?
NO.
THERE'S ONE PLACE HE CAN GO WHERE MAYBE HE CAN RESOLVE THIS...
GLISSSS
A PORTAL STANDS WAITING FOR HIM...

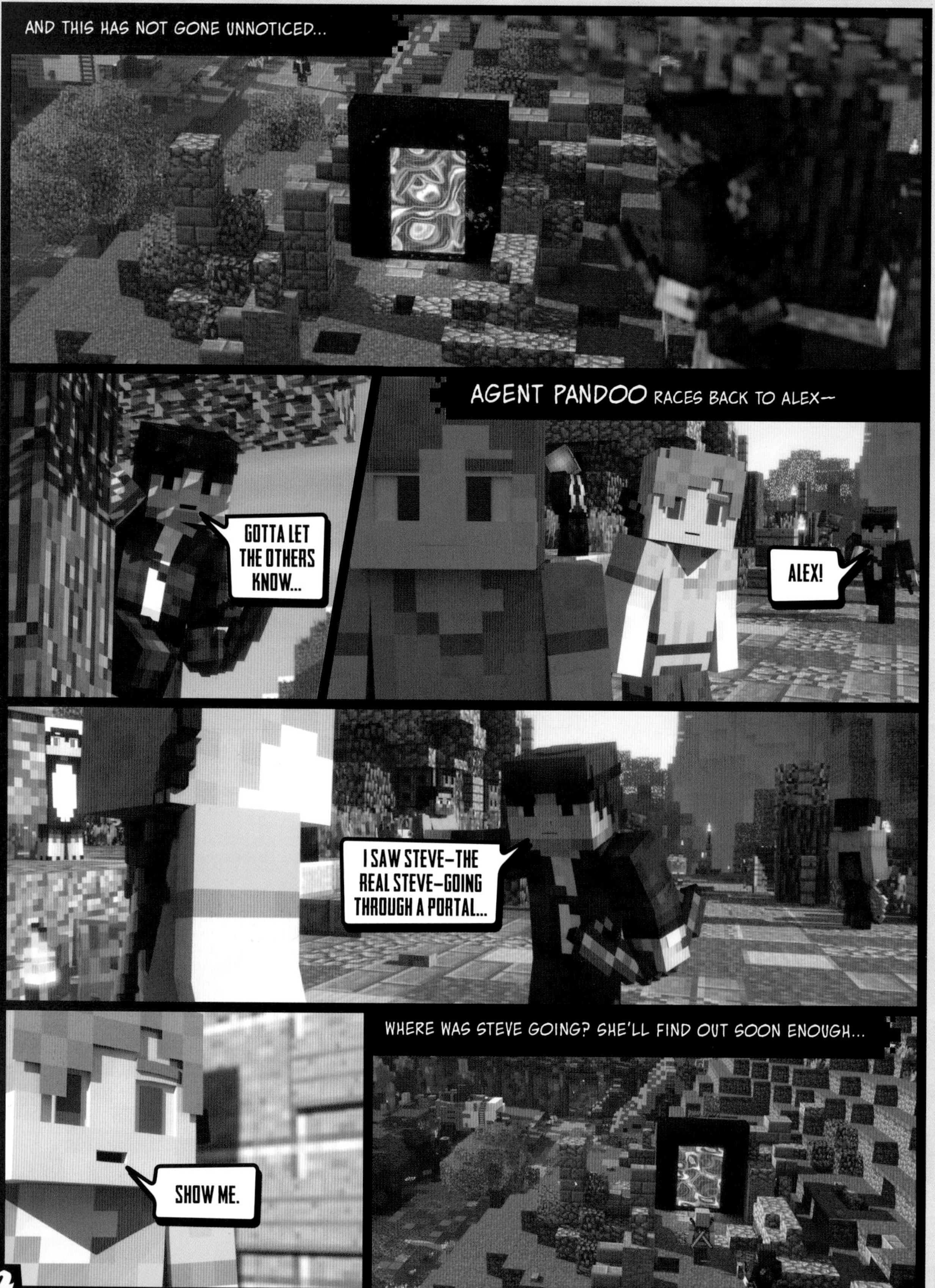
AND THIS HAS NOT GONE UNNOTICED...
GOTTA LET THE OTHERS KNOW...
AGENT PANDOO RACES BACK TO ALEX—
ALEX!
I SAW STEVE—THE REAL STEVE—GOING THROUGH A PORTAL...
SHOW ME.
WHERE WAS STEVE GOING? SHE'LL FIND OUT SOON ENOUGH...

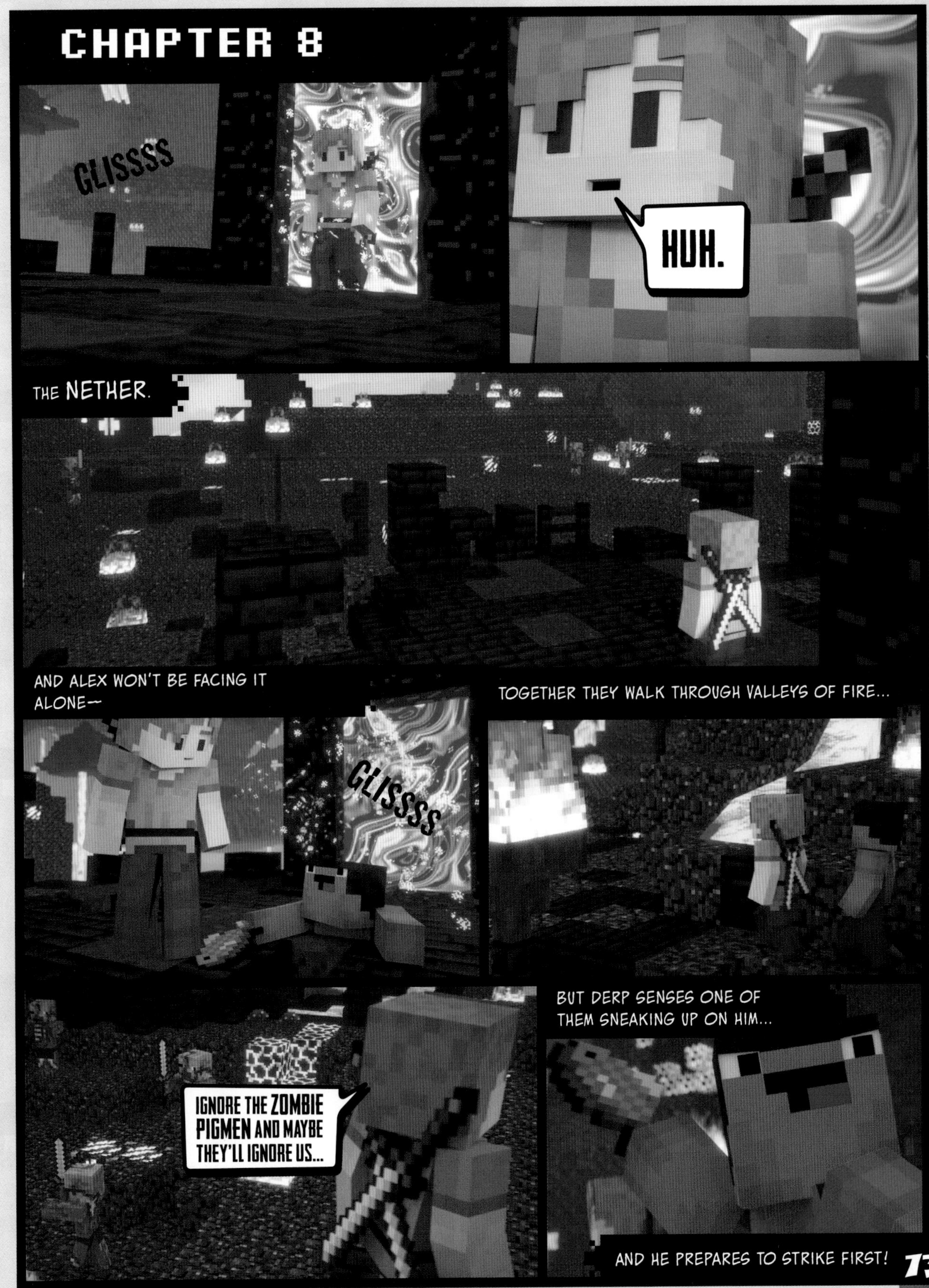
CHAPTER 8
GLISSSS
HUH.
THE NETHER.
AND ALEX WON'T BE FACING IT ALONE—
GLISSSS
TOGETHER THEY WALK THROUGH VALLEYS OF FIRE...
IGNORE THE ZOMBIE PIGMEN AND MAYBE THEY'LL IGNORE US...
BUT DERP SENSES ONE OF THEM SNEAKING UP ON HIM...
AND HE PREPARES TO STRIKE FIRST!

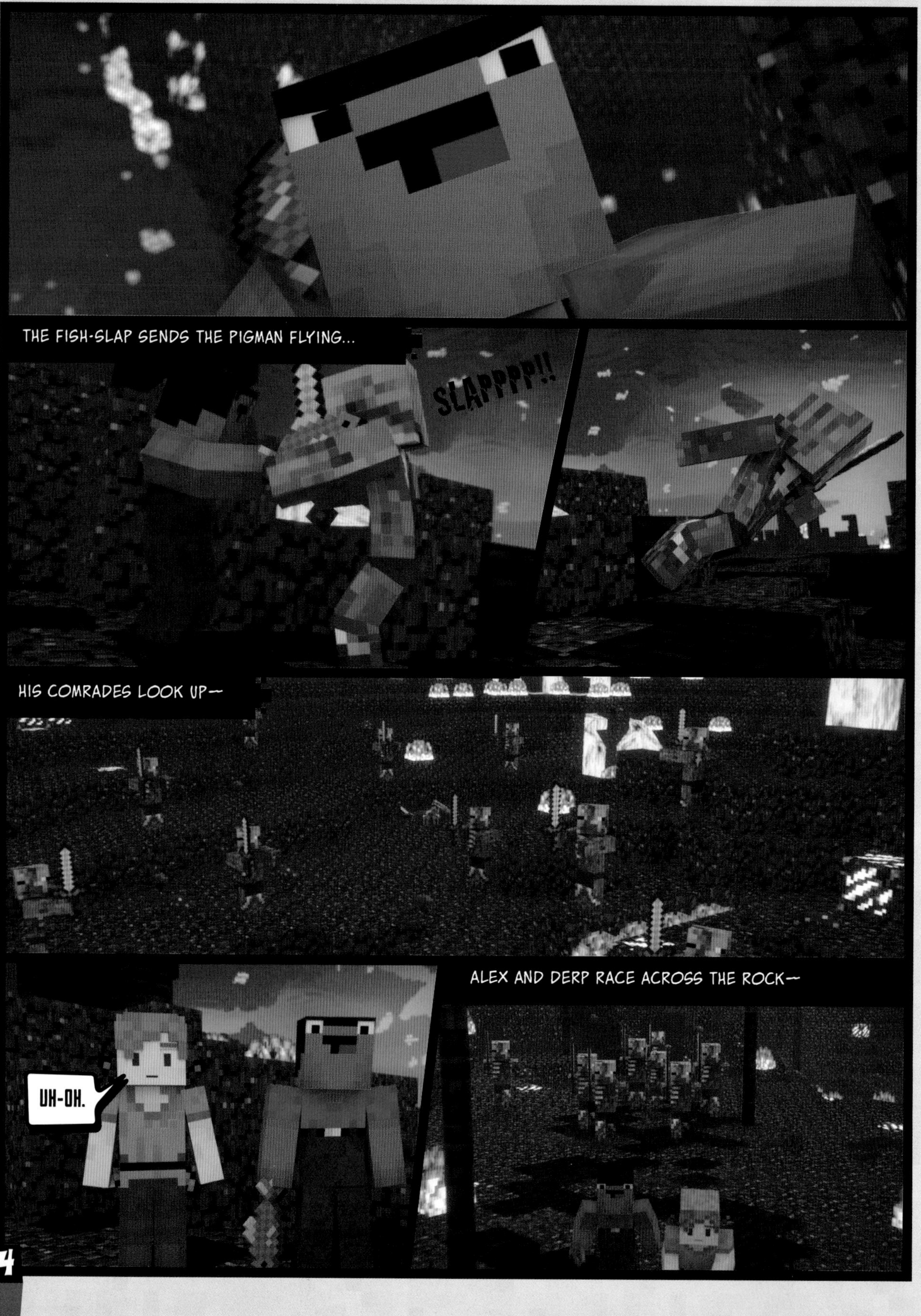

THE FISH-SLAP SENDS THE PIGMAN FLYING...
SLAPPPP!!
HIS COMRADES LOOK UP—
UH-OH.
ALEX AND DERP RACE ACROSS THE ROCK—

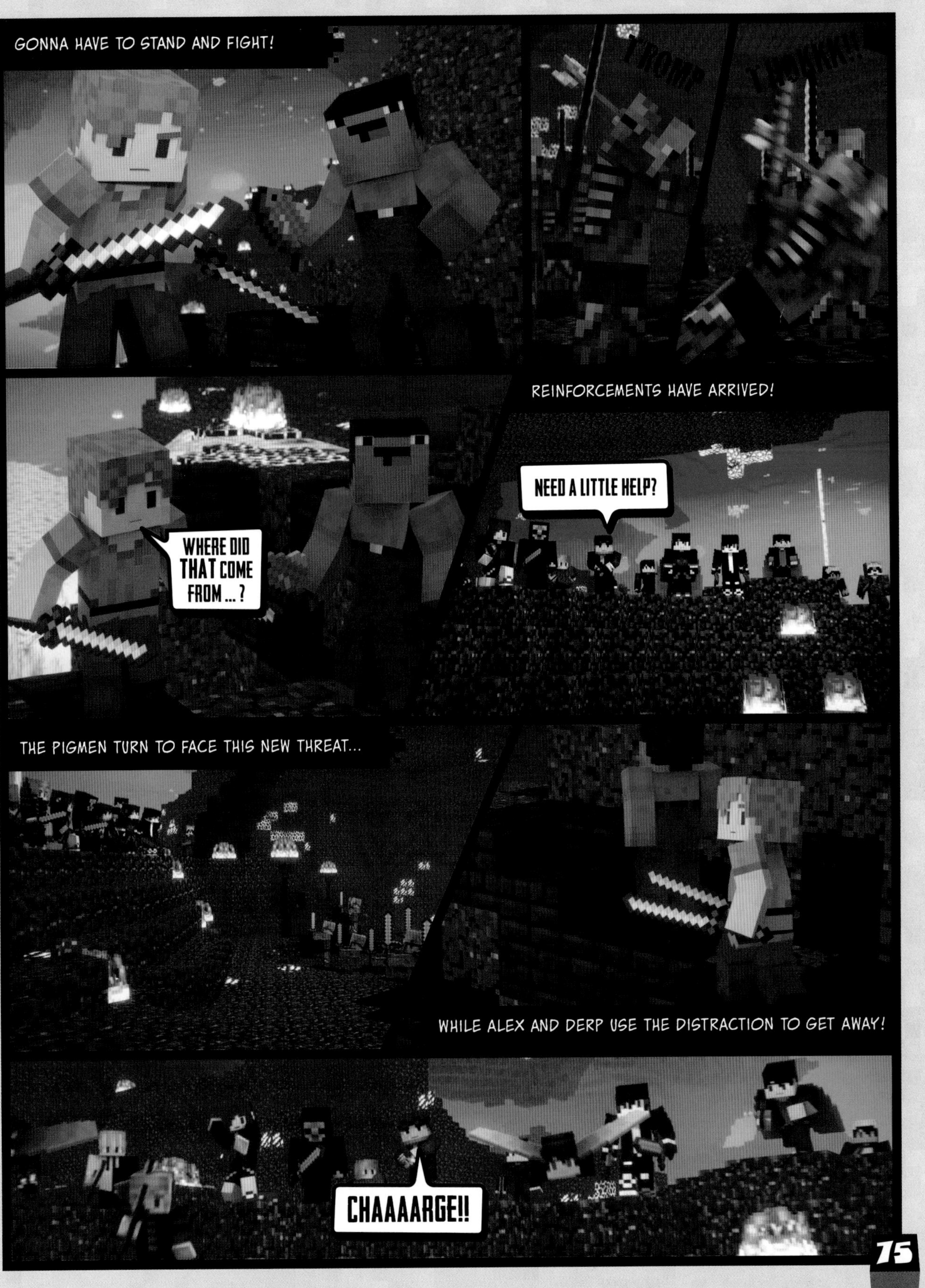
GONNA HAVE TO STAND AND FIGHT!
TROMP
WHERE DID THAT COME FROM ... ?
REINFORCEMENTS HAVE ARRIVED!
NEED A LITTLE HELP?
THE PIGMEN TURN TO FACE THIS NEW THREAT...
WHILE ALEX AND DERP USE THE DISTRACTION TO GET AWAY!
CHAAAARGE!!

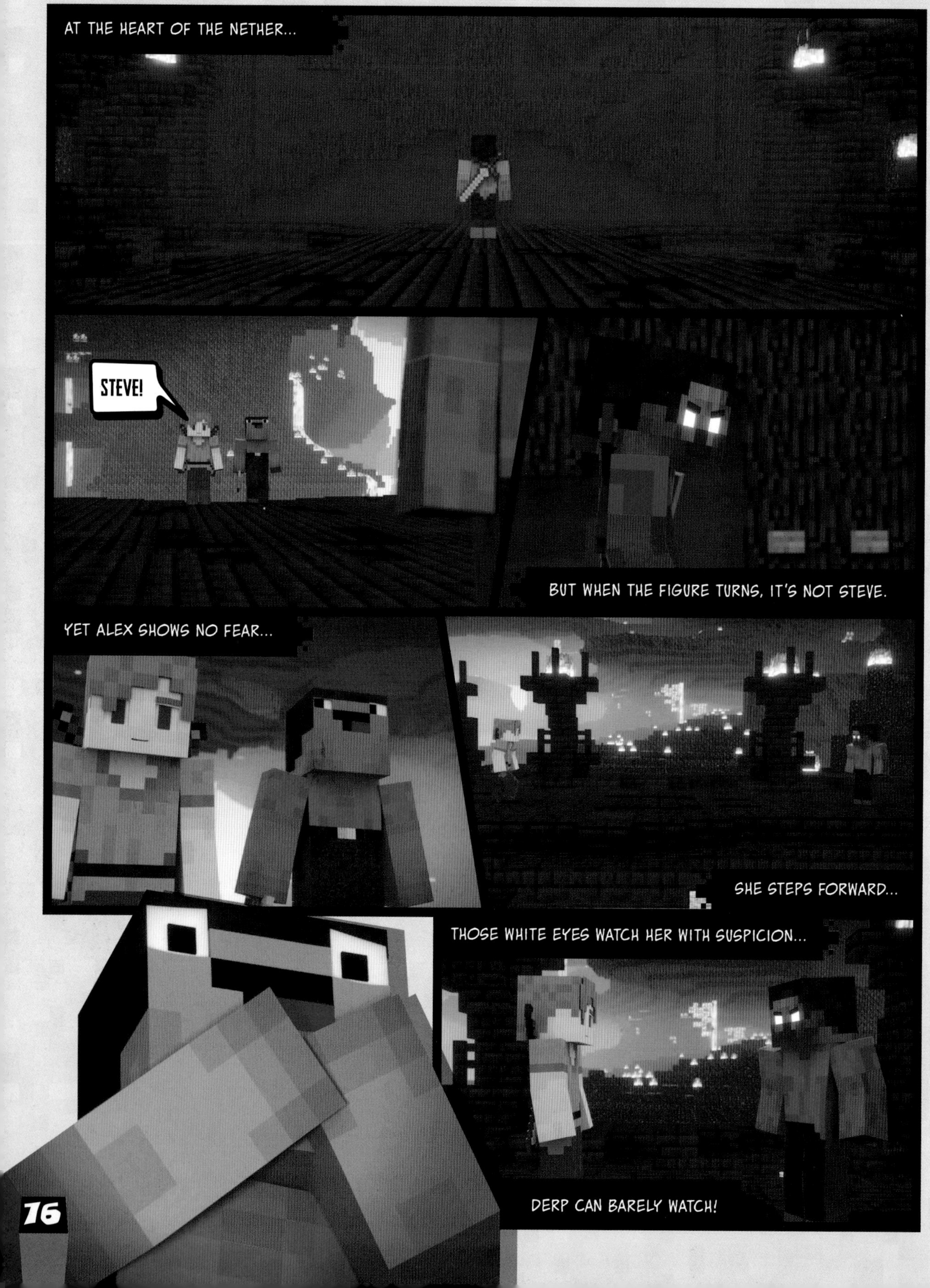
AT THE HEART OF THE NETHER...
STEVE!
BUT WHEN THE FIGURE TURNS, IT'S NOT STEVE.
YET ALEX SHOWS NO FEAR...
SHE STEPS FORWARD...
THOSE WHITE EYES WATCH HER WITH SUSPICION...
DERP CAN BARELY WATCH!

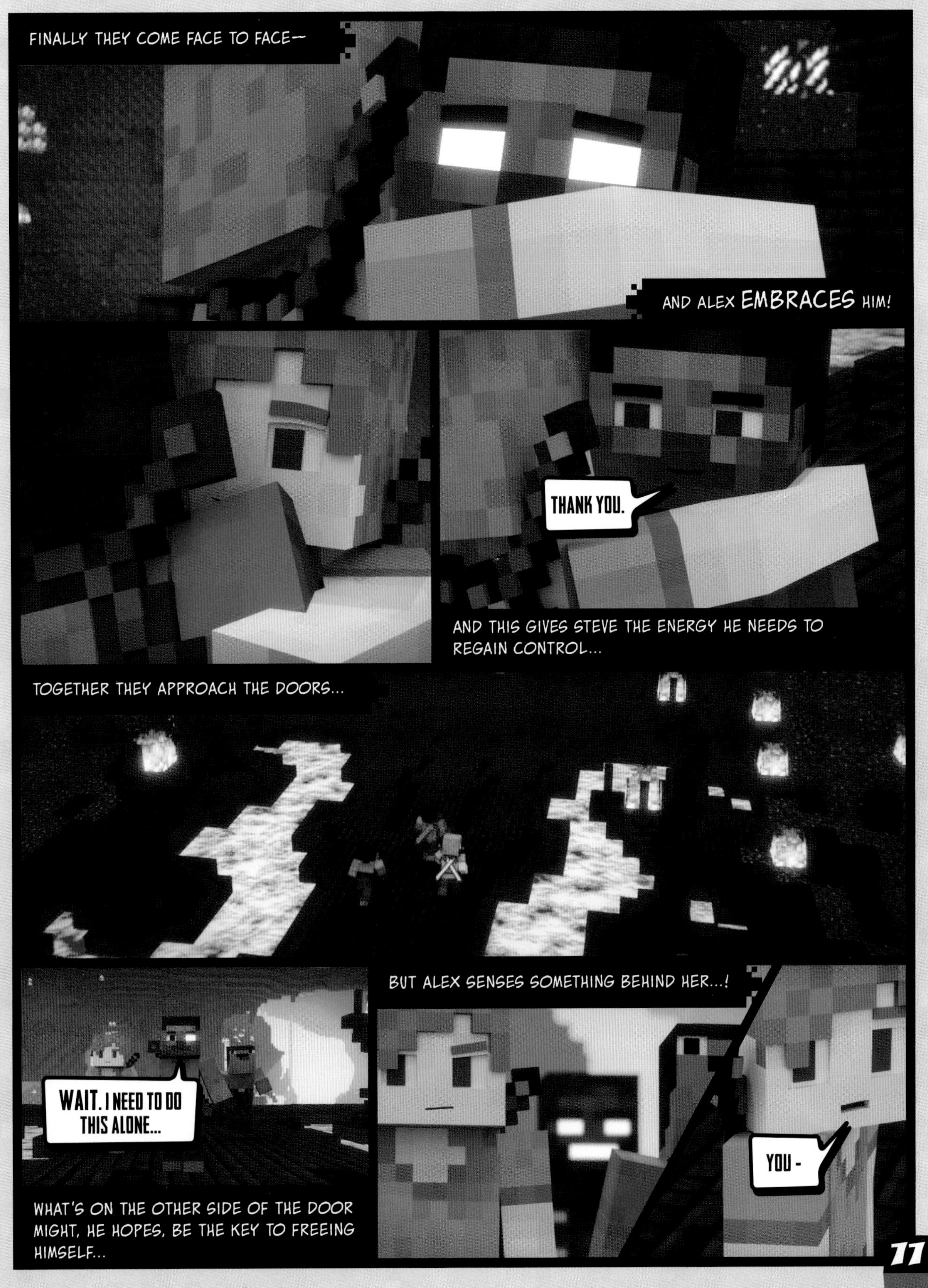
FINALLY THEY COME FACE TO FACE—
AND ALEX EMBRACES HIM!
THANK YOU.
AND THIS GIVES STEVE THE ENERGY HE NEEDS TO REGAIN CONTROL...
TOGETHER THEY APPROACH THE DOORS...
WAIT. I NEED TO DO THIS ALONE...
WHAT'S ON THE OTHER SIDE OF THE DOOR MIGHT, HE HOPES, BE THE KEY TO FREEING HIMSELF...
BUT ALEX SENSES SOMETHING BEHIND HER...!
YOU -

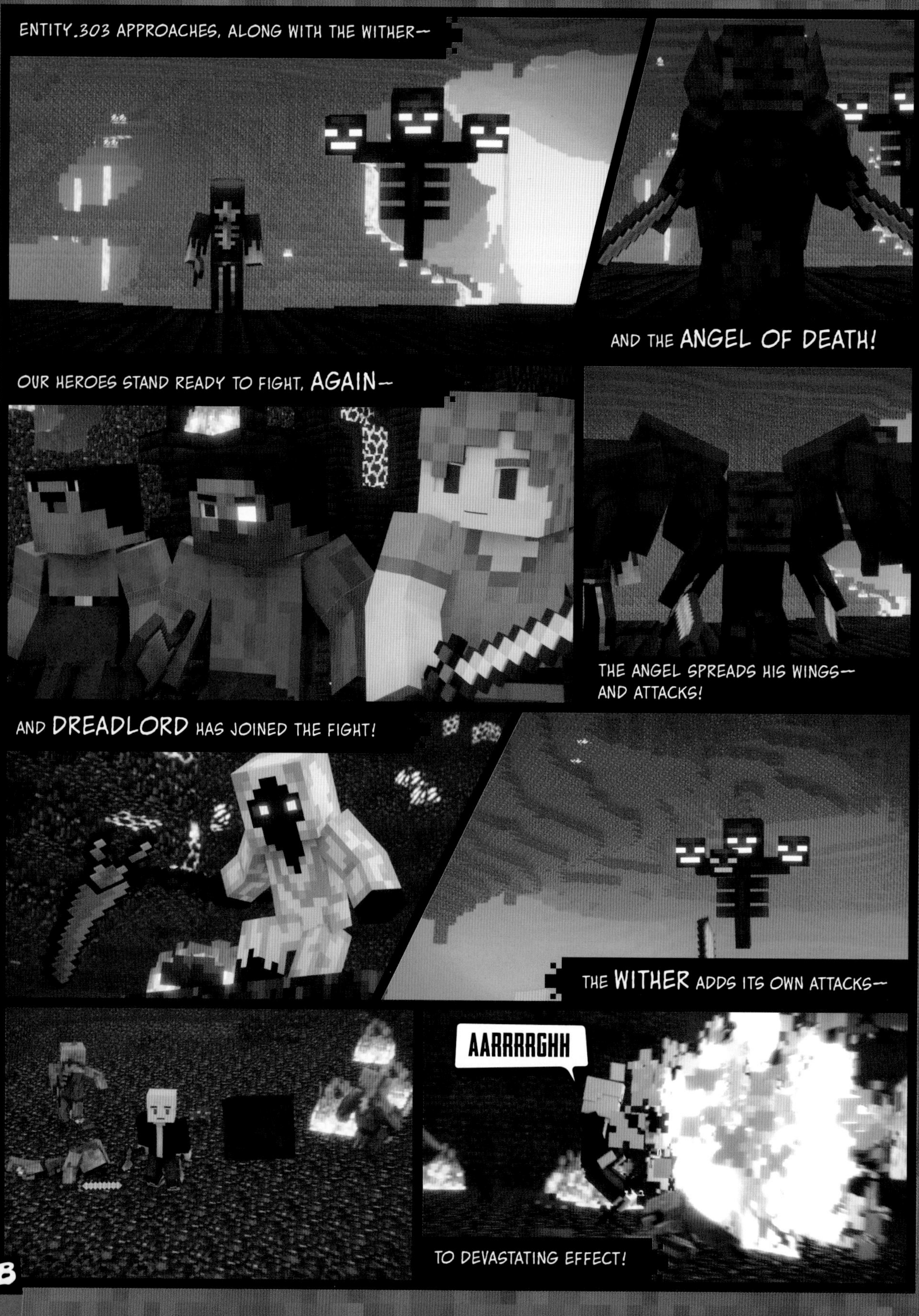
ENTITY_303 APPROACHES, ALONG WITH THE WITHER—
AND THE ANGEL OF DEATH!
OUR HEROES STAND READY TO FIGHT, AGAIN—
THE ANGEL SPREADS HIS WINGS— AND ATTACKS!
AND DREADLORD HAS JOINED THE FIGHT!
THE WITHER ADDS ITS OWN ATTACKS—
AARRRRGHH
TO DEVASTATING EFFECT!

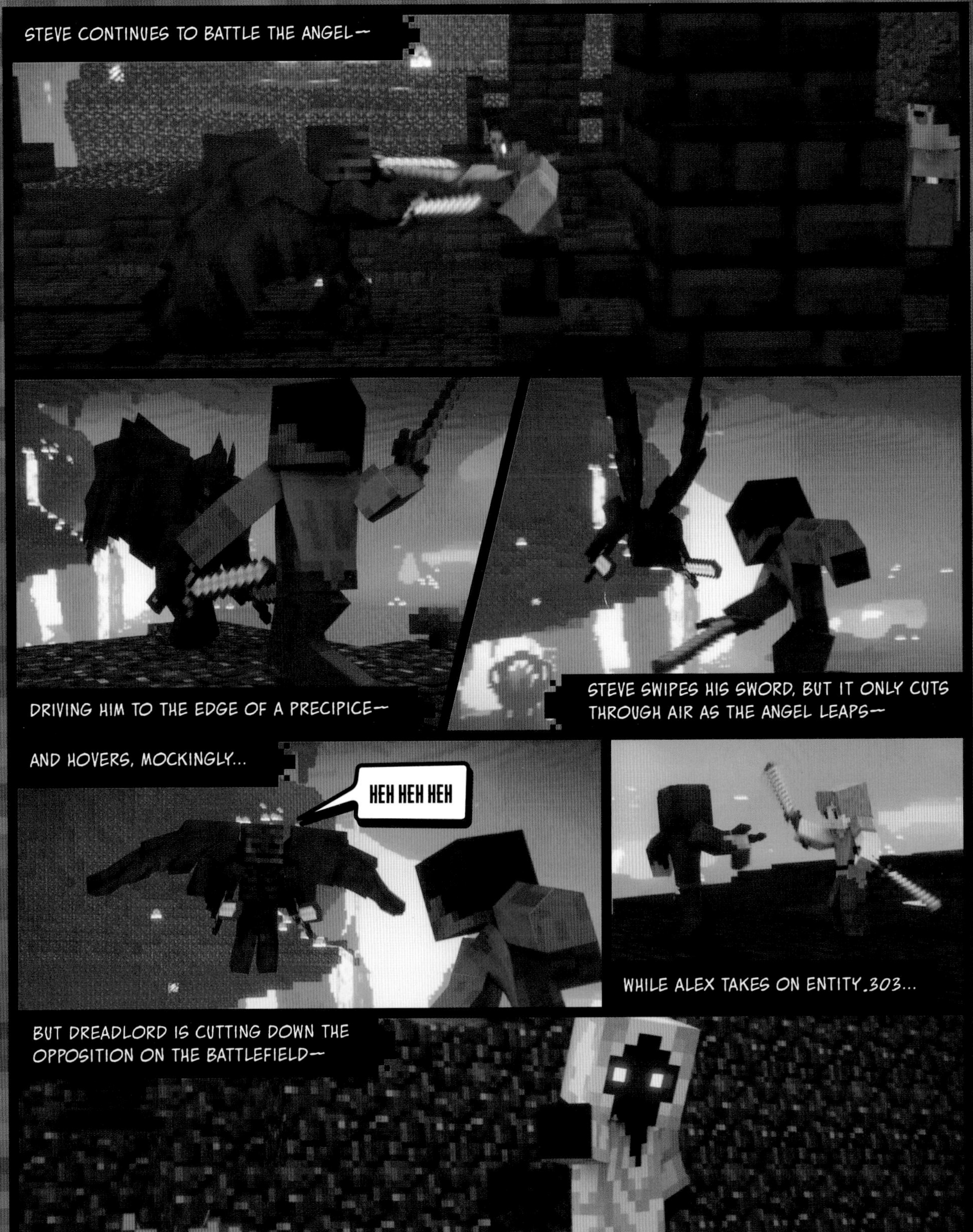
STEVE CONTINUES TO BATTLE THE ANGEL—
DRIVING HIM TO THE EDGE OF A PRECIPICE—
STEVE SWIPES HIS SWORD, BUT IT ONLY CUTS THROUGH AIR AS THE ANGEL LEAPS—
AND HOVERS, MOCKINGLY...
HEH HEH HEH
WHILE ALEX TAKES ON ENTITY.303...
BUT DREADLORD IS CUTTING DOWN THE OPPOSITION ON THE BATTLEFIELD—

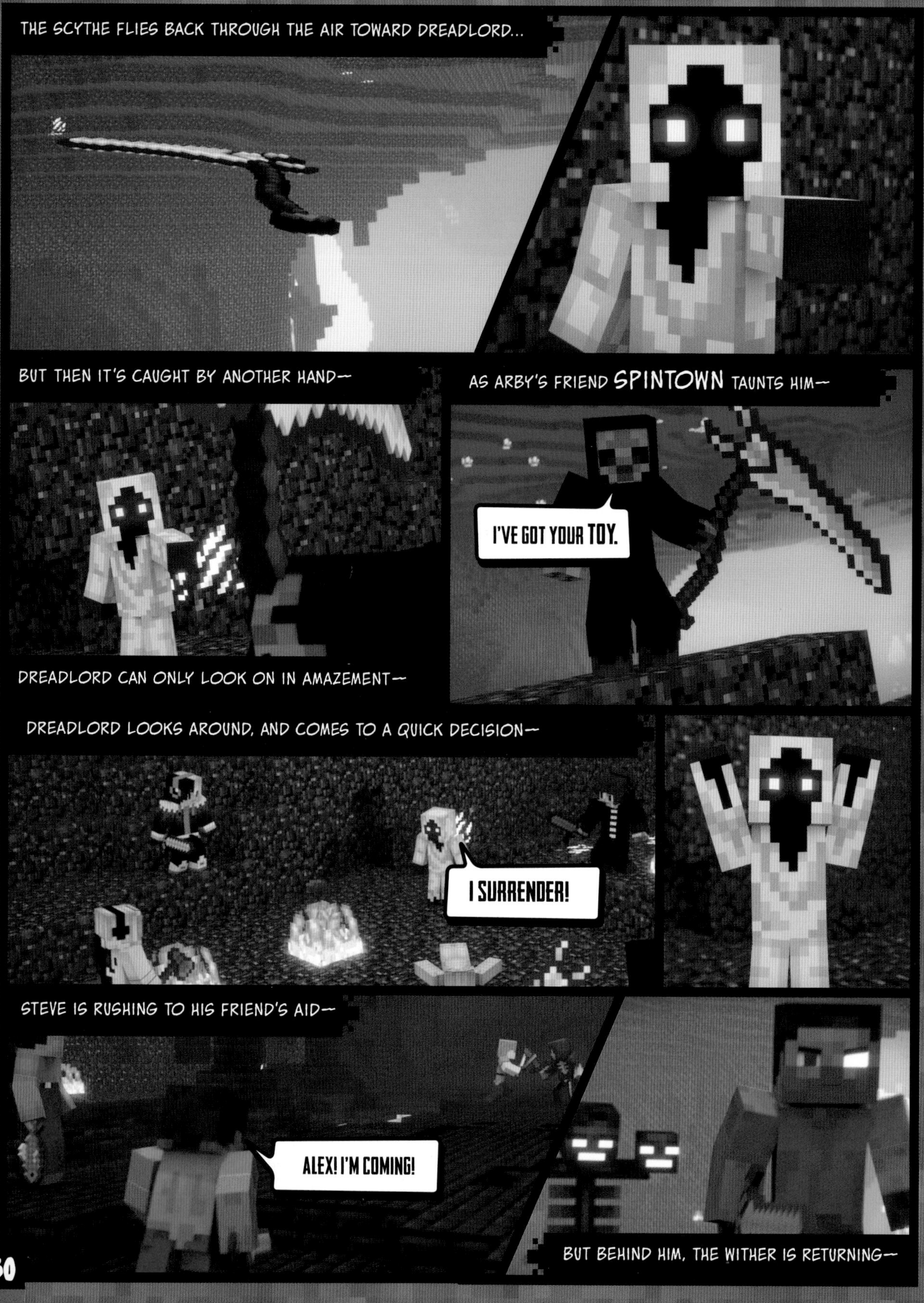

THE SCYTHE FLIES BACK THROUGH THE AIR TOWARD DREADLORD...
BUT THEN IT'S CAUGHT BY ANOTHER HAND—
DREADLORD CAN ONLY LOOK ON IN AMAZEMENT—
AS ARBY'S FRIEND SPINTOWN TAUNTS HIM—
I'VE GOT YOUR TOY.
DREADLORD LOOKS AROUND, AND COMES TO A QUICK DECISION—
I SURRENDER!
STEVE IS RUSHING TO HIS FRIEND'S AID—
ALEX! I'M COMING!
BUT BEHIND HIM, THE WITHER IS RETURNING—

STEVE TURNS—

BUT FINDS HIMSELF RIGHT IN THE LINE OF FIRE—

DERP DOESN'T EVEN THINK—HE **THROWS** HIMSELF IN FRONT OF STEVE—

POOOOMMFFF!!

DERP FALLS....

DERP...?

WE **ALL** KNOW THIS FEELING.

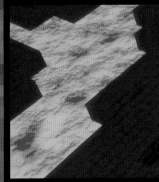

YOU DIED!

Score:0

RESPAWN

TITLE SCREEN

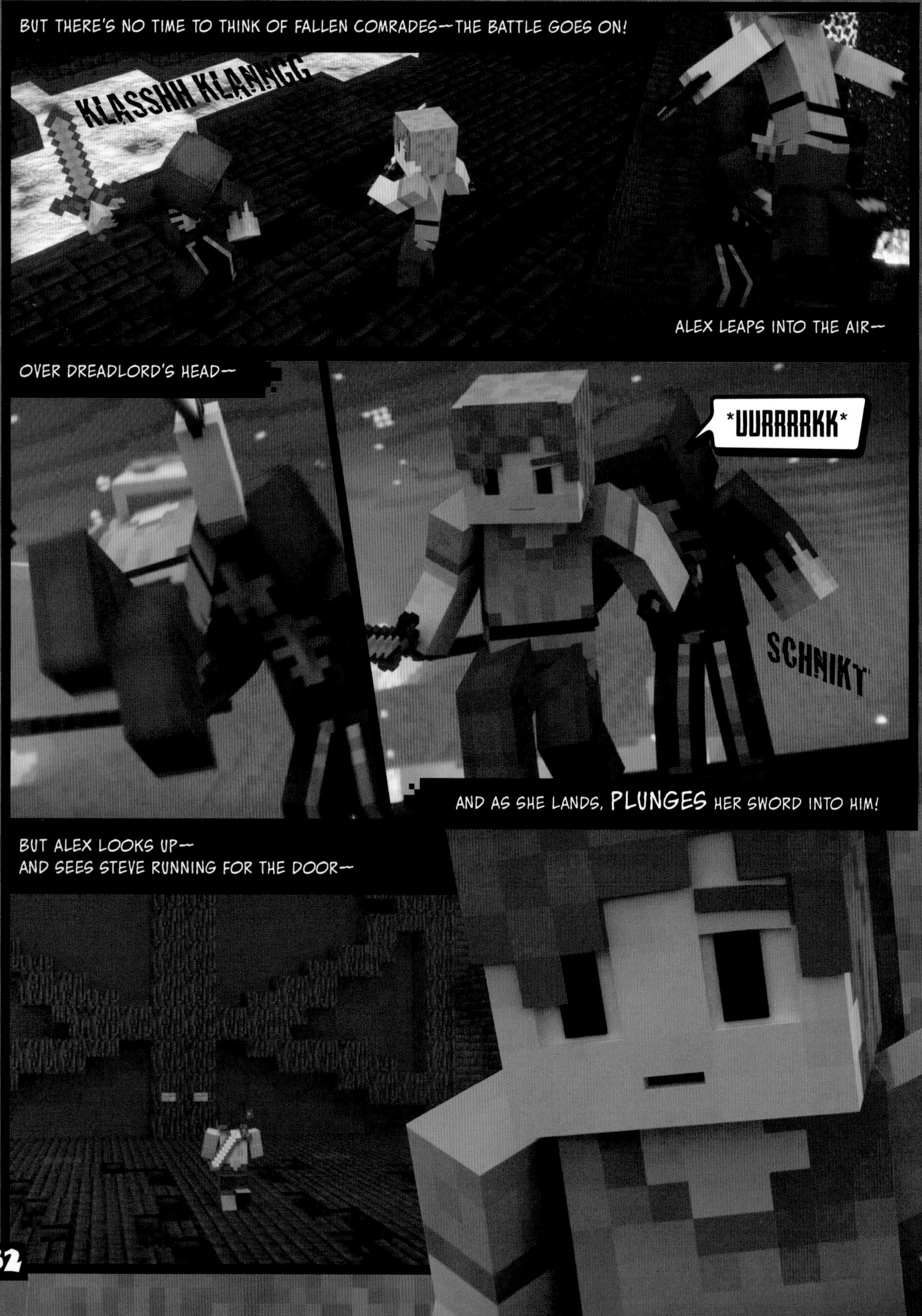
BUT THERE'S NO TIME TO THINK OF FALLEN COMRADES—THE BATTLE GOES ON!
KLASSHH KLANNGG
ALEX LEAPS INTO THE AIR—
OVER DREADLORD'S HEAD—
UURRRRKK
SCHNIKT
AND AS SHE LANDS, PLUNGES HER SWORD INTO HIM!
BUT ALEX LOOKS UP—
AND SEES STEVE RUNNING FOR THE DOOR—

CRRREEEAAAAAKK...

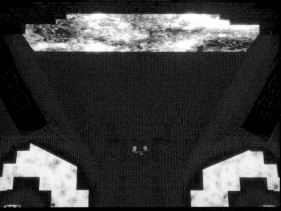

CAUTIOUSLY HE APPROACHES THE SHIMMERING WALL...

AND PLUNGES HIS HAND INTO IT—

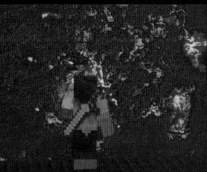

THE WALL GLOWS—

REFLECTS HIM BACK AT HIMSELF...

BUT IT'S MORE THAN JUST A REFLECTION!

TWO STEVES, BOTH HALF HEROBRINE...

BUT ON THE OTHER SIDE ... IS ANOTHER ALEX—HER DARK REFLECTION!

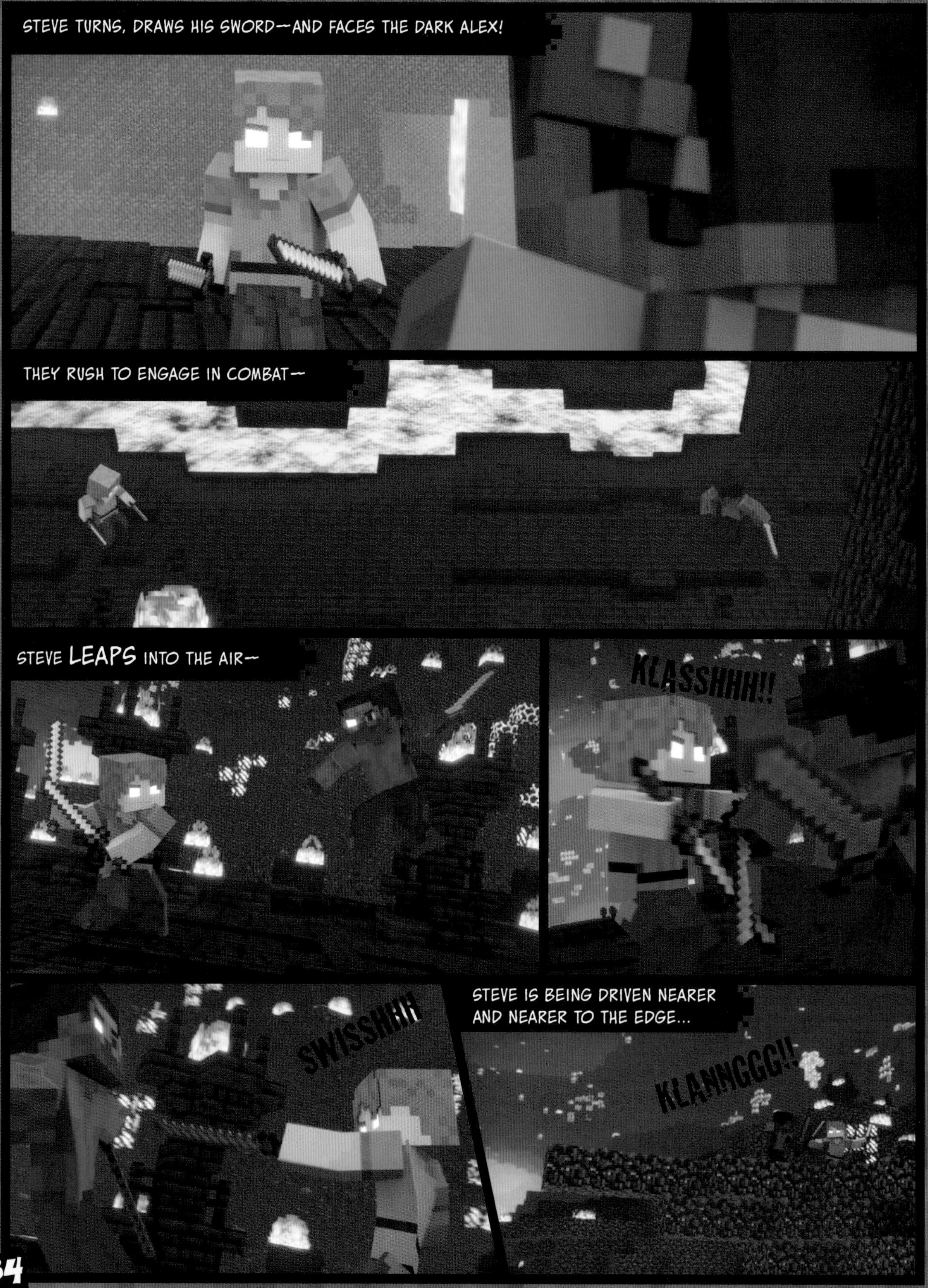
STEVE TURNS, DRAWS HIS SWORD—AND FACES THE DARK ALEX!
THEY RUSH TO ENGAGE IN COMBAT—
STEVE LEAPS INTO THE AIR—
KLASSHHH!!
SWISSHHH
STEVE IS BEING DRIVEN NEARER AND NEARER TO THE EDGE...
KLANNGGG!!

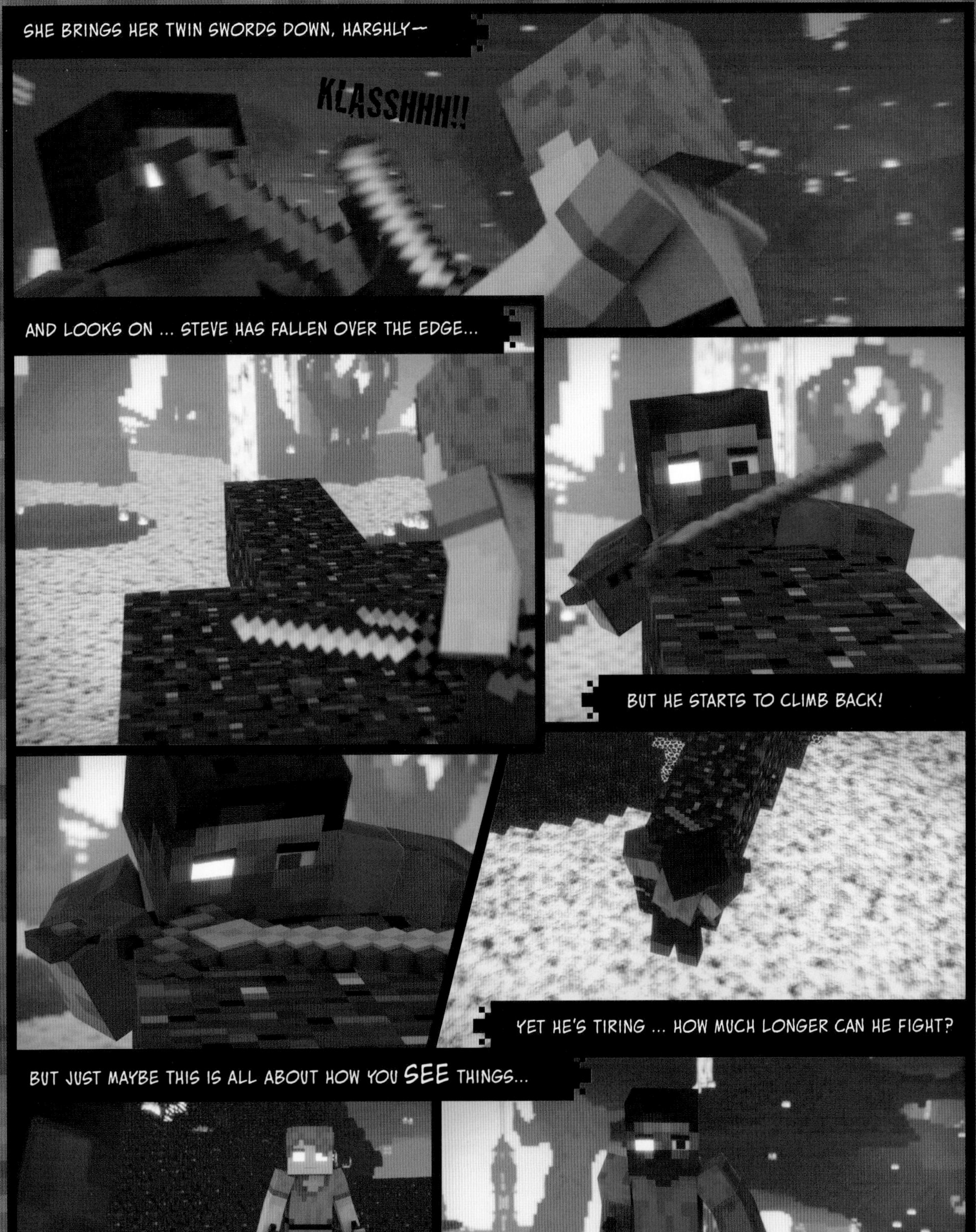
SHE BRINGS HER TWIN SWORDS DOWN, HARSHLY—
KLASSHHH!!
AND LOOKS ON ... STEVE HAS FALLEN OVER THE EDGE...
BUT HE STARTS TO CLIMB BACK!
YET HE'S TIRING ... HOW MUCH LONGER CAN HE FIGHT?
BUT JUST MAYBE THIS IS ALL ABOUT HOW YOU SEE THINGS...

WITH AN EFFORT OF WILL, STEVE SHIFTS HIS POINT OF VIEW...

AND THE ALEX HE KNOWS RETURNS!

STEVE...

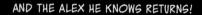

STEVE REALIZES HE'S BEEN SEEING THINGS AS THEY
APPEAR IN THE MIRROR—

THAT HE WAS **HIMSELF** WHEN ALEX HUGGED
HIM, NOT HEROBRINE—

THAT HE'S BEEN FIGHTING THE REAL ALEX
ALL ALONG ... AND NOW STEVE KNOWS
WHAT HE HAS TO DO!

BUT THEN—THE GROUND BENEATH HIS
FEET BEGINS TO SHAKE!

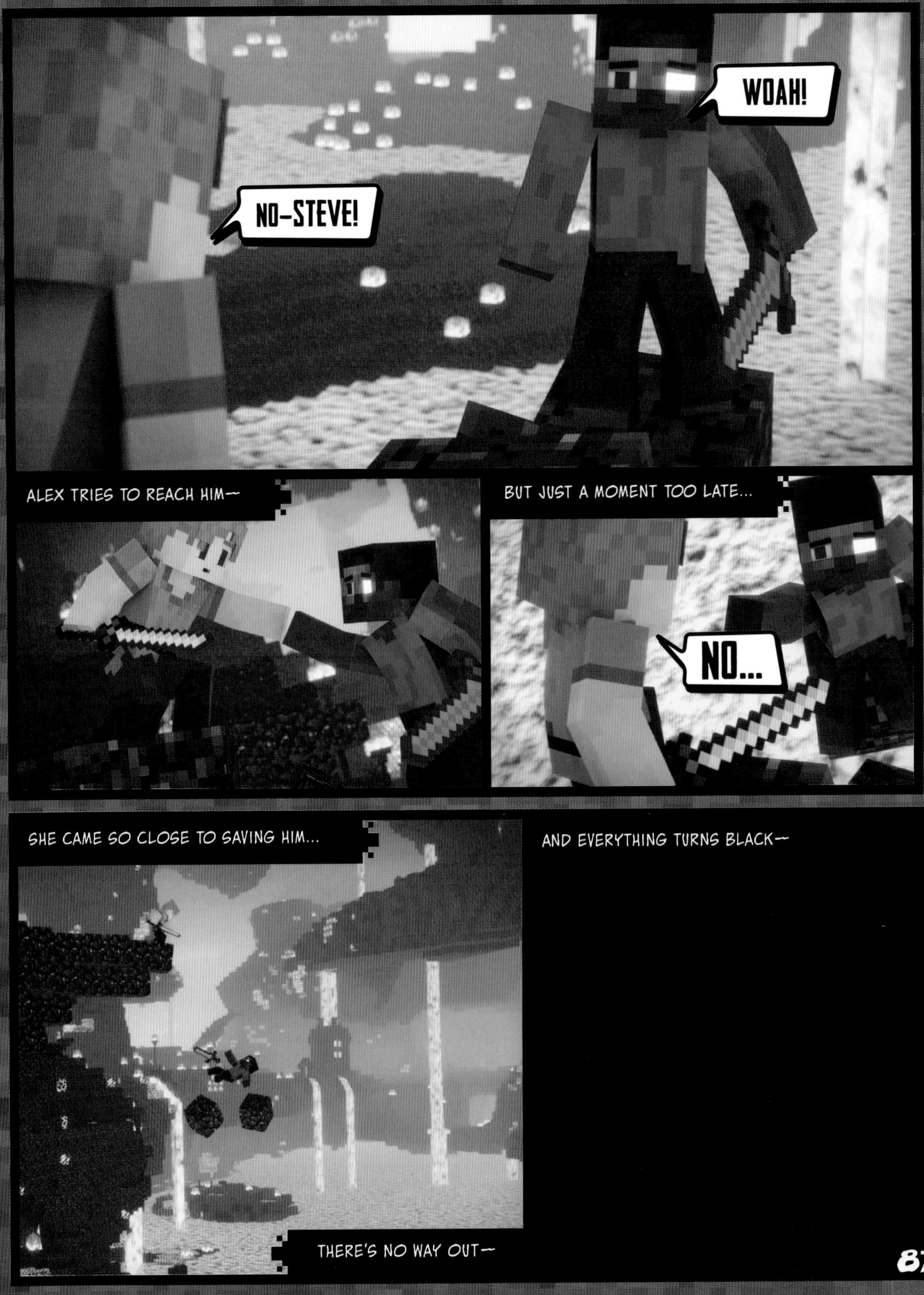
WOAH!
NO-STEVE!
ALEX TRIES TO REACH HIM—
BUT JUST A MOMENT TOO LATE...
NO...
SHE CAME SO CLOSE TO SAVING HIM...
THERE'S NO WAY OUT—
AND EVERYTHING TURNS BLACK—

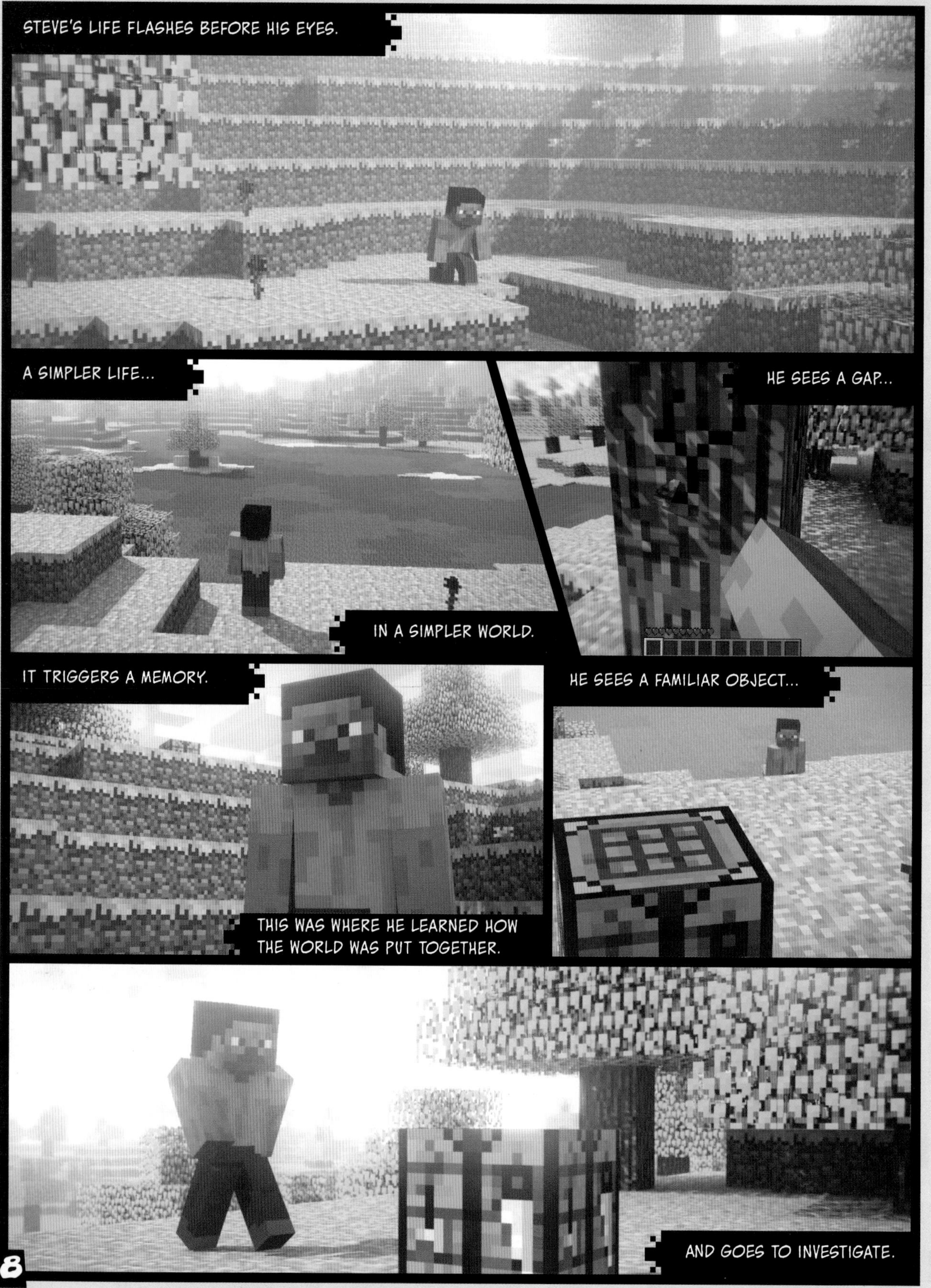
STEVE'S LIFE FLASHES BEFORE HIS EYES.
A SIMPLER LIFE...
IN A SIMPLER WORLD.
HE SEES A GAP...
IT TRIGGERS A MEMORY.
THIS WAS WHERE HE LEARNED HOW THE WORLD WAS PUT TOGETHER.
HE SEES A FAMILIAR OBJECT...
AND GOES TO INVESTIGATE.

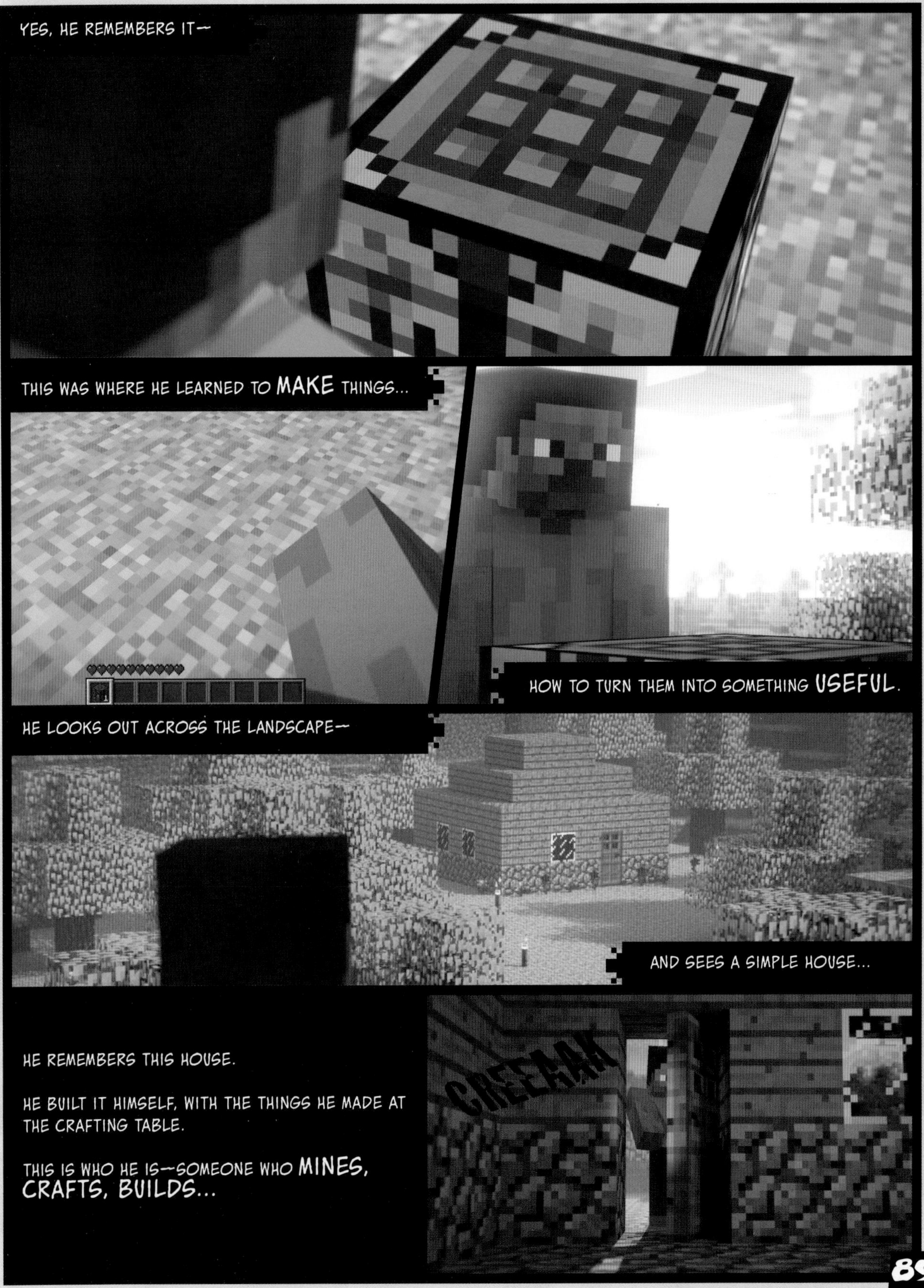
YES, HE REMEMBERS IT—
THIS WAS WHERE HE LEARNED TO MAKE THINGS...
HOW TO TURN THEM INTO SOMETHING USEFUL.
HE LOOKS OUT ACROSS THE LANDSCAPE—
AND SEES A SIMPLE HOUSE...
HE REMEMBERS THIS HOUSE.
HE BUILT IT HIMSELF, WITH THE THINGS HE MADE AT THE CRAFTING TABLE.
THIS IS WHO HE IS—SOMEONE WHO MINES, CRAFTS, BUILDS...
CREEAAK

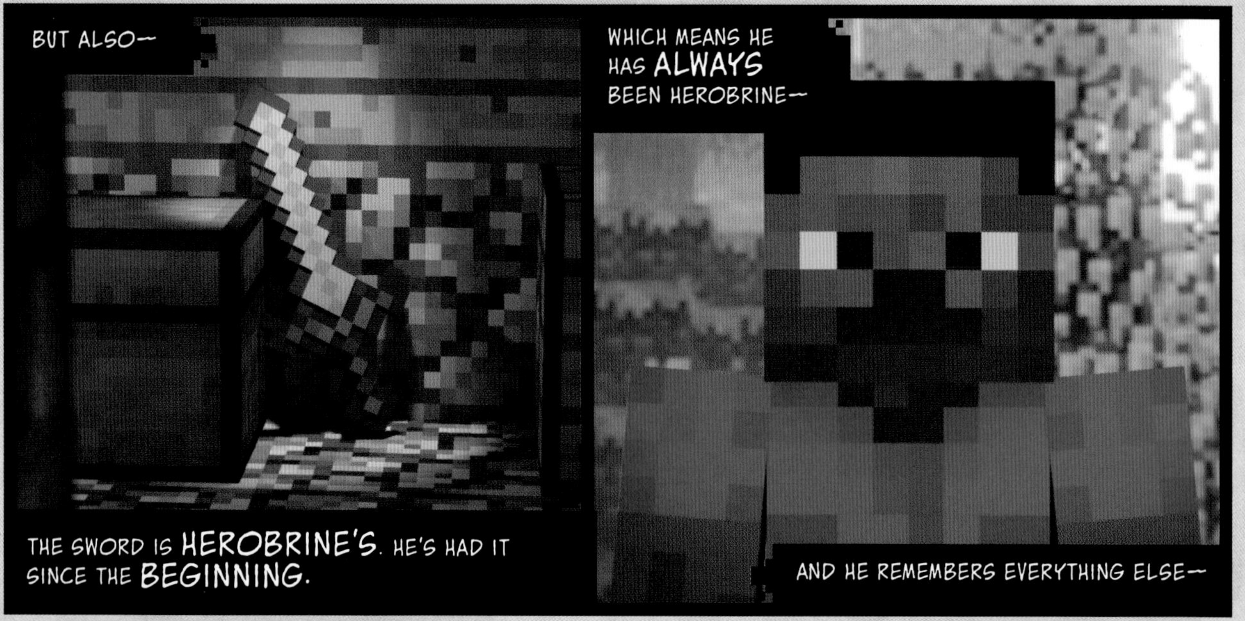
BUT ALSO—
THE SWORD IS HEROBRINE'S. HE'S HAD IT SINCE THE BEGINNING.
WHICH MEANS HE HAS ALWAYS BEEN HEROBRINE—
AND HE REMEMBERS EVERYTHING ELSE—

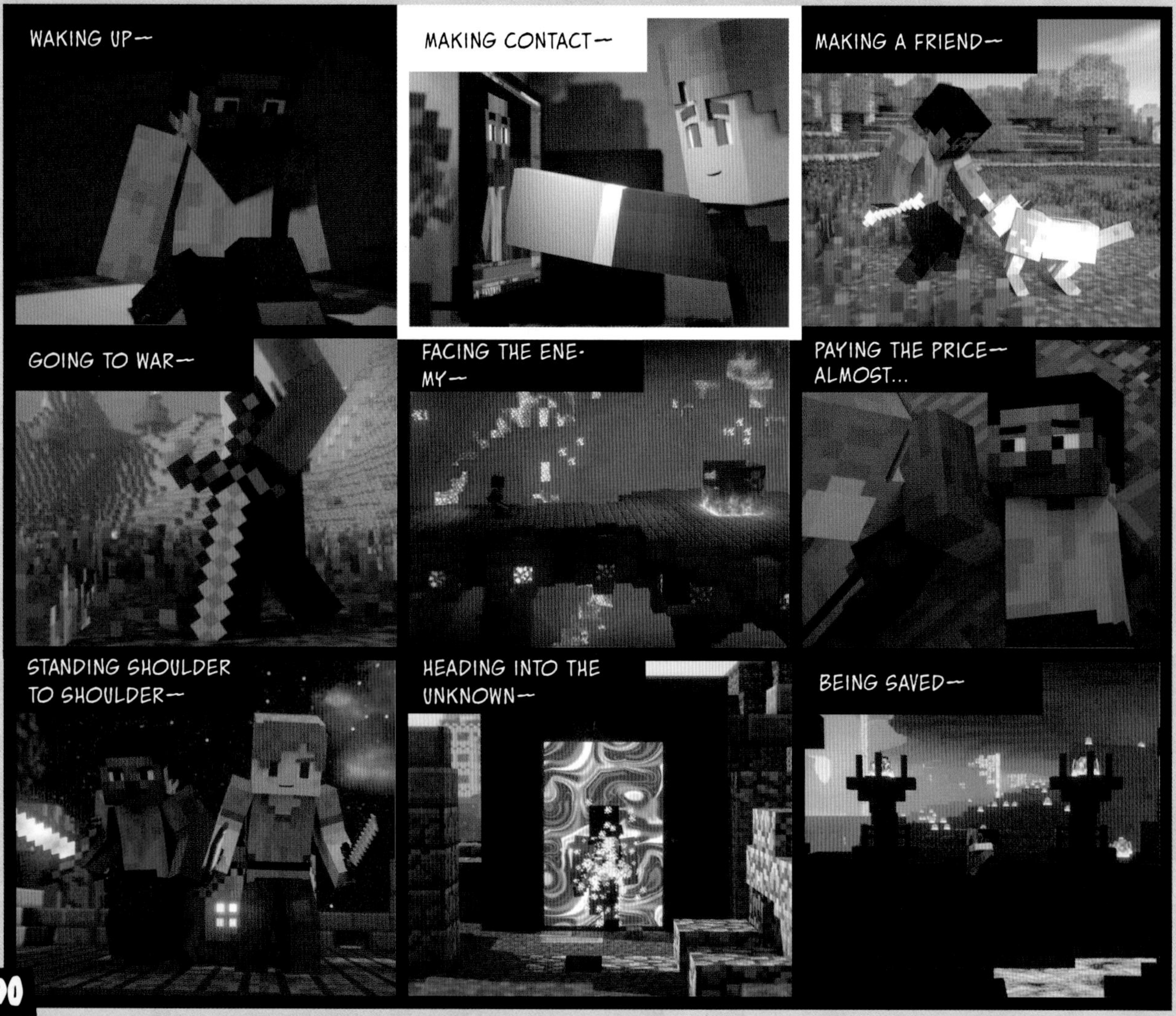
WAKING UP—
MAKING CONTACT—
MAKING A FRIEND—
GOING TO WAR—
FACING THE ENE-MY—
PAYING THE PRICE— ALMOST...
STANDING SHOULDER TO SHOULDER—
HEADING INTO THE UNKNOWN—
BEING SAVED—

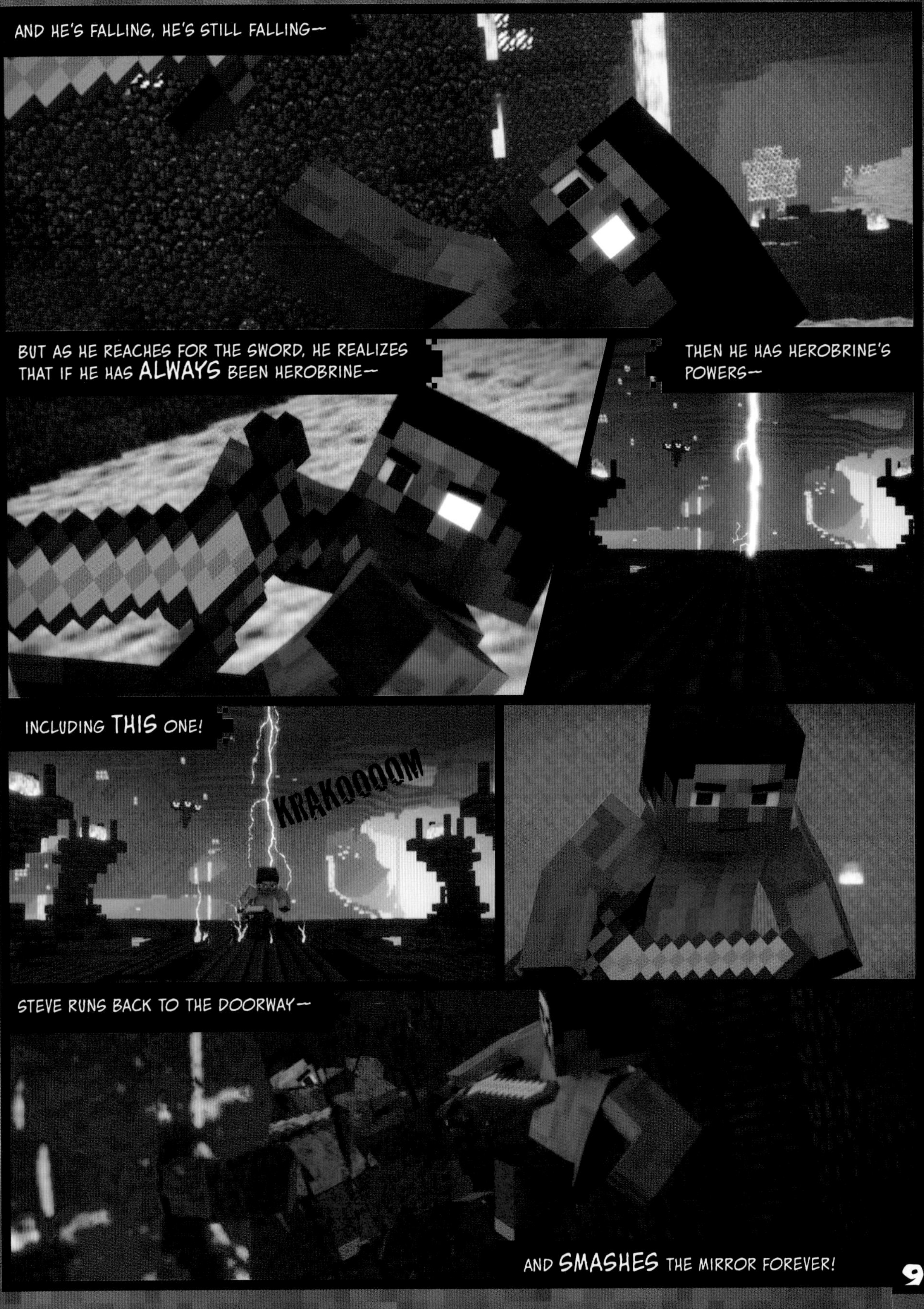

AND HE'S FALLING, HE'S STILL FALLING—
BUT AS HE REACHES FOR THE SWORD, HE REALIZES THAT IF HE HAS ALWAYS BEEN HEROBRINE—
THEN HE HAS HEROBRINE'S POWERS—
INCLUDING THIS ONE!
KRAKOOOOM
STEVE RUNS BACK TO THE DOORWAY—
AND SMASHES THE MIRROR FOREVER!

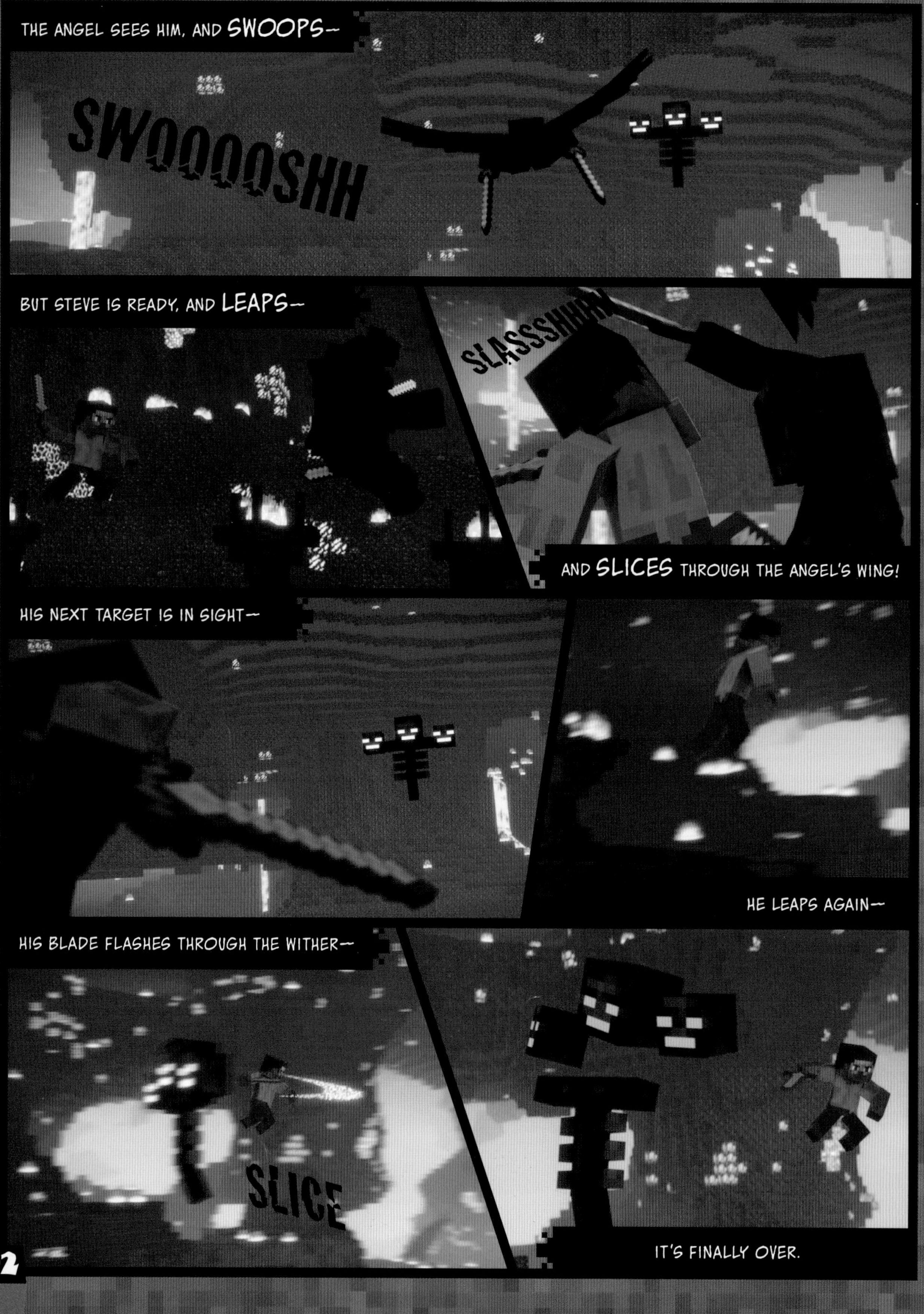
THE ANGEL SEES HIM, AND SWOOPS—
SWOOOOOSHH
BUT STEVE IS READY, AND LEAPS—
SLASSSHHH
AND SLICES THROUGH THE ANGEL'S WING!
HIS NEXT TARGET IS IN SIGHT—
HE LEAPS AGAIN—
HIS BLADE FLASHES THROUGH THE WITHER—
SLICE
IT'S FINALLY OVER.

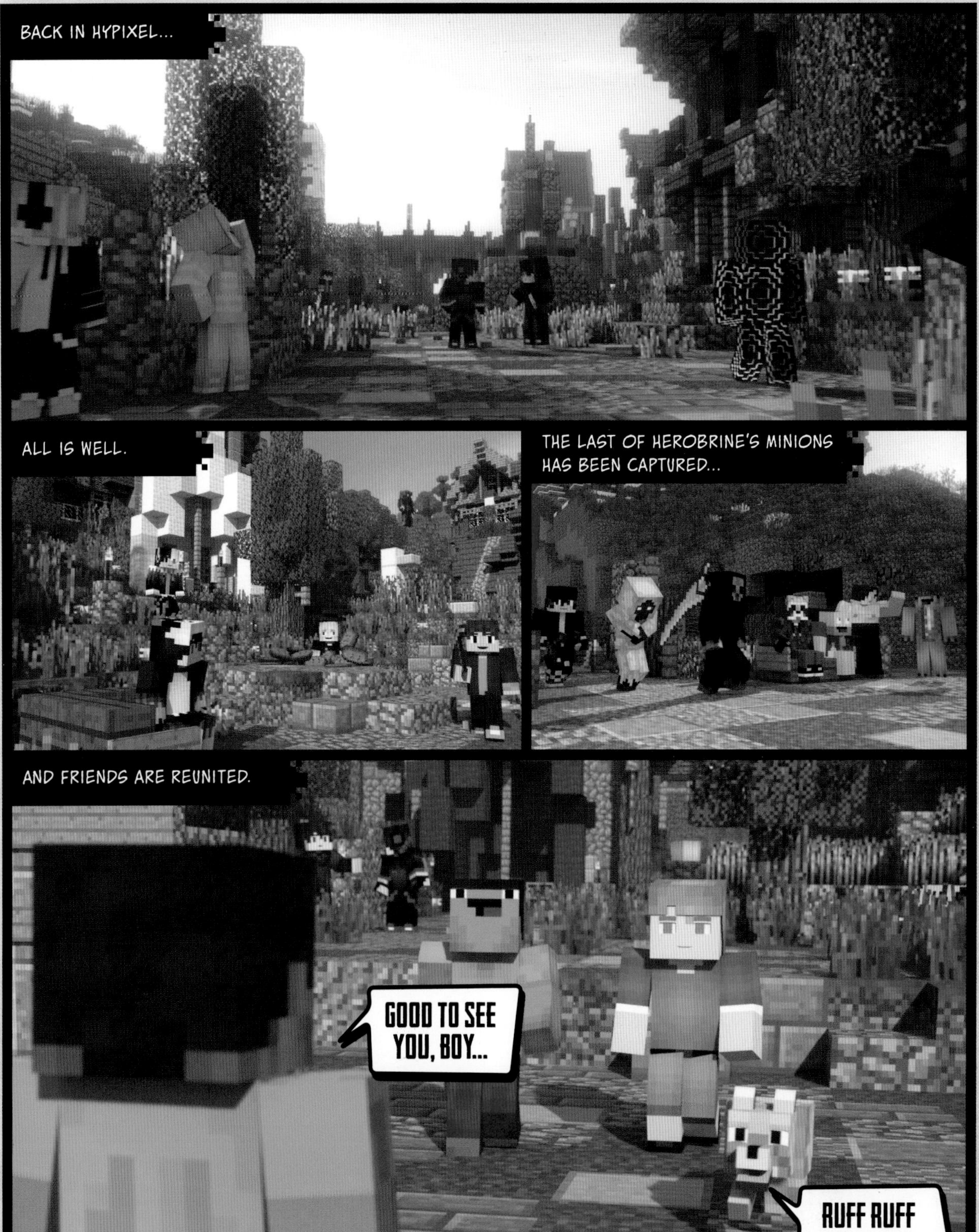
BACK IN HYPIXEL...
ALL IS WELL.
THE LAST OF HEROBRINE'S MINIONS HAS BEEN CAPTURED...
AND FRIENDS ARE REUNITED.
GOOD TO SEE YOU, BOY...
RUFF RUFF

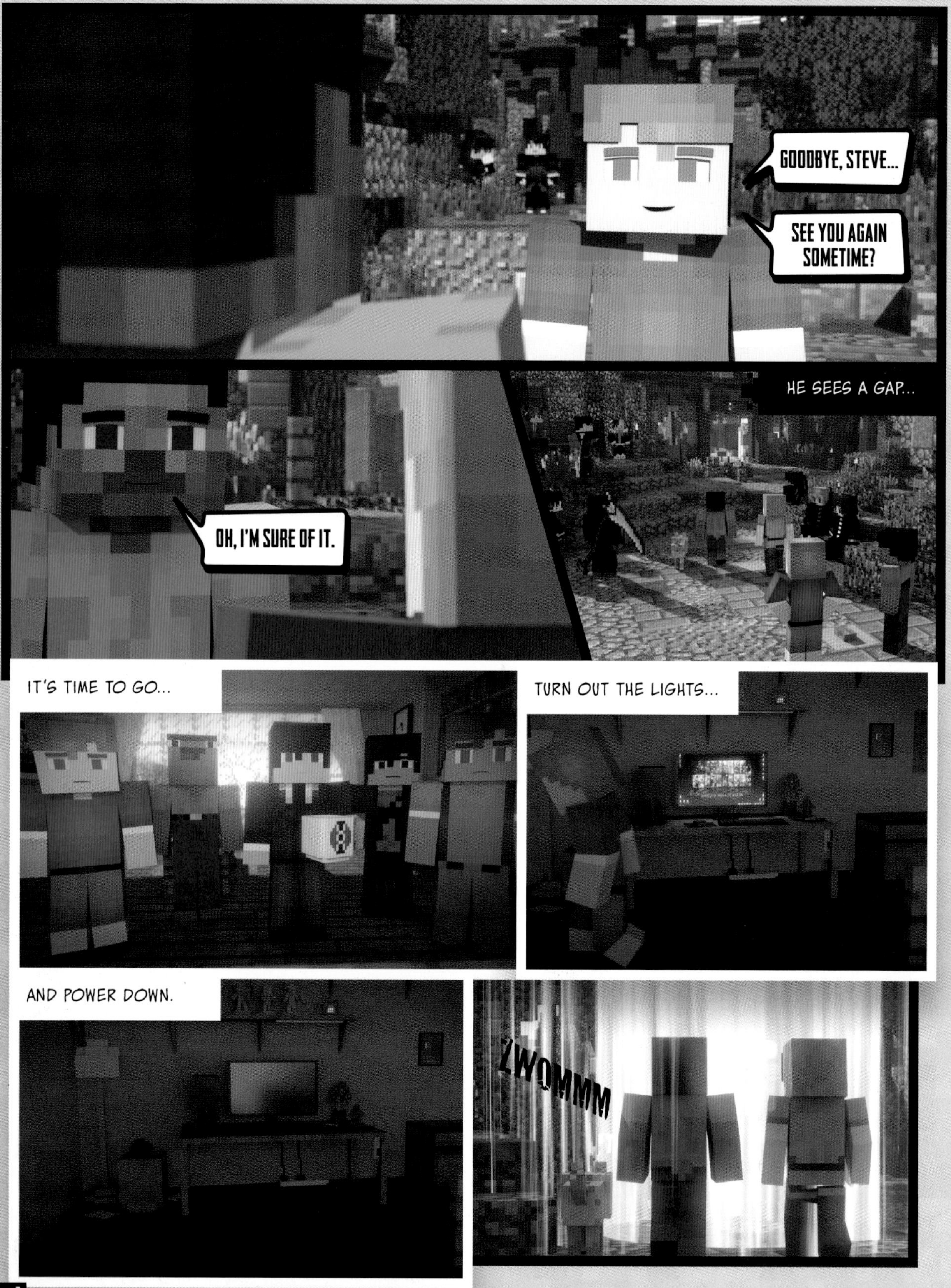
GOODBYE, STEVE...
SEE YOU AGAIN SOMETIME?
OH, I'M SURE OF IT.
HE SEES A GAP...
IT'S TIME TO GO...
TURN OUT THE LIGHTS...
AND POWER DOWN.
ZWOMMM

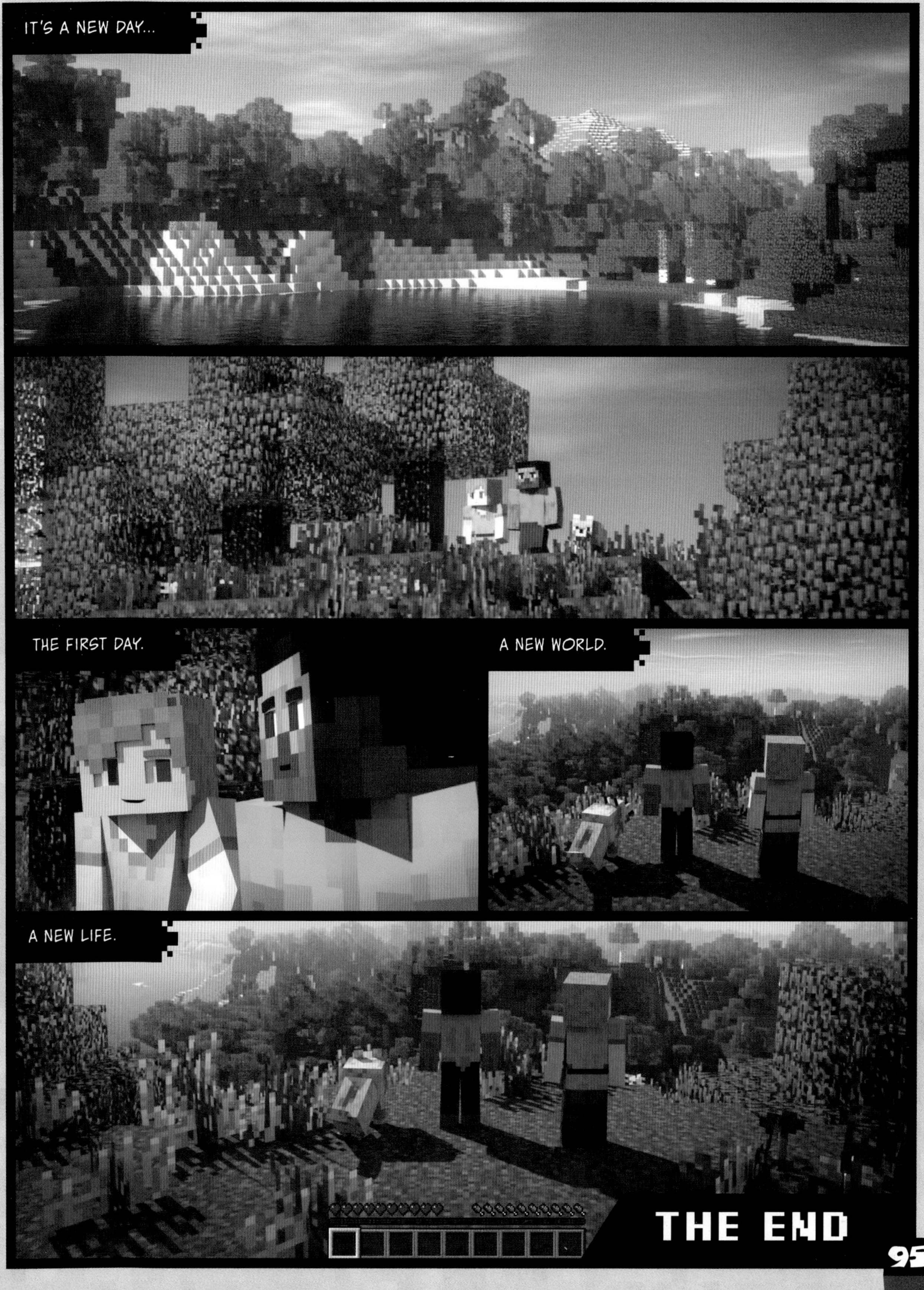
IT'S A NEW DAY...
THE FIRST DAY.
A NEW WORLD.
A NEW LIFE.
THE END